An excerpt from *Waking Kiss*

His kiss transformed then, from soft and gentle to something else. I tensed, fearful of the sudden change in his demeanor. He stood like a wall in front of me, his muscular, sculpted physique pressed against my much smaller body. He didn't paw at me. If he was rough or clumsy, I could have pulled away and said, *ugh, this asshole*, and regained control of the situation, but he was the opposite of clumsy. Each touch of his lips, his tongue, ignited a response in me. His fingers twisted in my hair, his tugs causing pain but something pleasurable too.

His arm slid around my waist and tightened in a hard clasp, and in that moment something inside me awakened, some part of me that I'd stuffed down and smothered for years. That thing— want, desire—stirred to life with a starving vengeance. I returned his kisses with uncharacteristic abandon, and the harder I kissed him, the tighter his grip became. He had me cornered, but I found I liked being cornered by him. I wanted to be trapped and restrained against the wall and kissed into submission. I'd avoided passion and sex for years because I feared force, because I was afraid to give up control, but somehow he took all of that out of the equation and made me *want him*.

The more he kissed me the harder I cried, because it felt so good and so scary, and because each kiss was changing me a little inside. I grasped his arm with my free hand, clutching the rose stem in the other. I had to stop him before I lost myself, before bad memories and bad feelings turned this dream into a nightmare…

Waking Kiss

by

Annabel Joseph

Other erotic romance by Annabel Joseph

Mercy
Cait and the Devil
Firebird
Deep in the Woods
Fortune
Owning Wednesday
Lily Mine
Comfort Object
Caressa's Knees
Odalisque
Command Performance
Cirque de Minuit
Burn For You
Disciplining the Duchess
The Edge of the Earth (as Molly Joseph)

Erotica by Annabel Joseph

Club Mephisto
Molly's Lips: Club Mephisto Retold

Coming Soon:

Fever Dream
Cirque Vivide

Note: This novel contains references to childhood abuse and violence which may disturb some readers. If you are struggling with the aftereffects of a past traumatic event, your first course of action should always be to seek the help of a licensed mental health professional, as did the characters in this book.

You can learn more about mental health services in your area by doing a web search or visiting nimh.nih.gov (U.S. National Institute on Mental Health) or nami.org (National Alliance on Mental Illness).

Chapter One:
Act Three

Since I was a little girl, I've wanted to be invisible. Not in a cool, magical kind of way, but in that way of *please don't look at me too hard.* Ballet has always been a compulsion for me, not a pleasure. It was something I got serious about because I had to, despite the trauma of being poked and prodded since my most tender years, judged and lambasted because my turnout was weak or my *port de bras* one degree off center. That stuff will drive you nuts, but it's always been worth it to me, like jumping upstream is worth it to a salmon. It's a survival thing.

That's why I really didn't want to dance center stage with The Great Rubio in our company's heralded production of *Sleeping Beauty.* I'm not being coy. I'm not pretending I didn't want to when secretly I would have killed for the chance. No. I really didn't want to, and it never should have happened in the first place. There was a clause in his contract with the London City Ballet to prevent such a farce. *Mr. Rubio will dance with prima-level ballerinas only. In the event a prima dancer is not available, Mr. Rubio shall not be compelled to perform and a substitution shall be made.*

But in this case, Princess Aurora pulled a muscle stretching backstage before her Act Three entrance and I was the only other dancer available with her shade of jet black hair. A stagehand yanked me from the palace set by the back of my ball gown.

"What are you doing?" I asked, pulling it from his grubby fingers.

"Do you know it?" His words didn't make sense until I saw Mariel, the injured Sleeping Beauty, sobbing a few yards away as a swarm of helpers stripped off her rhinestone-embroidered tutu.

"Do you know it?" He shook me, tugging at the straps of my "Fourteenth Wedding Guest" costume. Of course I knew it. Every corps girl knew the part of Sleeping Beauty from the opening *pas de chats* to the closing *arabesque*. Every one of us had watched Mariel dance it in practice over and over while imagining ourselves in The Great Rubio's arms. Fernando Rubio was a God to us—capital letter. He was a celebrity recognized by people who weren't even into ballet, a superstar we'd all been warned not to look at or talk to backstage.

"Yes, I know it," I said automatically, before I processed what that meant.

Four pairs of hands stripped off my ball gown costume and strong-armed me into Mariel's ornate white tutu. Oh, okay. Oh. *No.* I couldn't dance with Rubio, not center stage in front of a packed theater.

"I can't," I said in a panic. "I won't be able to do it. My shoes are too soft."

They twisted knots in the stretchy clear shoulder straps of the costume since Mariel was taller than me. I tried again. "Uh, really, I can't do this. My shoes aren't up to it."

See, the boxes, or tips, of pointe shoes are constructed of layers of fabric, material, and glue hardened into a molded point. If they're not broken in, those boxes sound obnoxious on stage, like the clopping of a horse. If they're very broken in, like mine, they're nice and quiet but it's impossible to do demanding pointe work—and Princess Aurora required demanding pointe work.

"My shoes are too soft, you guys." I think I said it two more times but everyone ignored me. "Why aren't you listening to me?" I finally cried, waving my hands at the stage manager.

A vein throbbed in his temple. "You've got to dance, shoes or not."

"Then I need to go grab a better pair."

"You're on in eight minutes." He looked around for someone to send but they wouldn't know which pair I needed. Hell, I didn't know which pair I needed. I didn't have a single pair of shoes that would make

8

me good enough to dance with The Great Rubio. "I'll be back," I said, darting away.

He trailed me for a second but then he stopped and hissed, "Seven minutes, or else!"

Shit. Shit. *Shit.* I banged through the door into the backstage corridor and barreled toward the dressing rooms. I took the corner so fast I almost slid into the opposite wall. I couldn't fall down in this five-thousand-dollar tutu, and I definitely couldn't dance Princess Aurora in these flimsy shoes. I reached the corps dressing rooms and yanked the doorknob to the women's door. No. Oh God, no. *Locked.*

"No, no, no, no," I pleaded with the universe. "Oh, no. No, no, no." Every time I said no, I yanked down on the doorknob, like maybe this time it might miraculously open. I turned in a panic. Someone had to have a key, but how long would it take to find that person? Oh God, I was fucked. I was going to have to dance the third act of *Sleeping Beauty* with my idol in the world's shittiest pointe shoes.

I ran back down the corridor and collided full speed into what felt like a brick wall but was actually a very solid man. "Hey," he said, catching me. "Where's the fire?"

"Key." I shook my hands at him. "Key, key, key, key. *Key!*"

"I'm sensing you need a key." His lips tilted into a half smile, and I gave myself a second—no, half a second—to appreciate how handsome he was. Designer suit, long honey-brown hair curling around his shoulders, wide, carved cheekbones and striking amber eyes. He looked thirty-ish or thereabouts, a few years older than me. He had a golden-tan complexion like Rubio, but based on his accent, he was a fellow American. I gave myself another half second to mourn the fact that this guy probably didn't have a key.

"I need to get into the dressing room," I cried. "It's locked."

"Show me. I'll open it for you."

"I need a key."

"Show me," he said again.

I took him to the women's dressing room and rattled the doorknob. "I only have about...I don't know...five minutes to get back to the wings."

He eyed my rhinestone-encrusted tutu. "Okay. Stand back."

For one wild moment I thought he was going to shoulder through the door. He looked strong enough to do it, but what he actually did was bop the doorknob with a quick, smooth movement of his palm. I heard a popping sound. He turned it and held the door open for me.

"Oh my God, oh my God," I babbled. "How did you do that?"

"It doesn't always work. It depends on the make of the knob. With this kind of door—"

"No," I said, cutting him off. "I don't have time."

"What can I do to help?"

"I need shoes. New shoes." I ran over to my carrel, crouched down and pulled out my basket of pointe shoes. I started knocking the toes on the floor, trying to find a pair that was adequately broken in, but they were all too loud and stiff. "I'm screwed," I wailed. "I can't believe this is happening to me. These are all too hard."

He took one in his hand and started kneading it. "Want me to help you soften them?"

I grabbed the shoe back. "No! Oh, God. There's no time." I sat in my chair and leaned forward, batting away a faceful of stiff, sequined tutu. "Oh, please. Help me," I said, trying to reach past the layers of tulle to the ribbons on my ankles. "Help me take these off."

I was barking orders to a perfect stranger but he complied, kneeling to untie the pink ribbons and unwind them from my ankles while I picked out the pair of shoes that was least noisy. I dug my toe pads out of the discarded pair, wrapped them around my toes, and jammed them into the new pair. He held my tutu down and out of the way while I bent to adjust the elastics and tie the ribbons.

"Hey," he said over the frantic rasping of my breath. "Everything's going to be okay."

"Everything's not going to be okay," I snapped. "I'm about to dance *Sleeping Beauty* with The Great Rubio. And listen to this." I clopped the toes of my shoes on the floor and then kicked my old, soft ones across the room in frustration.

"*The Great Rubio?*" he repeated, chuckling. I was almost to the door when I realized how rude I'd been to him.

"I only had seven minutes," I said, turning back. "I'm so sorry. I—"

He waved me off. "Fly free, little ballerina. Go."

I ran out the door, thinking I should have at least said thank you. It was too late now. The stage manager was a deep shade of scarlet when I skidded up to him. "Damn you," he said. "You're on in thirty seconds."

10

Grunts attacked my scalp with hairpins as they affixed Princess Aurora's aluminum and rhinestone crown to my head. At least my black hair would hide the blood. *Ouch.* There had to be blood.

"Shake your head," the lead costumer barked. The crown didn't budge. Some woman pushed past him, grabbed my face in one hand and used the other to apply a haphazard slash of the dark red lipstick Sleeping Beauty wore. Out of the corner of my eye I noticed the man from the dressing room observing this chaos. His long, tousled hair contrasted with his sedate expression, his cultivated bearing. He had a great body but he was too big to be a dancer. I wondered why he was hanging out backstage.

"Do your lips. *Do your lips!*" the makeup lady hissed, smacking her own together until I mimicked her, smearing oily crimson in what I hoped was an adequate outline.

Someone tugged at my back, fluffing the tutu. The waist and bodice fit like a second skin. Apparently Mariel and I were the same size in the middle if not in height, and in fact we looked very much alike, with pale complexions, black hair, and blue eyes. Only difference was that she was a principal who'd danced this role for weeks now, and I was a faceless member of the corps. Also, my shoes weren't broken in and I was about to possibly have a heart attack.

I looked around for my lock-breaking hero but he'd disappeared again. "Just get through it, Ashleigh," said a low voice at my side. The company director, Yves Thibault. Mr. Thibault was a great director because he understood his dancers. For instance, he understood that I danced best in a group, at the back of the stage out of the spotlight. I appealed silently for him to intervene and save me, perhaps by canceling the rest of the ballet or delaying it until another principal ballerina could be fetched.

It wasn't happening.

Rubio stretched on the other side of the stage, oblivious to the drama, deep in performance mode. He wasn't called The Great Rubio for nothing. Such focus, such artistic brilliance—and the body of a Brazilian Adonis. The twenty-six-year-old *virtuoso* had risen from the slums of Rio to the top of the ballet world on pure, glorious talent. Me, I'd scratched my way into the London City Ballet corps and that was probably as far as I'd ever go.

I scurried to my mark, or maybe one of the stagehands pushed me. I heard the cue to enter and looked up at the same moment into Rubio's dark, wide-set eyes. My inspiration, my idol—this was both a dream and a nightmare. We moved toward each other, arms outstretched. My smile said *oh God, help me*, while his was more *WTF?* He fixed his expression first, turning to the audience with a blazing smile. I did the same. We posed, the happy couple, Sleeping Beauty and her prince.

The orchestral cue straightened my spine like the demanding tap of a teacher. I could do this. I'd been dancing for twenty of my twenty-four years. I could do it—I just wasn't ready to. Rubio swept me forward to center stage and we struck another pose. His whole body tensed, vibrating beside me. I could sense his fury like a palpable thing and it shook my already-faltering confidence. *Don't mess up*, my brain screamed. *Don't do one thing wrong or your idol will hate you forever.*

The dance began with a sustained *développé* facing away from the audience. I had to extend my leg to the front and then lean backward in a very slow, graceful, controlled movement. One wobble, the slightest falter, and I'd fall on my ass in front of four thousand eyes. My balance depended solely on his skill as a partner. My hands were so sweaty I was afraid my fingers would slip, but his grasp tightened like a vise. He centered me, supported me. In those slow, panicked seconds he sent me a message with his stance, his grip, his balance.

I got you. This is yours to fuck up.

Oh God, I was going to fuck it up. I knew it. A quick turn and I was in his arms. His body was solid relief after balancing so precariously on one toe. *Arabesque... Graceful...graceful, Ashleigh.* His hands were there when I needed them, right where they were supposed to be. He hadn't become the world's premier dancer by being a clod.

He let go and we were free of one another, sweeping the length of the stage only to turn and make lovey eyes at each other. My toe shoes sounded as loud as gunshots. I clasped my hands to my heart in an exaggerated motion I'd seen Mariel do a hundred times. *Arabesque, sweep around.* Oh no, our timing was off. I strained to hear the beats in the music, but all I could focus on was the thumping of my shoes. Somehow Rubio managed to look both impassioned with love and livid with me.

"I'm sorry," I whispered as we came together for an *arabesque penchée.*

"Shut up," he hissed through his teeth.

On that note, we moved into another series of supported and unsupported *attitudes*. He could have let me fall on my ass. I'm sure he wanted to, but he was steady as a rock and I felt overwhelming gratitude.

Fresh on the heels of that trauma—a lift. Oh no, and another and another. I tried to remember what I'd learned in partnering class but I'd been in the corps so long that I wasn't used to being lifted. I wasn't any heavier than Mariel but I probably felt like a ton of bricks to him. He set me down with an illusion of weightlessness but I could feel the effort in his arms. There was nothing to do but smile and pirouette. I accidentally whacked his thigh with my knee during the last turn.

"Asshole," he grunted as I arched into a fish dive. My form was so bad he almost dropped me. Through the next three series of supported pirouettes I was careful not to touch him, but that threw off my balance so his hands had to rescue me, extra effort for him.

Another eye contact moment. Both our smiles were forced. His gaze looked demonic. I skittered downstage left. *Thunk, thunk, thunk, thunk, thunk.* One of the ball guests actually broke character to grimace. *Ignore her, Ashleigh. Pose, smile.* Rubio pulled me into a sweeping *arabesque*. More pirouettes, another lift, fish dive. Somehow I survived it.

"Thank you," I said under my breath as he led me forward for the bow or *reverence*.

His reply came through a tight, fake grin. "Get off the fucking stage."

I waited in the wings while he did his solo, trying to process the emotions I felt. Part of me was giddy to have been partnered by The Great Rubio, while another part of me was devastated by his scorn. I took slow, deep breaths as I watched him perform. His solo was a parade of soaring leaps and intricate steps—and he made it look effortless. I was supposed to follow this? I felt a sense of panic, of being trapped. It was like being strapped into a roller coaster car, heading straight up the tracks even though you'd decided on second thought you didn't want to ride. *Click click click click.*

But I had to ride this one out, especially with Mr. Thibault staring at me from the other side of the stage. Rubio swept through his bows to a rising din of applause. As soon as he exited, I took a deep breath and made my entrance. The applause died. The audience surely realized by now that I wasn't Mariel, the much-loved ballerina who'd danced the previous two acts.

The orchestra launched into my solo, the conductor watching my cues to guide the tempo. I didn't know if I was dancing too slow or too fast. I performed leaps, *attitudes, battements* in my sparkling white costume and crown, mentally ticking through the combinations. I focused on executing each step and tuned out my clopping toes. I nailed the technique out of sheer desperation, and halfway through I realized I was going to survive. After the last racing slew of pirouettes I rose *en pointe* and halted in perfect concordance with the music. No toppling over, no weak ankles. My spine was tempered steel. I smiled joy out of every pore in my body and was rewarded with louder applause this time. I wasn't Mariel, but they recognized my effort.

Rubio came sweeping back and we pranced through the last few lifts. I felt lighter this time, or maybe we were getting used to each other. "*Jesus Cristo,*" he muttered. "You whale." Maybe we weren't getting used to each other. His hands bruised my thighs with a death grip and he bit out something else in Portuguese that I was glad I couldn't understand.

One last pose to this set of dances, and the gracious, swoon-like bow. He held my hand, dipped down into *reverence* like silk. Applause bloomed and rose to a roar of sound. Wow. This was fame, glory, adulation. It wasn't adulation for me, of course. I understood that, but a smile still stretched across my face. Rubio was furious—I could feel it in the rigid set of his arms as he led me offstage. We waited in the wings as the corps, minus one member, moved through the formations of Act Three's final number.

"Where is Mariel?" he spat.

"She got hurt. I had to fill in." I'd lived so long with the injunction against talking to him that I didn't dare say more.

He moved past me, advancing on Mr. Thibault, who'd joined us at the side of the stage. "Why?" he barked, flicking a finger to indicate me. "Why this?"

"There was no one else. It was an issue of time."

"She is..." He threw up his hands as if adequate criticism escaped him. "Terrible balance. She kicked me." He glared at my offending toe shoes. "The noise of her. I will never forget."

"She got through it." Mr. Thibault looked briefly at me, tension hardening his blue eyes.

"Come," Rubio ordered, holding out his hand. "Finale." We joined the company onstage for the closing tableau, and I executed my final graceful *arabesque* as we gazed adoringly at one another. It was all I could do to maintain the necessary eye contact. In the glare of the stage lights his eyes were black as the depths of hell.

The music ended and the audience exploded into applause. I felt more like a side of beef than a ballerina as Rubio hauled me through an endless series of bows. Roses flew at us like projectiles. "This is Mariel's applause," he snapped when I stayed a little too long *en reverence*, "and those are Mariel's flowers."

"They're your flowers too," I said. "They're well deserved." His only response was an irritated snort. For my part, I'd never fake-smiled so long or so hard in my life, but I didn't dare stop, not here at his side with flowers raining down and the spotlight on both of us like some waking dream. *Rubio, Rubio, Rubio, bravo!* The chants came from every corner of the theater while the living legend bowed and flashed his signature megawatt grin. Finally the curtain fell, bringing the performance to a close.

My smiling, princely idol turned on his heel and walked away. *Thank you, Mr. Rubio. I'll never forget this.* I didn't say it. I wasn't contractually allowed to say it.

My fellow corps members surrounded me as Rubio stalked down the backstage hall spouting foreign expletives. He slammed his dressing room door with a resounding crash. "You did a great job, Ash," said my friend Desiree, tucking me against her side. A few other corps dancers congratulated me and made wry comments about my big break, but they were just being polite. I didn't feel happy or celebratory about my performance, especially after Rubio stormed off cursing. I didn't know how I felt. Maybe numb.

Desiree dogged me to the dressing room, where I surrendered Mariel's beautiful costume to a stagehand.

"I can't believe how lucky you are," she sighed.

I made some vague, equivocal sound, throwing on a robe. She parked herself next to me while I removed my makeup. "How did he smell?" she asked. "Did he smell really virile? How did it feel when he smiled at you?"

But he hadn't smiled at me, not once. "It felt great to dance with him," I lied, only because I knew that was what she wanted to hear.

"How did his hands feel? Did they feel strong? Warm?"

I put down my towel and gripped the edge of my carrel. "Des, can I tell you about it later? After I've processed it for a while?"

"Sure. Hey, where are you going?"

I waved a hand at her and ran for the bathroom. She trailed behind me. "Ash, what's wrong?"

I threw open the stall door and leaned over the toilet. Everything in my stomach came up.

"Oh God, hon. You're sick."

I retched again, an awful, grating sound. Tears oozed from my eyes. When I felt able, I reached back to shut the stall door.

"I'll go get help."

"No. Desiree—"

But she was gone and I didn't feel strong enough to stand up yet. I gripped the edge of the seat, unsure if I was crying from sadness, nerves, or throwing up so hard. I heard someone in the bathroom whisper, "She wasn't that bad."

Asshole! Whale! The words, with his accent's inflection, sounded over and over in my ears. I retched again and I think I brought up some of my stomach lining. I felt devastated, completely emptied out. I heard a crisp knock on the stall and Mr. Thibault's voice.

"Ashleigh, when you've finished vomiting, I would like to have a word."

I bunched up a handful of toilet paper and held it to my mouth. "Are you going to fire me?"

"I have no plans to fire you." His French-inflected words were low and reassuring. "You haven't practiced the role of Aurora. I appreciate your attempt. It was adequate, things being what they were."

Out of everything he said, I only heard two words. *Attempt* and *adequate*. It was a kind way of saying my performance sucked. I wiped my mouth again, dried my eyes, flushed the toilet, and opened the stall door. He held out a bottle of blue-tinted sports drink.

I flinched and shook my head.

He had bottled water in his other hand. Like I said, he was a good company director. I opened it and took a drink. "I'm sorry I didn't do better. I'm sorry my shoes were loud. I wasn't prepared."

Mr. Thibault smiled, his brow crinkling behind wire-rimmed glasses. "None of us were prepared. I never saw such a fast costume change."

"How's Mariel?"

"I don't think the injury is as serious as we feared."

"Will they save the flowers for her? From the curtain call?"

He patted my arm. "I'm sure they'd mean more to you than to her. They're collecting them right now to donate at the hospital. Before you leave, run and fetch an armful. Take them home and put them in a vase for a job well done."

I felt a sudden impulse to hug him, and squelched it just as quickly. One did not hug the tall, slim, ultra-reserved ballet director. I didn't believe even Rubio could hug him. I showered quickly, dressed, and packed up my dance bag, but by the time I reached the stage someone had already gathered all the roses. Then I noticed a small pink one shuffled under the edge of the curtain.

I tucked the rose into my bag and headed backstage, past the entourage of pretty women and well-dressed men spilling out of Rubio's dressing room. They weren't dancers. He had a posse. I tried to duck by, only to come face-to-face with The Great One himself.

"Ah, look," he said, opening his arms to me. "My partner. Such beauty and grace."

His voice dripped with sarcasm. I might have cowered. It wasn't my finest moment. I was afraid he'd see the rose in my bag and take me to task over it, maybe call me an asshole again. His friends barely spared me a glance before turning back to their conversations, half in English, half in Portuguese. I opened my mouth to say good night, only to be pulled into the crook of his arm.

"You come to the party, eh, girl? Come on."

I was about to refuse when I glanced into the half-open door of his dressing room. The tall man from backstage was hanging out in there, leaning against the far wall. In a weird, flashback-y way, I remembered the feel of his fingers brushing over my ankles as he untied my shoes. I hadn't really taken it in while it was happening, but I remembered it so vividly now.

I had no business partying in my condition, but it might be the only opportunity to talk to the guy and express my thanks. I let Rubio sweep me along with his group, past the milling eye-contact-restricted dancers, past Mr. Thibault, who raised one finely manicured eyebrow. He seemed to ask, *What on earth are you doing?*

And honestly, I didn't know.

Chapter Two:
Lifestyle

The babble of British-English mixed with Portuguese thickened as the limo crawled downtown streets to the glitzier part of London. Rubio had settled beside me on one of the velvet-upholstered benches, but now he ignored me completely. I couldn't say at that point if he was still my idol. In a sad, sick way I think he was. I made silent excuses for him as I stared down at my hands. My loud shoes had annoyed him. The theater had broken his contract, making him dance with me. I was heavy to lift. He didn't like surprises. I made up a lot of excuses for him because I didn't want to admit my long-time object of adoration was an obnoxious jerk.

Down the opposite bench, the lock-breaker sprawled in his seat, his button-down shirt open at the top, revealing a triangle of bronze, lightly furred chest. He'd been handsome backstage, but here in the muted glow of the limousine he was gorgeous, all long legs and sexy hair. The woman beside him laughed at something he said and pressed her ample cleavage against his arm. I felt a stab of jealousy. Why not me? Where was my ample cleavage, my ability to throw my head back and flirt and bandy words around with a suave, handsome man like Mr. Lock-breaker? I was quiet and awkward, skinny and merely adequate in so many ways.

"Get your bag off me," Rubio said, pushing it over into my lap. "Why you bring your dance bag? You won't need it for the party."

My rose chose that moment to shift inside and poke its petals from the top. I moved my hand to hide it, but not fast enough. He pulled it out. "Ah, bad girl! You stole Mariel's flower."

He was kidding, teasing me, but like an idiot I shook my head.

He crowed with laughter. "Why you even care about flowers?" he asked. "You a romantic, girl? Such a beautiful rose…"

He said it with a mock dramatic flourish, waving the bloom in front of him. He brought it to his nose and took a giddy sniff. Then he opened his mouth, closed his straight white teeth on it, and started ripping the petals out like a rabid dog. I watched, traumatized. Everyone howled at his antics as pink petals flew everywhere. He gnashed a few between his teeth and spit them out with exaggerated coughing and choking sounds.

It was silly to feel upset. It was only a rose, but it was a rose from my Princess Aurora performance. It was special. I had planned to take it home and dry it, frame it between two panes of glass and keep it forever so I could tell my grandkids about the time I danced with The Great Rubio. Or the Not-So-Great Rubio.

He handed me back the half-bent stem, bored with it now. I put the broken stalk in my bag because it was all I had left. I stared out the window, feeling hurt and humiliated even though no one seemed to care about my shredded rose past the thirty seconds or so it had been in his hands.

A moment later he nudged me away so a bosomy, big-mouthed woman with purple-streaked hair could sit beside him. I stared past her knees at the carpet of petals on the limo floor. The reek of her perfume triggered nausea again, not that I had anything else to bring up. The ride came to an end a couple minutes later. Rubio and his friends poured out, heading for a gated, towering white house set back from the curb. Wow, Rubio had an amazing place. The perks of stardom. I dawdled and exited last. Mr. Lock-breaker waited by the door to assist me.

"Thanks," I said, sliding from the car. He pulled me up while I stared at his hands. Big hands. Huge feet. Six-foot-four at least, maybe six-six. I was short so it was hard for me to judge. I looked up at him and his eyes widened in recognition.

"Oh, it's you! I almost didn't recognize you without the…" He gestured toward his face.

"Garish makeup?"

"Yes. And the tutu."

I glanced down at my department store cardigan and faded black leggings. "We aren't allowed to wear them home."

"Too bad," he joked. "They look really comfortable."

Handsome *and* funny. I shouldered my rumpled dance bag even though no one else in this crowd had dance bags. No one else had a scrubbed-clean face and wet black hair pulled up in a messy twist. Might as well do what I'd come to do so I could bail out of here. "I meant to tell you earlier in the dressing room...thank you. I'm sorry I was so short with you."

He shrugged. "You seemed pretty frantic. I understood."

"I don't know how you unlocked that door but I'm glad you knew how to do it."

"I work in security. I know some tricks." He leaned closer to me. "I told you everything would be okay."

Everything was not okay, not to me, but I smiled at him like it was. A male voice that sounded a lot like Rubio's called from the house. "Wilder! Come on, man! What you doing?"

He looked back at me and thrust out his hand. "Liam Wilder. It's nice to meet you."

"Ashleigh Keaton."

His clasp was warm, his handshake firm. His stance was relaxed but his gaze held an intensity that unnerved me. "I'm glad you're here, Ashleigh. It's been too long since I've talked to an American girl." His voice was silken, deep with a slight lilt. He nodded back toward the door. "You ready to go in?"

This incredible specimen was asking me to go in. *Puhleeze, Ash. Forget it.* I backed away from the invitation in his gold-amber eyes. "I better head home. I don't think Mr. Rubio meant for me to come." I looked around for a cab but this was a residential area. Nothing. That would have been too easy. I dug in my bag for my phone.

"You're not staying for the party?"

"I'm not really in the mood. It's been a long, crazy night for me."

His smile widened. "That's exactly why you should stay. You look like you could use a few drinks."

I stopped searching for my phone long enough to grin at him in exasperation. "A few drinks would put me under the table."

Again Rubio called from the house. "*Liii*-am!"

He sighed. "I'm being paged." His voice took on a firm, compulsory note. "Come to the party. Otherwise I'll feel obligated to see you home and we'll both miss out on a lot of fun."

Was he flirting with me? I didn't hang with many guys, and never guys who looked like him. What if I stayed at the party? In fifteen minutes he'd get bored with me and blow me off. The perfect ending to a soul-crushing night. "The thing is, I'm not really a party person."

"There's no pressure to do anything," he said. "It's fine to just watch, or hang out. There are people who come here and never do anything at all."

I thought about Rubio's laughing, chatting posse and found that hard to believe. "I'll bring everyone down, just sitting around doing nothing."

"That's where you're wrong." He jabbed a finger back at the house. "They're a bunch of unapologetic attention whores. They love putting on a show. Come in, have a drink. Otherwise, literally, I'll have to take you home and be all white knight about it."

I swallowed hard. He was definitely flirting. I could picture him as a knight, actually. I could picture him in a suit of armor, rearing back on a horse with a battle cry.

"Um," I said, pushing the knight-on-horseback imagery from my mind. "I don't know."

Rubio yelled out the window again, but Liam ignored him and smiled at me. "The attention whores are getting restless."

"You're not an attention whore?"

He shook his head. "No. I'm more of a watcher type. I observe, I analyze. If I do things, it's not for attention."

His answer captured my interest. If what he said was true, he was a lot like me. Maybe... Maybe this was one of those moments in life, one of those karmic incidents you had to embrace. Maybe the universe had put this man in my path for a reason. Maybe it wasn't coincidence that he'd been there to unlock the dressing room door.

Liam gave a little bow and gestured toward the house. *Take a chance*, said a small voice inside me. *He could be the one.* Even if he wasn't, he was so sinfully, ridiculously beautiful to look at. If he ditched me inside, I'd call a cab and go home. No harm done.

I squared my shoulders and took a deep breath for courage, and followed him through the gates and up the stairs to the heavy wooden door of Rubio's house.

* * * * *

I didn't know what it was about Ruby's dancer friend that turned me on so much. I didn't care. I just wanted to play with her strong, sleek body and fuck her all night. It was partly her cute, bashful thing. I didn't meet a lot of shy girls, but when I did they were almost always closet freaks.

At the same time, she was a dancer, a performer. That intrigued me. I'd gotten an up-close-and-personal look at her trim ankles and sculpted legs when I helped take off her toe shoes. I thought it was pretty cool that she'd stepped in and danced a lead role at the last minute, even if Ruby ranted about her performance afterward. I thought her dancing was great.

Or maybe I just thought her cute little ass was great. Either way.

I took her past the bouncers and into my house, where the night's festivities were in full swing. She hugged her bag to her side until I showed her an out-of-the-way place to stow it. I assured her that no one here stole shit, which was true, because none of my friends were suicidal enough to steal shit in my home.

She looked around at the marble floors and ornate molding. The main floor of the house was one large open space in neutral tones, ivory and white and taupe, with a kitchen set into the corner. I entertained a lot so I had a bunch of leather chairs and couches and fancy end tables and four-foot-high urns my interior designer had picked out. Why did anyone need four-foot-high urns in their home? Fuck if I knew, but I had five or six of the things. There was a tall fireplace at the far end of the room, gleaming staircases in either corner, and an eclectic collection of art decorating the walls. I was proud of my place but I hated the way it echoed when it was empty. So I had parties, probably too many. One every Saturday, at least.

"What are you drinking?" I asked her.

"I better not have anything."

"No?" I got a beer so I wouldn't end up too buzzed. I didn't drink much in general, but with a new prospective play partner, sobriety was a good thing. Ashleigh asked for a Coke. Cute.

I introduced her to a few people, but the majority of my guests were already heading downstairs to the play room. Ashleigh needed more time to get comfortable, judging by the way her gaze darted around the room. I led her over by the fireplace to avoid Trina. Trina was as aggressive as

Ashleigh was shy, and she'd been wanting to bottom to me for a while. Trina didn't do it for me, though. I was ridiculously picky about my submissives, for good reason. When I played, I liked to play hard.

Not that I was going to go balls-to-the-wall with my dancer this evening. The best partners were the ones who made me slow down in the beginning, who revealed desires and vulnerabilities like the petals of an opening flower. Trina would be more like the rose Ruby had ripped up in the limo, a quick shower of petals with a mess left behind. I hated messes.

I turned my back to Trina and focused on Ashleigh.

"So, first things first. Where are you from?" Before she could answer I held up a hand. "Wait. Let me guess. The Midwest."

She gawked. "How did you know?"

"I didn't know. It was a guess, like I said. The city is harder." I pulled at my lower lip, pretending to concentrate. "St. Louis?"

She shook her head.

"Chicago? Milwaukee? No. Cleveland?"

She shook her head again. "You've never heard of the place I'm from."

"Small town?"

"Extremely small."

"What brings a small-town Midwestern girl to London to dance?"

Her eyes drifted over my shoulder to where Trina was doubtless giving her the *get lost* glare. She looked back at me. "Rubio brought me here."

Damn, she was Rubio's? I hadn't gotten that message at all.

"I mean," she said at my confused look, "I came here because he was dancing here, even though it was a step back professionally. I had more options in New York, but I wanted... I decided I needed to be here."

Her hair was so pretty and dark, the color of blackberries. "Do you regret it?" I asked.

"What?"

"Taking a step back?"

She thought about that for a moment. "I don't think so. Being part of City Ballet is more important to me than advancing through the ranks of some lesser company."

"What about tonight?"

If she held her glass any tighter she was going to break it. "What do you mean?"

"I mean, tonight you had a chance in the spotlight. Did it make you question whether you made the right choice?"

She took a deep sip of her drink as Trina moved into my line of sight, standing so her breasts were displayed to maximum effect. I ignored her, concentrating on my thoughtful ballerina. "No, I never question," she said. "Honestly, I didn't start dancing out of some desire to become a star. I just enjoy doing it. My body enjoys doing it. I came here to work with Fernando Rubio and Yves Thibault, no matter the cost and sacrifice. It seemed worth it to me."

My body enjoys doing it. That's all I heard. I thought very intently about how my body would enjoy dragging her down to my play room, cuffing her to a spanking bench, and going to town on her marvelous ass. I wondered if she would be loud or quiet, if she'd want lots of sex with her play or if she'd prefer to concentrate on impact and pain. I wondered if she had any naughty piercings or tattoos hidden under her non-descript black clothes.

Oh shit, she'd asked me a question. "I'm sorry," I said, pretending I couldn't hear her over the music.

"Where are you from?" she asked a little louder. "And how did you end up over here?"

"Business brought me here. I'm from California, by way of Cuba and Ireland."

She blinked, looking up from her drink. "How does that happen?"

I moved a little closer, out of Trina's line of sight. "My mother was from Cuba and my father was a Dublin lad." She laughed when I said *Dublin* with an Irish accent. "I grew up just outside L.A. so, obviously, I've got a lot going on."

"Obviously." She had such a pretty smile. I hoped she was one of those girls who liked sex with her BDSM, because there were a lot of things I wanted to do to that mouth. I put my beer on a nearby table. It was time to move things along.

"So," I asked in my best *I'm-a-trustworthy-dominant* voice. "How long have you been in the lifestyle?"

"The lifestyle?" She blinked at me. "Forever, I guess. But I've only gotten serious about it the last couple years. When I left New York and decided to come here."

"I see." *Forever* sounded promising. I wondered what she meant by getting serious in the last couple years. Was she into edgier play? Hardcore slavery? I hoped she didn't belong to some other dom, some online motherfucker or something. Only one way to find out, and that was to make my move. "Can I be honest with you?" I said, very close to her ear.

She nodded. "Uh, sure."

"There's something about you that intrigues me. Your eyes, or your body. I like little girls."

Shit, that sounded so wrong. She made a squicked face.

"No, I mean, petite women," I amended. "Women who are small enough to manhandle a bit. Just for fun, of course." I slid a hand up her arm, a light, seductive touch. "Ruby's never invited one of his ballet friends here before. You fascinate me."

She stood very still beneath my full-force invitation stare. Her expression wasn't welcoming. I didn't know if it was due to shyness or disinterest.

"Where's Rubio?" she asked, looking around. Shit. Disinterest.

"Downstairs in the play room, I imagine."

"This house has a play room?"

This house? Didn't she realize this was my house? And why did she think everyone came here to party? I had a basement full of BDSM furniture and equipment—and soundproof walls.

"Want to check it out?" I asked. I'll admit it, I was proud of the play room I'd put together. Maybe it would change her mind about hooking up with me. I took the glass out of her hand, set it on the table next to my beer. "No drinks allowed down there."

I held out a hand and her fingers closed around mine. Trina scowled and finally seemed to accept defeat as Ashleigh and I crossed the main room and headed for the stairs. There were tons of other guys here who'd be happy to play with Trina, but Ashleigh didn't seem to be generating much interest. Well, she was wearing black, shapeless clothes, but her eyes... Her eyes were so wide and pretty, light blue or maybe gray with dark lashes. There was something in the way she moved too, some sensual or ethereal quality that made me want to touch her and hold her in my arms. And she was an American. Midwestern girls. Heh.

To the play room then. I walked ahead of her down the stairs and into the darker, lower floor of the house. We were enveloped by the warm glow of candles and the beautifully erotic sounds of pleasure. Rhythmic thuds accompanied shrieks and muffled screams.

"There's Ruby," I said, pointing to a rack near the corner, where his curvy, screeching partner writhed in chains. Rubio was naked, his cock hard and jutting out. He sidled up to his play partner and rubbed his junk between her ass cheeks. I grinned as he ran a groping hand down between her legs and ripped off her g-string, then stepped back and accepted a whip from a nearby assistant. The implement was perhaps three feet long, black braided leather. I turned to Ashleigh, to make some crack about whether she still wanted to talk to him.

My words died at the look on her face.

"Oh my God," she whispered. Her eyes were wide, her cheeks pale. She looked around the play room in shock.

"What's wrong?"

"Nothing." She tried to act cool and nonchalant, but I could tell this wasn't what she'd expected. In that terrible moment, I realized I'd misunderstood every one of her signals, realized that we'd been speaking two different languages, fellow Americans or not. Ashleigh Keaton was vanilla, and she was completely freaked out by what she was seeing. I looked over my shoulder and tried to imagine the play room through her eyes. Grasping, whipping, screams and laughter, naked people bound in all kinds of positions on all kinds of equipment, all of them going out of their minds.

I got her attention with light fingers placed at the small of her back. "Hey, you want to go back upstairs? Finish those drinks?"

She nodded. "It's hot down here, isn't it?"

We started up the stairs. Her back was ramrod straight and her mouth curved in a fake smile. I wanted to tell her it was all right, that she didn't have to pretend to be okay with all the hedonism she'd just seen. I'd exposed her—nonconsensually—to some pretty hardcore shit. "Go sit on the couch," I said when we reached the first floor. "I'll be right back."

I stormed down the stairs and did something I never allowed anyone else to do at my place. I interrupted a scene in progress. I grabbed Ruby from behind just before he drew back to throw a whip stroke.

"You fucking prick," I said, taking his feet from under him and pinning him to the floor. "Why'd you invite her here?"

His play partner grinned over her shoulder, her back a canvas of red-pink whip bites. Ruby grinned too, like this was some kind of joke. "I did it for fun," he said. "She was standing there in the hall and I

26

brought her. What, she's not kinky?" He tried to throw me off but I wasn't having it.

"I thought you knew her," I said. "I thought she was a friend of yours, that she was in the lifestyle."

"Oops. No. I never see her before tonight." He took in my embarrassment, my disappointment in one perceptive glance. "You like her, huh? I hate to tell you, she's a shitty dancer."

I wanted to punch the snark right out of him but I'd tried it before and it never worked. I let him go instead and apologized to his partner for interrupting. My energy would be better spent debriefing Ashleigh, if she hadn't already fled my place and called the cops. But no, she was sitting on the couch like I'd told her. Like a good sub...only she wasn't a sub.

I got a fresh Coke for her on the way over. She shifted to make room for me.

"Here," I said, thrusting it into her hands like a peace offering. *I'm sorry, Ashleigh. Of all people, I know what's seen can't be unseen.*

"So..." I leaned forward to catch her gaze. "I gather you ended up here by mistake."

"I— Well—" She shrugged. "Yes."

"When I asked you about the lifestyle you thought I was talking about...?"

"Ballet."

"And when I mentioned a play room, you thought..."

"Pool tables, maybe. Pacman." She rubbed her forehead. "I'm disappointed about the Pacman."

And I'm disappointed that I won't get to play with you tonight.

I didn't dare tell her that. She might decide to give it a go, and there was nothing worse than breaking in a vanilla girl. Well, I assumed there wasn't. I hadn't been with a vanilla girl in...well...ever. I clicked into concerned-friend mode. "I'm sorry. I wouldn't have taken you down there if I'd known you weren't into the lifestyle. Honestly, I thought you were a sub. I mean absolutely no offense by that."

"Uh..." She put down her Coke and rubbed her forehead again. "I'm not even sure what lifestyle you're talking about. Or why I might be offended. What's a sub?"

Sigh. "A sub is someone who submits. A submissive likes to surrender and let another person take over. There's, you know..." I paused, spreading my fingers. "A dominant counterpart. Who does things to the sub."

"Like Rubio?"

"Yes, like Rubio, but Ruby's a top, not a dominant."

"Oh, I see," she said, even though I could tell she didn't see at all. How to condense everything down into understandable sound bites?

"See, tops are mostly into the sensation and pleasure of it. They play casually, for fun. Dominants are more serious about roles and rules, and usually more into the power exchange."

"Power exchange?" she asked, wrinkling her nose.

"It's complicated to explain." And pointless, at the end of it. I watched her luscious, non-kinky lips while she took a drink. What a waste of those lips. I frowned and scratched the back of my neck. "I'm afraid our mutual friend may have brought you here to be cruel."

She looked around and I wondered what she was thinking. There was almost no one left in the room now. A few people idled near the top of the stairs. From below, I heard Rubio's voice, Rubio's laugh, along with more screaming. "He enjoys being cruel," I said quietly. "Perhaps you already knew that."

She poked at the ice in her drink. "Tonight on stage, he called me a whale and an asshole."

"He did what?" She looked so sad. I wanted to kiss her. *Vanilla. She's vanilla.*

I leaned back from her while she stared at me, biting her lip. "Do all dominants...or tops, or whatever...enjoy being cruel?" she asked.

"I wouldn't say that. Nothing in this lifestyle is ever all or nothing."

"Do you enjoy being cruel?"

"Jesus. That's a really loaded question."

"It's a yes or no question."

"And one I'd rather not answer if nothing's going to happen between us."

If nothing's going to happen? Apparently some part of me was still holding out hope, most likely my half-erect cock. Could something happen between us? I stared at her shapely, strong legs beside mine. I wanted to hold her and touch her. I groaned inwardly. "It's too bad you're not a sub."

"A guy spanked me once, but..."

"But?"

"It was nothing like the stuff going on down in that dungeon."

28

"Play room."

"Play room, whatever."

A shrill scream carried up from below, followed by Ruby's shouts of encouragement. Ashleigh looked deeply disturbed. "Is that safe, what he's doing to her?"

"Believe me, she likes when Ruby pushes her limits. They're perfectly matched in that way. They're lucky." *Unlike us.* "Did you enjoy it?" I asked to draw her attention from the screaming. "Getting spanked that one time?"

"Not really. But I didn't like the guy very much."

"Why? Because he was a dominant?"

She shook her head. "No, because he had bad breath and he always tried too hard. And he...he wasn't a dominant, I don't think. He was kind of a pussy."

I stifled a smile. "Dominants are never pussies. No, wait. Sometimes they are."

"But not you." We both started laughing, at the awkwardness, the hopelessness of me and her.

"I don't like people hurting me," she said, as if that settled things between us. "And you like to hurt people."

I turned my head a little in rebuttal. "Yes and no."

"So you're not a 'dominant' or whatever?"

"I am. But whether I want to hurt someone depends on the circumstances. It depends on wants and needs, observation and negotiations. Consent. It's hard to explain to someone who's never exchanged power. I assumed Ruby invited you here because you were in the lifestyle, or because you were curious."

"Oh."

I was determined not to utter the words but they spilled out anyway. "Are you curious? At all?"

She looked around the room and then fixed her eyes on some point in the middle of my chest. "Honestly—"

"There you are!" We both turned as Rubio swaggered over. "Why are you still dressed, girl?" He grabbed Ashleigh in a hug and rubbed his dick against her stomach. His posse gathered around in a half circle, laughing and gawking as he pressed his lips against the side of her neck.

"Let her go," I snarled.

"But she's my Sleeping Beauty." He turned, playing to his pals. "Don't you think we make a perfect pair?" They snickered as he forced her into a clumsy turn. "Her balance isn't too great. I hold her here—" His hand closed over one of her breasts. "And here." I lunged for him as his other hand clamped hard on her crotch. "And then we do the lift!" He swung her into the air just out of my reach, then slid her down the front of his body, groping her again.

I pulled her away from him and held her against me. "You're an asshole."

"No more so than you," Rubio shot back.

His friends chortled as music throbbed in the background. Ashleigh pushed away from me and stalked toward her bag beside the couch. Her hair had tumbled down from her careless twist and flew back from her shoulders as she moved. Graceful, angry ballet dancer.

I went after her. "Ashleigh, wait."

"No. I'm gonna go."

I sucked at playing the white knight. I didn't deserve her or her pretty blackberry hair, or her kissable, shy lips. I corralled her in my arms and led her to Rubio. "Tell her you're sorry," I said to him. He made a face and balked. I felt dangerous anger. "Apologize or leave my house."

Ashleigh turned to stare at me. I should have told her it was my house from the beginning. I should have been honest about what I wanted from her outside on the curb, so none of this would have happened.

Rubio squirmed, scratching his balls. He knew I was a hair's breadth from losing my shit, and he knew me well enough to know it would be a bad scene. "I was just playing, being silly." He appealed to Ashleigh. "You knew I was only joking. Yes, girl?"

"Apologize like you mean it. Use her name, you dumb fuck."

"I'm sorry, okay?" Rubio threw up his hands. "I am very, very sorry... What's your name?"

I hissed, but Ruby protested, "I don't know her. I never saw her before today."

Ashleigh wiggled away from me. "I'll find my way out."

I followed, pushing past Trina, who never fucking gave up. "Ashleigh, please stop."

She halted and spun to face me. "Why didn't you tell me this was your house? Your party?"

"I don't know. I didn't want to freak you out."

"Oh, because everything else here isn't freaky enough." She rolled her eyes and walked away. I didn't want her to leave this way, storming out in a huff. I didn't want her to leave at all, damn it. I wanted her to transform into what I'd fantasized she was, but that seemed unlikely to happen.

"Will you at least accept a ride home?" I asked, catching her at the door.

"I'll take a cab."

"I'm calling my driver. He's just down the street." I pulled out my phone and paged Travis, vaulting after Ashleigh when she slipped outside.

"I'll walk," she said. "I'll find a cab along the way."

I stepped into her path. "No, you won't." I stared into her eyes, very intensely, very directly. *Liam Wilder, lifestyle dominant.* "I won't let you walk. Tell my driver where you live and he'll take you right to your doorstep. It's the least I can do."

Travis eased up to the curb but I kept my eyes locked on hers. I'd call her a cab if I had to, but she wasn't going to walk.

"Okay," she finally said.

"Okay. Or you could go out for a drink with me," I heard myself say. "We could talk. You could calm down and we could talk about…whatever." *What?*

As soon as the words were out I wished I had them back again. She wanted to say yes. I could see it in her eyes, but then she looked up at the house and something in those eyes shut down.

"Thanks for the ride home," she said. "I appreciate it."

I stood at the curb and watched the car until it turned the corner. She watched out the back window too, pretty, shy Ashleigh Keaton, who wasn't kinky. Of *course* she wasn't.

Fuck me.

Chapter Three:
Dangerous

I danced the afternoon matinee the next day, Sunday, in the back of the corps again. One of the principal ballerinas filled in for Mariel, who was out for the season to rest and rehab. Suzanne did a great job as Princess Aurora. I don't think Rubio whispered an expletive to her once.

I was over Rubio, though, over the trauma of our brief, ill-fated partnership. I convinced myself I didn't care about losing him as an idol, about learning the truth of how awful he really was. I was determined not to care, but then he passed me backstage and looked right through me, and well, I cried a little. I cried squeezed-off, secret tears because I didn't want my friends to notice. I pretended I had makeup in my eyes, poked and prodded at the corners until the emotion passed. That's what I got for trying to make eye contact with The Great Rubio when it was against the rules.

I tuned out the post-performance chatter in the dressing rooms and begged off when a group of friends invited me to dinner. My Sunday nights were sacred. After I showered I put on worn, comfy sweats, gathered my laundry and shoes and left the theater without speaking to anyone. I had the rest of the day off, and all of Monday and Tuesday. The free time stretched before me, the greatest amount of time before my next class or rehearsal. I normally loved that feeling of freedom, but today I was grieving. For what? For Rubio's attention? He was an asshole. For Liam Wilder?

Maybe a little for Liam Wilder, who lived in a big house and threw parties with cavorting, naked people who enjoyed BDSM. When he'd invited me downstairs to his "play room" I was thinking video games, pool tables, maybe a trampoline. That would have been awesome. *Yeah, this is not a play room. This is a sex dungeon. Not the same thing, Liam Wilder. Jesus Christ, these people are naked. And what—what the fuck are they—?*

I knew about BDSM, vaguely. I'd even let a guy spank me once when he was trying to get me in the mood. It hadn't worked. I had a complicated relationship with sex, unlike Liam Wilder, who threw parties in his personal home dungeon. He must have thought I liked to do those kind of things, maybe even imagined doing them with me. After I left, maybe he'd hooked up with that hovering woman who'd shadowed him all night, whose boobs and sex appeal put mine to shame. A guy like him could probably have any woman he wanted.

I told myself I didn't care, that I'd dodged a bullet with Liam Wilder, but I knew I'd always wonder what might have been if I was his type. If I was a *sub*. If I'd taken him up on his drinks invitation. Well, it was too late now.

I kept my head down all the way home, not wanting to draw anyone's attention. I sought solace in invisibility like I always did. About halfway there it started to rain, making big dots on my heather-gray hoodie and tee shirt. The sky darkened and a full storm swept in, complete with lightning and thunder. I stalked on, letting the rain soak me while everyone around me ducked into shops and under awnings. By the time I got to my building I was drenched down to my bra and panties. My hair plastered in wet streaks across my face as a freak gust of wind propelled me through the building door and into the cement stairwell that led to my apartment.

"Fuck you," I muttered as the door crashed closed behind me. How dare the wind slam the door on me? It felt like another insult, not as bad as Rubio ignoring me, but close. I pushed the hair back from my eyes, shouldered my dance bag, and started up the stairs to the third floor. I turned the corner and was digging for my keys when the shape of a man moved out from the shadows.

"Oh my God!" I wasn't sure if I screamed it or mouthed it. My heart kicked into overdrive and my hands came out to ward off the intruder. It took a few seconds to process the fact that the intruder was Liam, looking taller and more imposing than ever in the claustrophobic hallway of my low-rent building.

"What are you doing here?" I asked. My breath huffed out in a gasp. "How did you know this was my place?"

He blinked, staring at the front of my soaked hoodie. "My driver has an excellent memory."

Oh yes, the silent, uniformed driver. He'd walked me right to this door, and it hadn't occurred to me that in his insistence to do so, Liam would know where I lived.

"You're soaked," he said, taking a step closer. He was in jeans, the expensive, weathered kind that cling to a man's body in all the right places. He'd paired them with a sage pullover and an equally weathered, caramel-colored leather jacket that probably cost two months of my dancer's salary. He was completely dry.

I clutched my sodden bag closer to my side. "Why aren't you wet? How long have you been here?"

"Not long. I would have called but I didn't have your number. I wanted to bring you this." He held out a single rose. "It's from last night's performance, to replace the one Rubio…ate."

I stared at it, awed by his thoughtfulness. The rose was velvety pale pink, just like the other one. "Where did you get it? I mean, how—"

"The flowers were still in the back, in a box. Yves was very helpful."

"You know Yves?"

"I know Yves." He frowned. "And Ruby too, although it pains me sometimes to call him a friend."

I took the flower and held it to my nose, swallowing back emotion as I stared at him. He'd gone to the theater to find a replacement rose for me. It was the nicest thing anyone had done for me in months. "Thank you," I said. "I felt bad about the other one."

"I know. I felt bad about a lot of things that happened yesterday. I made Ruby apologize to you, but I should have apologized too." He ran a hand through his hair and looked at the floor, then back at me. "I should have listened when you said you weren't a party person. I should have read your signals better. I should have seen you home myself after I kicked Ruby out. I should have done a lot of things I didn't do. I guess my main concern is whether you're okay."

It was my turn to talk. To say I was perfectly fine, that it was no big deal. I wanted to say all the right words but they wouldn't come. I could feel my face breaking. I didn't want to start bawling in front of him—I was so ugly when I cried. No graceful, pretty tears here. More like awful, miserable, emotional-weirdo tears, so it was really, really important that I get away from him. I clutched the rose to my chest and searched for my keys.

"Ashleigh."

"What?" My voice sounded thick and weird. Maybe he wouldn't notice since he didn't know me that well. And why the fuck were keys as elusive as unicorns when you needed to find them in your purse? I saw him reach out in my peripheral vision, and then he took my face in one of his hands, just gripped it between thumb and fingers. Our gazes met and locked. His eyes were liquid amber, even more beautiful than I remembered. He came close, so close to me, and I realized he was going to kiss me. He tilted my face and brushed his lips across mine with the barest hint of pressure.

It wasn't a lucid decision—*okay, I'm going to cry now*—but as his lips moved over mine, the tears that had been building up all day spilled out of my eyes. My face scrunched up and my mouth trembled uncontrollably. He brushed his fingers through the wet trails, nuzzling me, dropping warm, light kisses on my cheeks. "Don't," he whispered. "Don't cry."

I didn't want to, but I couldn't seem to stop. I touched his waist when he drew back, my silent plea for him to continue even if I was falling apart in his arms. He answered with a deeper kiss, a skillful, attentive exploration that had my fingers tightening against the softness of his sweater. While he nibbled and teased and slipped his tongue between my teeth, he slid a hand back to cradle my nape, then he walked me backward, pressing me into the corner of my door.

His kiss transformed then, from soft and gentle to something else. I tensed, fearful of the sudden change in his demeanor. He stood like a wall in front of me, his muscular, sculpted physique pressed against my much smaller body. He didn't paw at me. If he was rough or clumsy, I could have pulled away and said, *ugh, this asshole*, and regained control of the situation, but he was the opposite of clumsy. Each touch of his lips, his tongue, ignited a response in me. His fingers twisted in my hair, his tugs causing pain but something pleasurable too.

His arm slid around my waist and tightened in a hard clasp, and in that moment something inside me awakened, some part of me that I'd stuffed down and smothered for years. That thing—want, desire—stirred to life with a starving vengeance. I returned his kisses with uncharacteristic abandon, and the harder I kissed him, the tighter his grip became. He had me cornered, but I found I liked being cornered by him. I wanted to be trapped and restrained against the wall and kissed into submission. I'd avoided passion and sex for years because I feared force, because I was afraid to give up control, but somehow he took all of that out of the equation and made me *want him*.

The more he kissed me the harder I cried, because it felt so good and so scary, and because each kiss was changing me a little inside. I grasped his arm with my free hand, clutching the rose stem in the other. I had to stop him before I lost myself, before bad memories and bad feelings turned this dream into a nightmare. I forced myself to stop responding, to push him away. His kiss gentled and his arm at my waist loosened. He drew back—only slightly—and pressed his forehead to mine.

"What is it?" His thumb caressed my cheek. "What's wrong?"

You brought me a rose. You kissed me. He wouldn't understand why that called for tears. He didn't understand anything. Instead I said, "I had a terrible day," which was mostly true.

He rubbed behind one of my ears, a light touch that made my breath shudder. "What was so terrible about it?"

"I don't know. I felt bad about last night."

"Bad in what way?"

I swallowed and turned my face from him. I shivered with cold, or anxiety, or perhaps the shock of his proximity. He drew away with a soft sound. "Where are your keys? Let's go inside and get you out of those wet clothes."

I understood from his words exactly what he wanted me to understand. *Let's go inside and fuck on some horizontal surface.* His gaze communicated it, along with the pitch of his voice and his gentle but possessive grasp on my arm. I understood—but old fears die hard. I wanted him but I didn't. I fumbled around in my bag, my fingers useless and heavy with nerves.

Waking Kiss

"I can't— I—" *I can't do this. I'm embarrassed. I'm afraid.* "I can't
let you in. My apartment is a mess."

His hand stroked up and down my arm. He watched me with far too
much attention. "Are you okay?"

I shrugged and flailed around in my bag for the keys. If I didn't
come up with them soon I was going to fling the whole damn thing
against the wall. "I'm fine."

He took it from me and within five seconds came up with the keys.

"Thank you," I said. "I'm sorry. I have to go change." I could really
feel the cold now that he'd let go of me. I stared at the middle of his
chest, wondering how to turn the closeness of this moment into a
goodbye. The idea of it started my bottom lip trembling again. Why not
me? Why couldn't I have this man and the things he offered? Why
couldn't I be different?

"Ashleigh." He said it light and slow as I stared at his lips. "Let me
come in, just until you feel better. We don't have to do anything."

I leaned back against the door, gripping the knob. "The thing is..."

"The thing is...?"

"I— I don't usually let anyone in my apartment."

"Why, what's in there?" he asked in a bemused voice. "Piles of dead
bodies?"

No, I thought. *Just one dead body. My own.* I turned back to the
door, opened the lock and edged myself inside. I intended to close it but
something in the way he stood there stopped me.

"I don't want you to come in," I said. "I'm just... I'm just too
weird."

He stepped forward, right into my apartment, and smiled at me.
"Too normal, I'd worry about. Too weird is perfectly fine."

* * * * *

I'd been with a lot of women in my life. I'd seen a lot of strange
things over the course of my adventures, but one thing I'd never seen
was a blanket fort in a grown woman's apartment.

At first we both ignored it. She put the rose on her kitchen counter
and ducked into the bathroom to change out of her wet clothes. She
emerged in a tiny tee and form-fitting sweatpants that I wanted to peel
right back off her, but then she pulled on a drapey cardigan that

37

swallowed her whole. She faced me with a look that said *you're still here?* She offered me coffee and I accepted. I didn't want to leave.

While the coffee brewed, she showed me around her studio apartment. *Here's the kitchenette. Here's the bathroom. Here's the closet. Here's the window.* There was no bed. Believe me, I looked.

But there was a blanket fort. I was having second thoughts about what I was doing here.

I'd come here to fuck her, in case you hadn't figured that out yet. Kinky or not, her graceful, unique ballet body attracted me. I wanted to grope her all over and work out my curiosities with some prolonged and athletic sex. I wanted to pull her glossy hair, pinch her small, pert breasts. After I fucked her, I could stop wondering what it would feel like to fuck her. I could walk out of here in the morning and sleep a lot better tomorrow night.

That was the plan. I just hadn't expected a blanket fort in the corner.

But she ignored it and drank coffee, and so did I.

"Where did you say you were from again?" I asked.

She half-smiled at me. "I didn't, remember? You guessed."

"But you never actually told me."

She stared down into her coffee cup. "I grew up in Wyoming. In cattle country." She made a face and looked back up at me. "To this day, I can't stand to eat beef. I don't like anything from a cow."

I stared at her. "No steak? Hamburgers? Roast?"

She shook her head firmly. "I don't eat beef."

I pointed at the cream she'd set out for our coffee. "That comes from a cow."

"It's not the same."

"Leather jackets?" I asked. I'd slung mine over the back of my chair.

"I don't care about those so much. It's the food that makes me sick. The taste." She shook herself a little. "There's a smell in Eastern Wyoming that makes me sick."

"One nice thing about London—there aren't a bunch of cattle ranches stinking up the place."

That made her smile. A little.

"Tell me about your security job," she said, stirring her coffee. "And your talent for opening locks."

"I only work on the right side of the law, I promise. I own a personal service agency with my dad. Ironclad Solutions—discreet personnel for the rich and famous. Bodyguards, PAs, travel security. Business is pretty good." That was an understatement, but she'd seen my house. She knew. I was past apologizing for my money. I gave away as much as I could and enjoyed my life with the rest of it, although I felt a pang of guilt sitting in her tiny, bed-less apartment.

"Bodyguards, huh?" She glanced at my well-developed biceps. "Is it ever dangerous?"

"Sometimes. It depends on the situation. Sometimes it's just escorting a client around an unfamiliar city, or babysitting celebrity kids. When Rubio travels, he uses our agency's protection to ensure his...personal space. We serve high profile clients who need security and management, but in most cases it's not a life or death thing."

"In most cases?" She shook her head. "Wow."

"Are you worried about me?" I teased. "About my agents? Believe me, they're well trained. Like you, only a different set of talents."

"Is that how you found out about Rubio's...uh...proclivities? You had to follow him into some sex club?"

"Not me, no. My employees probably have, a time or two. But I knew Rubio in BDSM circles before he ever used Ironclad." I fell silent a moment, my gaze trailing off over her shoulder to her slouching blanket fort. "Can I ask you a personal question, Ashleigh? Where is your bed?"

A flush crept across her cheeks. She thought for long moments, like she was putting together some big, enlightening answer. I waited patiently to be enlightened, but in the end all she said was, "I don't have one."

I leaned closer and whispered, "Do you sleep in the fort?"

She got the same look on her face that she had when Rubio pulled the rose out of her bag. Embarrassment, guilt. A bit of horror.

"If you do," I said a little louder, "I'll pretty much think it's the coolest thing I've ever heard. I guess it's possible that you sleep on your couch, but the fort would be so much edgier."

"It's not edgy," she said, fighting a smile. "I can explain it, actually."

"I'm all ears."

She looked over at the pile of blankets. "I grew up in a super religious family. My mom and dad always threatened me about the devil. They said he wanted to possess me, that he was always watching me and making me do bad things." She bit a fingernail and looked back at me.

"At some point, I got this idea that the devil lived under my bed. After that, I couldn't stand to be in one."

This was all kinds of fucked up. "So you don't have a bed because a devil might be under it?"

"I just don't like beds. Anything could be under them. Devils, monsters. Spiders."

Your parents, I added silently. I glanced at her fort. "So, blankets have devil-repelling qualities?"

She shrugged. "A devil hasn't gotten me yet."

Ha. You're sitting across from one.

"Can I go inside?" I asked, standing and crossing to check out the sprawling structure. The sides were propped up with hinged gymnastics mats, one red, one blue. A white and yellow floral quilt spanned the top, along with a couple smaller fleece blankets. There was only one pathway to crawl in.

She hustled over and got in my way. "I don't think it's big enough for you."

I leaned down, peering through the opening. There were more blankets and a small mattress inside. "Oh, I could squeeze in there, but then there wouldn't be much room for you."

She stared at me. She wasn't blushing anymore but had paled almost to the color of her quilt. "You really want to go in?"

"Yes."

She let out a breath, and her hands opened and closed. She had to know what I wanted to do to her under those blankets. I didn't think I'd made much of a secret of it, especially after the way I'd kissed her out in the hall. She looked like she wanted to invite me in, but was too embarrassed—or nervous—to do it.

I straightened, giving her some space, and walked around the sides like an appraiser doing an inspection. "We can make it a little bigger, can't we?" I knelt down and started pushing the mats to the side. At first I worked alone on the renovations, then she joined me, lifting the quilt and repositioning the fleece blankets to fit the new, wider layout of her fort...or her bed.

God knew I didn't deserve to go into her safe place, but when she slipped through the curtain of the entrance I dropped down and crawled in behind her. I'd come here to fuck Ashleigh Keaton. There was no way in hell I was staying out.

Chapter Four:
Rough

I couldn't remember if I made blanket forts like this when I was a kid. I did know that I'd never been afraid of the devil. I'd been at home with darkness and violence from an early age, but this was not a violent space. There were flowers printed on the quilt-roof and more blankets to cover the inside walls. We both squeezed onto the narrow mattress. I was a clumsy, ill-fitting intruder but she accommodated me as best she could.

Once we'd situated ourselves, she reached above her head to a small shelf behind the pillow. She clicked on one of those LED lights made to look like a candle. It flickered and everything. I could see the glow of it in her eyes. Then I noticed the photos of Rubio pinned to the sides of the blankets.

"Oh, no," I said. "Some devils got in."

She reached out to touch one of the pictures. "I used to really like him."

"Do you still like him? If you say yes, I'll lose a little respect for you. Just keeping it real."

"I don't, I guess. He almost made me cry today at the theater."

My teasing mood darkened. "What did he do to you?"

"He ignored me. He's always ignored me but…" She let out a long, shuddering breath. "Today it made me feel pretty bad."

"Down they come." I started yanking them loose, being careful not to mess up the blankets. "You have a pen or a marker? We could draw faces on them."

She laughed, even though it was a miserable laugh. She took a scrapbook from under her pillow and pulled a pen out of it. The scrapbook was bursting with clippings and photos of Rubio.

I forgot all about drawing faces and stared. I could tell the scrapbook had been put together with care and looked at a lot. I'd sensed last night that she was sad about Ruby, disillusioned, maybe even heartbroken, but in that scrapbook I saw the physical manifestation of all she had lost. "I'm taking this book," I said gently. "Throwing it on a bonfire or something. Because I know him, and he doesn't deserve this. No."

"But he's a legend. He inspired me." She gave me a pleading look. "Where am I going to get my inspiration now?"

I tapped her chest. "How about here? You have a thousand times more heart than him. I bet you could dance a thousand times better than him if you tried."

I could tell she thought I was talking shit. Maybe I was. I hunched over and flung the photos and scrapbook out the doorway of the fort. I didn't want anything of Ruby's in there while I was finessing my way between her thighs. I lay back down and looked around the soft walls. "This place is growing on me, Ashleigh. It's very cool."

She smiled, a sweet, shy smile that made my cock jump. "Your house is cooler."

"It is not." I touched the tip of the fake candle. "I like your retro lighting."

"I used to have real retro lighting, real candles, but fleece isn't as fire retardant as you'd think."

"Oh God."

"No, there wasn't a fire. Well, just a small one."

I put a finger to her lips. "Hush. I'll have nightmares. I'll have to buy you a real bed for my peace of mind."

She rolled a little away from me. "I wouldn't sleep in it."

"You just need to find a bed that feels as safe as this place," I said, pulling her back toward me. "They make them, you know. Beds with curtains and canopies."

I was surprised how much I wanted her to feel safe. I didn't kiss her anymore but I left my hand where it was, cradled near her waist.

"Tell me about you and Rubio," I said. "What happened onstage to make him so angry with you?"

She shook her head. "Every bad thing happened. Everything that could possibly go wrong."

"I didn't notice anything bad from the theater seats. You should have told him to fuck himself."

She stared at me like I was speaking a foreign language. "I'm not allowed to talk to him. I'm not supposed to make eye contact with him. None of us are."

"You're kidding."

"No, I'm not."

I took her hand and brushed my fingertips against her palm. "I thought he was only an asshole at my parties. I didn't realize he was an asshole at work too."

"It's hard to believe, isn't it? When his dancing is so inspired?"

I ran my fingers up her arm, pulling her closer. She stiffened but she didn't do anything to stop me. "Sometimes it seems that talent is given indiscriminately," I said. "Money too. Sometimes it seems that the least deserving people have it." I fell squarely into that group. I curled a bit of her black hair around my thumb. I wanted this girl, entitled asshole that I was, but I didn't deserve her. "For the record, I think your dancing is inspired."

She turned her head to avoid my gaze, and her hair pulled around my finger. I might have released it then but I didn't. Our bodies were so close, her slender one aligned to my solid frame. I was ridiculously erect. I'd never raped a woman and I never would, but if I could have, I would have ripped off her tight little sweatpants and buried myself to the hilt inside her.

In the midst of my lurid fantasies, she reached back and switched off the flickering candle. We were plunged into blanket-covered darkness. Was it an invitation? I let go of her hair and glanced around, and then I saw the stars above us. Not stars—flowers. The flowers of Ashleigh's quilt were luminescent, irregular dots of light over our heads. She was so close beside me. I felt warm and amorous, and utterly detached from the world. It was just me and Ashleigh in our dark universe with flowers for stars hanging over our heads.

"Can I ask you something?" she said.

"Anything."

"At your party, when you said you wanted to play with me…"

I went very still. *Don't ask. Don't ask what I wanted to do to you.* Ashleigh's delicate nature spurred my vilest fantasies. Force and restraint, torment and invasion. I wanted to fix her to a rack and flog her until she was sobbing, and then pillage every one of her holes until she begged me to stop. Then I wanted to lock her away where no one could touch her, where I wouldn't even let her touch herself. I wanted to take away her safety and make her long for her mats and blankets. I wanted to clamp her and plug her and chain her and train her to grovel at my feet. When she was completely broken, when her will and soul were mine, then I'd give her mats and blankets back. That's what I wanted.

I didn't know how we got to that place from this little enclave of flower-stars. It didn't even seem worth it to try.

"If I played with you," I said instead, "what would you want me to do? It's dark," I added when she didn't answer right away. "That means you can say whatever you want. What are your fantasies?"

"I don't..." She sounded breathless. "I don't have any."

"Tell me. I won't judge you."

She turned toward me in the darkness. I could barely make out her features. "You're the dominant, aren't you? Why don't you tell me?"

"Tell you what to fantasize about? That's pretty hardcore submission, but we can start there if you like." My fingers threaded through hers. "Now, what kind of fantasies should I force on you? It can't be anything too scary. You're new at this."

"You're making fun of me."

"I'm playing with you," I corrected her. "Forced fantasies. Very hot. But if you're not into that, let's try again. What would you like me to do?"

"I don't know. Maybe...make me do things. Tie me up?" She sounded uncertain, like she needed me to judge her answer.

"Okay." My fingers slipped from hers to circle her wrist. "That first 'B' in BDSM stands for bondage. Being tied up or restrained is a common kinky fantasy. Do you think you'd like that?"

"I don't know. I thought the dominant decided everything in BDSM. I didn't think you'd give me so many choices."

"Does that appeal to you? Not having choices?"

She shook her head. "No. Yes. I don't know."

"Let's try it out and see." It only took me a second to grab both her hands and trap them over her head. "Struggle for me. Try to get away."

She pulled with her arms first. For a small woman she had surprising strength, but she was no match for a guy my size. When she couldn't escape my hands she used her body to try to wrench away. Before she started using her legs I cinched them under one of mine. She really started fighting then and while I let her squirm around a little, she couldn't get very far. The more she struggled, the harder I got. "Okay, enough," I said when I reached critical mass. "Be still."

She was breathing fast and so was I. I leaned down and kissed her, and she smiled against my lips. "You're strong," she said when we parted.

"So are you." My eyes were used to the darkness now. My leg was still slung over hers and my erection was about two inches from her hip. I desperately wanted to jab it between her legs but she was jittery and I doubted she'd welcome it. This seduction was turning out to be a marathon, not a sprint. I sighed and scooted back from her. "That's physical bondage. Pretty exciting, right? Especially when you're having other things done to you at the same time. There's also mental bondage, which can get even more complex."

She traced her wrists where I'd held them. "Is that like, messing with people's minds?"

"In a way. It's like saying, I'm going to touch you wherever I want and you're not allowed to move a muscle. Or working your partner into a frenzy but not allowing her to come until you say she can. I like to set up situations where my sub has to use her own willpower. Her desire to submit. To obey."

She was silent a moment. "That's really intense."

"Some people play really intensely. Dominants, submissives, masters, slaves, even ponies and toys and fucksluts. You name it. Other people just top and bottom for pleasure and call it a day."

"Like Rubio?"

"Yes. He's too impulsive and selfish to get into the lifestyle-role stuff. But he's a responsible top. He finds like-minded people and makes sure they enjoy themselves." I shrugged. "Different strokes."

"You're not like that." It wasn't a question.

I sighed and rubbed my forehead. "No, I'm not like that. I prefer to engage with my partners on a deeper level."

"You fall in love with them?"

Whoa. How did she leap from D/s to love? *Because she's vanilla, idiot.* "Love is... Love is another thing. People who exchange power don't have to be in love. Or love isn't...you know...central to the proceedings."

"Oh." I could see the wheels turning in her head, I just didn't know which direction they were going. "So you could..." She paused and tilted her chin. "So you could develop a deep BDSM relationship with someone, play with them, have sex with them, and still have no strings attached?"

I couldn't tell from her tone what she thought of that. "Some people do it that way," I hedged. "A lot of people in my social group. Rubio does it that way."

"What about you?"

"Yes," I admitted. "I prefer it that way. I prefer to play with no strings attached." I hoped she wouldn't ask me why, or expect me to spill out explanations and excuses.

She didn't. What she said was, "Can you do that with me?"

Jesus Christ. Could I do that with her? I'd be glad to. *Should* I do that with her? Probably not. I'd never tried to "turn" a girl before, never attempted to bring a vanilla girl into the fold. I didn't know if I had the skill or the patience, and more importantly, I didn't know if she had the strength to stand up to me if I pushed her too fast.

But she was so, so beautiful. I looked up at the stars that were really flowers and thought about vanillas who were really kinky folks waiting to be born. I wanted her, ached for her here in our little haven from the world. I wanted her sex and her submission, her kinky innocence and nervous fidgeting. Her beautiful full lips and her soft voice and everything that made her different and compelling to me.

"Yes," I said. "I could do that with you. But it might not turn out the way you expect."

"I hope it doesn't," she said under her breath. I should have taken a moment to figure out what she meant by that, but I was busy drawing her willing, hot body into my arms. I was glad now I'd brought that rose over here. Genius idea, although it wasn't from the performance, just a florist. She'd never know. I was glad I'd managed to soothe her nerves and seduce her into this crazy little fort. As I kissed her, I traced up the contours of her back to her nape and pulled her closer into my embrace. I wanted to feel her skin against mine. I pushed her sweater back and eased it off. My cock was so hard it was about to bust through my jeans.

"Liam," she whispered.

I stopped and inclined my head to hers. "Yes, baby?"

"I want you to do what you did before." She bit her lip. Our faces were inches away. "I want you to hold me so I can't get away."

Hot excitement arced through me. I didn't see us developing any serious D/s thing in the future, but if holding her down got me inside her faster, I'd play along. "Give me your hands."

I took them in mine and pinned her with my chest. She lifted her hips against me, sending jolts of arousal to my balls and cock. I used one hand to trap her wrists over her head, and the other to caress down over her lithe body. Her hips were curvy but firm and when I moved, they moved. I licked her neck and nibbled at her jaw, daydreaming about the things I could do to her if she was as kinky as me.

"I love the way you feel, baby." I kissed her lips again, delving inside to taste more of her hesitation, her curiosity. My hands tightened on her wrists. "I'm going to touch you everywhere, wherever I want, and you won't have a choice in the matter. We've already figured out that you can't get away from me."

She murmured something sweet and acquiescent against my mouth while I moved my hand lower, over her form-fitting sweatpants to the vee between her legs. "I wonder how you like to be touched," I said. "I wonder if you like to be fucked hard or soft. There are so many things to discover about you." I cupped her mons, gave it a little squeeze.

She tensed. "Don't let go of me."

"I won't."

She made lovely, aching sounds while I groped her through her pants. My hand could practically span her pelvis, she was that petite. There was a novelty to our disparate sizes that excited me. I felt like a giant around her and I had to subdue the urge to be more brutal than she could take. I thought I'd die if I couldn't feel her and taste her. I dipped a few fingers into the edge of her waistband and when she didn't stop me, I slid my whole hand in there, inching down to discover hot, welcoming wetness. She made a sobbing sound as I traced a finger over her clit. "Do you like that, baby? Does it feel good?"

"Please... Don't talk to me. Just... Please do something to me. Anything."

I lowered myself on top of her, letting her feel every inch of my cock through the barrier of my jeans. I unbuttoned my fly with one hand and wrapped the other in her hair, nuzzling my lips against her cheek. "I want you," I said, even though I wasn't supposed to talk. Who was the dominant, anyway? I tore myself away from her to tug a condom from my pocket.

Turning back, I pinned her wrists over her head and sucked in a breath as she struggled under me. Struggling females drove me wild, they always had, and this one was exceptionally strong. With a growl I reached down and pulled at one of her thighs so I could burrow between her legs. I gritted my teeth against the agony of my desire, palming the condom so I'd have it close at hand. I didn't want to rush this, but I couldn't hold out much longer.

"No."

I almost didn't hear it at first, my blood was rushing so hard in my veins. But then she said it again, louder. "No, please." Her wrists struggled with sudden fervor against my palm.

"What's wrong?"

"Please get off me. I'm going to be sick if you don't let me up."

I moved and she vaulted up and through the mats and blankets and everything. I sat blinking in the sudden light as one of the mats fell against my shoulder. The bathroom door slammed and I heard awful noises. Coughing. Retching?

I stood and refastened my jeans, pocketing the condom. Maybe it was a virus. Food poisoning. Overexcitement? She was crying, I could hear it from across the room.

I righted her decimated fort in a haze of shock. What had happened? Was it my fault? I thought back over the things I'd done. Up until the last few moments she'd seemed totally into it. Could extreme arousal cause nausea? That wouldn't explain the sobbing. I went to the bathroom door and checked the knob. Locked. I could pop it in a heartbeat but she wasn't acting like she wanted my company.

"Ashleigh?" I rattled the doorknob. "What can I do to help?"

There was silence for a moment, then she flushed the toilet. "I'm all right. I just need a minute."

I spread my fingers against the door. "I'll be out here, okay? If there's anything you need."

"I don't need anything. You can go."

There wasn't a chance of me leaving, not while she was so distraught. "Can you open the door so we're not talking through it?"

Silence. After a few minutes I walked back over to the hastily-restored fort and twitched at the blankets and quilts. I wanted to crawl inside and turn the flickering candle on, or maybe look up at the glow-in-the-dark flowers again. Mostly I wanted to go back in time about half an hour and do something to make this all turn out differently.

I should never have tried to seduce her. She was way too sweet. I'd come over here with my false rose to fuck her and now she was crying in the bathroom. I looked over at the pink bloom, at my jacket thrown over her chair. I could have visited ten other women to get my rocks off, no seduction necessary. It was going to take a long time to get over the image of her busting through those blankets to get away from me.

I walked back over to the bathroom door. "Ashleigh, please. There must be something I can do."

"You can leave," she said, her voice muffled by paint and pasteboard. "I'm not trying to be rude. I just want to be alone right now. I'm really...really not feeling well. I'm sorry."

"Please don't apologize. Come out and say goodbye to me and I'll leave, if that's what you want. Or rather than apologize, just explain to me—"

The door whipped open. She stood there gripping the frame, her eyes and nose red with tears. "You're right. You deserve an explanation but I don't know how to explain it to you. It wasn't your fault."

Then whose fault was it? She was fine until I climbed on top of her. I felt a little sick to my stomach thinking about what might make her react that way. I swallowed hard, wanting to touch her and comfort her. Afraid to reach out for fear she'd start retching again. "What happened to you?" I asked.

She shook her head. "Don't."

"Ashleigh—"

She shut the door in my face and clicked the lock. I pressed my forehead to the wood. Who had hurt this girl so bad that sex made her freak out like this? Whoever it was, I wanted to plant a fist in his face.

"Ash?" I tapped on the door one last time. I spoke low, not really expecting her to answer. "Is there anything I can do?"

Silence. Complete and utter silence as if she'd ceased to breathe. I walked back across the room and twitched her blankets into place one last time. Floral quilts would forevermore be the stuff of nightmares for me. I grabbed my jacket, scrawled my number on the notepad on her counter, and called out to her from the door. "Okay, I'm leaving. I'm going to close the door behind me and then I'm going to stand outside until I hear you lock it. My number is on the counter if you need me." I thought a minute. "Please call, at least to let me know you're okay."

I opened her door and stepped through and closed it hard behind me so she would hear. About a minute later I heard the deadbolt turn, so, so quietly.

I never should have come. Sometimes you showed up to fuck a girl, and things didn't end up at all the way you hoped.

Chapter Five:
Help

Liam fixed my bed before he left. He placed my mats and blankets almost exactly as they'd been before he arrived. His rose laid on my counter, so beautiful, and next to it, his name and number, which was beautiful too. He'd been concerned. He hadn't wanted to leave me. I put my fingers over my lips, remembering his kisses, his thrilling touches, the silken way he spoke. He'd blame himself for what happened, but my issues with sex and intimacy were long-held and deeply entrenched. He couldn't have understood what I felt when he climbed on top of me. My father's weight. My father's bulk.

No, I couldn't think about it. I'd be sick again and I'd been sick enough.

I paced my apartment, angry, confused, disappointed. Defeated. If anyone could have fixed me, it would have been Liam Wilder. I thought this time it would be different, especially with the BDSM factor. For a while his force and confidence had worked and I felt swept away in the moment. But then…no. No, no, no, no, *no*.

I knew I should call to let Liam know I was okay, but I didn't want the questions. This had happened five or six times already, when I'd thought, *this* is the one who can make it work for me. *This* is the guy who can make me forget the rasping breath and heavy weight, and the raw, grinding pain between my legs.

If Liam Wilder couldn't do it, then that was it for me. It was time to give up and accept my lonely, solitary life. At least I'd have work to fill my days. Well, until I got too old to dance. I'd have my friends and acquaintances, and my comfortable apartment where I felt safe.

I would have to forget everything that had happened between us. I'd have to forget him, as hard as that would be. I was a dancer. I was used to enduring pain and denying myself things I wanted. I ripped the paper with his number on it into a million pieces so I wouldn't be tempted to call, then I took a shower and crawled into my flowered retreat to sleep, but once I was under there, I couldn't stop thinking about him. After a couple hours I pulled off the blankets, kicked down the mats, and slept on the couch.

Monday and Tuesday were hard, but I woke up Wednesday feeling better. I was focused again, or maybe just resigned. I took class at ten, concentrating on each step, blocking out any thoughts of Liam. I performed that night better than I'd performed since *Sleeping Beauty* began. When I watched the prince kiss Princess Aurora to life, I reminded myself it was only a fairy tale. I felt no regrets about Liam, no desire for Rubio to notice me or acknowledge me backstage. In fact, I was relieved he didn't. My world was restored to normalcy and I felt peaceful and calm. I walked home with a group of friends who lived on my block, looking forward to some tea and a good book.

My peaceful mood evaporated, though, the second I opened my door. At some point during the time I was away, a large bed had materialized in the middle of my apartment. Not just a bed, but a gorgeous work of art. What had Liam said to me? *You just need to find a bed that feels as safe as this place. They make them, you know.*

Oh my God.

The headboard and footboard were designed to look like bunches of woven-together branches, while each of the four posts resembled tree trunks. The trunks reached to the ceiling and supported a canopy of more intertwined iron branches. Light silk curtains hung down from the canopy, enclosing the space inside. The effect was undeniably, overwhelmingly protective, like a hideaway in a forest bower. I'd seen a bed like this before, on the set of *Sleeping Beauty*. It was similar to the one the princess slept in as she waited for the prince to awaken her, but that bed was made of painted plywood and aluminum, constructed by set designers. This bed was real, for sleeping in. The mattress and box spring were still in plastic, with two sets of new queen-size sheets and fluffy down pillows propped against the decorative headboard.

I walked closer, and then I paused, my eyes darting around the room. There was only one way this bed could be standing here in all its magnificence. Liam had broken into my apartment. I knew from experience he had no problem with locks. He'd come here when he knew I'd be performing at the theater, and probably brought delivery people too. Was he still here, spying on me from the bathroom or some hidden corner? I did a quick, nervous inventory of all the possible hiding places, but no, he was gone.

I traced the etching on the vine-like footboard, trying to quiet the alarm bells in my head. It wasn't normal to break into someone's place and leave a bed like this without asking. He barely knew me. Or did he? He'd kissed me and held me in my blanket shelter, and talked to me about intimate, personal things. About bondage, and dominance and submission. Hell, I'd pretty much begged him to fuck me. I'd also cried in front of him—twice. So maybe he thought he knew me well enough to make a grand gesture like this, or maybe it was an apology for upsetting me. Maybe he was so rich he was out of touch with what was considered normal.

I climbed onto the mattress and lay back, luxuriating in the soft pillow top, and inspected the pair of plastic-encased sheets. Eight-hundred thread-count luxury in crisp white Egyptian cotton. There was a note card slipped down inside one of the packages with a *W* embossed on the front. I pulled it out and flipped it open.

This bed will keep the devils away.

That was it. Nothing else, no signature, no elaboration. I stared at the silk curtains enveloping me, and the detailed, twisting ironwork of the frame. This was the most beautiful, extravagant gift I'd ever received—but it came with a bunch of uncomfortable memories, memories of his hands, his lips, his arms around me. My psychotic breakdown and his freaked-out retreat. He would expect me to call him and gush over this, but I didn't have his number anymore, and I couldn't find his house if I tried. He'd probably wait all evening for me to contact him in gratitude. What would he think when I didn't?

He'd think I wasn't worth this beautiful gift. Maybe he'd come and take it back as stealthily as he'd delivered it.

No, he wouldn't. Before he did that, he'd come over here to see why I didn't call. What if he came tonight? I made up my new bed and changed into my pajamas, and crawled behind the curtains in a mild panic. For two, three, four nights I waited for him to knock, or just pop the lock and come in, but he didn't come.

All that came were vivid dreams of Liam at my bedside, leaning down to kiss me in my forest bower like Sleeping Beauty's prince.

* * * * *

I didn't buy the bed with any ulterior motives. It was a gift, freely given, but I was disappointed not to hear from her that night. Or the next night. Or the next. Maybe she was pissed that I'd broken into her place, but I'd only wanted to surprise her and cheer her up. She must have thought I was a world-class psychopath.

It was probably for the best. She was a damaged, delicate person. She needed help, not extended sessions of kinky sex. I used company resources to look into her past, to see if there was something I could do, some anonymous way I could help her. I was 99.9 percent sure it was God-fearing daddy who'd hurt her so badly. What I didn't know was what he'd done to her or how long the abuse had gone on. It had been sexual in nature; that seemed an obvious assumption. The rest of it, I didn't know.

What I did know with one hundred percent accuracy was that I had to let go of my fantasies about sleeping with Ashleigh. She had a lot of issues to take care of before she'd reach a place where we could connect. She wasn't even into BDSM. *Well, not yet anyway...*

No. I couldn't daydream about breaking her to the lifestyle. I didn't have the time or the skill to fix a woman as messed up as her. Oh, there were messed-up chicks in the scene, sure, and sensitive, white-knight guys who loved to try to heal them. I'd never been one of those guys.

December arrived, *Sleeping Beauty* became *Nutcracker*, and she traded her poufy ball gown for a sleek snow-fairy tutu. I told myself that if she really wasn't okay, she couldn't dance as beautifully as she did, but I knew that for a lie. If she was anything like Ruby, the more miserable she was, the harder she pushed herself. As for me, I continued to struggle with an unholy urge to possess her. I ached for her slim, muscular body as I lay alone masturbating in bed. I distracted myself with work and parties and girls whose names I couldn't remember an hour after they left.

By mid-December, I weakened in my resolve to leave Ashleigh alone. I started going backstage after shows to hang with Ruby, but really to catch glimpses of her. I'd see her for mere seconds before she disappeared into a hallway or dressing room. It felt like spying, or stalking, but she never saw me because she never looked up and around her. She was a ghost in a white tutu, and after she changed, a fragile dancer in black sweats. She seemed to have friends...that reassured me...but she never left to go anywhere with them after the shows. She hid in the corps dressing room and left the theater long after the other dancers. I asked Ruby what she was doing and he shrugged.

"She work on her shoes, maybe. Sewing ribbons. Maybe she practice or work out. Whatever. Why you care?"

He'd long ago sensed my interest in Ashleigh, and it annoyed him. "Why don't you care?" I said back. "You danced with her once."

"Once." He looked up from his phone. "Once was enough."

"I didn't think she was that bad."

He grimaced so hard his face looked like a raisin. "Her technique...not so bad. But her shoes were awful. And she had this smile." He made a fake, bright pseudo-smile. "It freaked me out."

"You do that same smile onstage, brother."

He grinned at his phone, snapped a picture of himself and showed it to me. "This smile, yes?"

"No, that's the smile you use when you're about to be an asshole to a woman. I'm talking about this smile."

I did his oily-ballet-prince smile and he took a picture of me. "I send that to everyone," he said, nodding. "You look like an idiot." He pushed more buttons on his phone, scratched his chest and leaned back in his chair. "Ah, Brandi. She text me sexy photos. You care if I play with Brandi?"

I wasn't going to admit that I couldn't remember who Brandi was. "Go for it, if you want."

He waved his phone. "She's texting me looking for you. Maybe I send her that idiot-looking picture."

I could tell by his grin that he'd already done it. "When are you going to settle down with a respectable girl?" I asked as he showed me Brandi's extremely explicit photos. Oh yes. I remembered her now, based on her labial piercings.

"Soon as you do," he retorted. "You're much worse than me. Maybe you settle down with Ashleigh, eh?" He snickered, flicked through Brandi's photos a few more times, then threw down his phone and picked up his bag. "You call Brandi if you like. Tonight I'm busy."

"With who?"

"With life. Why you still here, Li-am? Why you hanging out at an empty ballet theater? Call Brandi, have fun. You break her in and maybe next time I'll join you and we do her together." He illustrated his suggestion with an interlaced mélange of poking fingers.

Brandi had already been broken in by most of the guys in our group. Both of us knew that. He left without a backward glance while I sprawled in his dressing room's plush recliner. *Why you still here?* I knew the answer to that question, but I wasn't a person Ashleigh needed in her life right now. I was a player, a pig, and frequently an asshole. She had emotional issues which I may or may not have exacerbated. Those intertwined branches on her bed were there to keep me out, not in.

I thought about Brandi, and Michelle, and Raine, and Bubbles, and all the other girls I could fuck any time with no repercussions and no stress. I would probably call Brandi later. Probably.

Why was Ashleigh hanging out at the theater all hours of the night?

I vaulted out of Ruby's recliner and paced his room once or twice. Then, against my better judgment, I headed down the deserted corridor toward the corps dressing rooms.

* * * * *

Since my *Sleeping Beauty* debacle with Rubio, I'd become obsessed with doctoring my toe shoes. I'd developed an exacting ritual to prepare each pair so I had three or four ready to go at any given moment. First I sanded down the satin tips of the toes for traction, then bent the shank in a slow and careful process. I sewed my elastics and laces on at a specific angle and only then did I go to work on the boxes, alternately kneading them and banging them on the dressing room floor until they lost their echoing "knock." *Bang, bang, bang.*

My practice behavior grew equally compulsive. Dance was all I had now; I had to make it count. I came early to class and warmed up twice as long as my fellow artists. I grimaced through each exercise, needing every movement to be flawless. When I had a bad class, I fell into a funk for hours. Performances were a little easier to deal with, since adrenaline distracted me from all but the worst faults. *Bang.*

But after the performances, I had to go home. *Bang, bang, bang, bang.*

I didn't know if it was the bed that kept Liam Wilder on my mind or if I was just cursed to never forget him. I stopped mid-bang, running my fingers over the gathers of satin under the toe. My memories of him were so vivid, I could practically smell the scent of his cologne.

I lifted the shoe to bang it again but then I sensed someone behind me. I whipped around, preparing to scream. A hand clamped over my mouth as I stared into wide amber eyes.

I'm not proud of it, but I clocked him on the side of the head with the shoe. Hard. He let go of my mouth to rub the spot.

"Jesus, Ash. Hello to you too."

He was dressed for the theater in a tailored charcoal coat and navy blue tie, his hair cinched back in a loose ponytail. He looked amazing.

"You gave me a heart attack," I said, trying to hide my physical reaction to his hotness. "Why are you here?"

"I heard banging. I thought someone was being beaten to death."

I twisted the satin ribbons around my fingers. He was smiling, teasing. Beautiful. All I could think of was the way we'd left things, my abrupt meltdown and the fact that I hadn't called him in all this time. "I'm working on my shoes," I said. "Did you come to see Rubio dance?"

"Not Rubio. This pretty ballerina I know." He advanced a step for every step I retreated. "How have you been, Ashleigh?"

I crossed my arms over my chest as he stalked me into the corner by the costume racks. "I've been really busy. I'm— I— I have classes, and sews to shoe—I mean, shoes to sew— and…spring rehearsals, and…a lot of dance stuff."

"A lot of dance stuff, huh?"

I considered running away from him, but what was he doing to me? Just talking in a soft, friendly voice. Handsoming me to death. A lock of hair had escaped his ponytail and curled over the shoulders of his expertly fitted suit. The quality of the garment reminded me of the sheets he'd bought, the sheets I'd slept on for weeks now.

"Uh, thanks," I said, flushing. "Thank you for the bed."

"You're welcome."

"I'm sorry I didn't call and thank you before now. I lost your number." I took another step back, squelching the urge to hide behind a row of tulle skirts hanging to the right of me. "The bed's so beautiful, but…you know…you didn't have to do that."

"I wanted to." He gave me an apologetic smile. "I'm sorry I broke into your place to deliver it. I wanted to surprise you."

"You definitely surprised me." *Yes, and broke the goddamn law.* I looked up at him from under my lashes. "If you did it because you felt guilty about that night—"

"It was a gift. It had nothing to do with anything except me wanting to give you a bed without any devils under it."

His words were easy and affectionate, but the memories were killing me. "I can't sleep with you," I blurted out. "I'm sorry. I can't."

"You don't have to sleep with me."

"But the bed—"

"Was a gift."

"If you want to take it back, that's okay. I'll understand. You should give it to someone else. A woman…who's…you know, really sexy and deserving and—"

"Tell me about your life in Cowskull."

His words hit me like a backhand slap. I decided to pretend I hadn't heard them. "Well, I'm pretty busy," I said, looking past him. "I should get back to my shoes."

"Your shoes can wait a minute." He leaned down until I met his concerned gaze. "I have to assume something really bad happened to you."

I stared at him. "How do you know about Cowskull?"

"It took about thirty seconds to do an Internet search for East Wyoming, cattle ranches, and Keaton. Your father's a piece of work, by the way. Monopolizing land, forcing bankruptcies—"

"I don't give a fuck about my father." I shot a wild look at the door as he boxed me further into the corner. "Why are you spying on me? You don't have anything better to do?"

"I have lots of better things to do, but I worried after I left your apartment. I've been worrying for a while now."

"Why is it any of your business?"

"Because I think someone hurt you," he said, reaching out to steady me. "I think it was your father. I don't want to upset you, but—"

"It doesn't matter anymore, any of that stuff. I've moved past it, way past it, and I hate that you—" I caught my breath and pushed away from him. "I hate that you're throwing all this in my face."

He followed me to the other side of the room, cutting me off at the door. "I'm not throwing anything in your face. I'm angry for you. I want to help you, if there's anything I can do."

I backed away from him, throwing up my hands. "Help me? How could you possibly help me?"

"I could arrange for your father to die in an 'accident.'" He emphasized the air quotes. "I'm thinking a bull stampede would be sufficiently gory and painful."

I couldn't tell if he was serious. Part of me wanted him to be serious but another part of me couldn't believe he'd pried into my private history. I felt exposed, and I hated feeling exposed.

"None of this is your fucking business." My voice wavered so I didn't sound as assertive as I'd hoped. "I don't want your help. I don't want your concern. I didn't even want your goddamn bed and now I'm stuck with it."

"Ashleigh—"

I brushed off his hand and slipped past him to get my bag. "Just, please...leave me alone. That's the best way to help me." The more he stared at me with his pitying, sensitive look the more livid I felt. Before I could duck out the door, he stepped in front of me, blocking my way.

"Have you thought about bringing charges against him? Or, I don't know? Confronting him and—"

"What? Doing whatever it takes to get past it so *we* can eventually have sex? So you can get what *you* want? It's not happening."

"This isn't about what I want. It's about this pain you're living with."

He was so beautiful. So disgustingly beautiful. I stood there, frozen, rigid, unable to reach out to him even though I wanted to.

"It's not fair for you to carry all this around," he said quietly. "It's not."

"I don't carry anything around. I've done counseling and all that shit. I'm fine this way. I avoid sex by choice."

"Choice? Is that what it was when you ran to the bathroom to throw up? Are you really happy?"

Was I really happy? What a nasty fucking question to ask someone like me. I shoved against the hard planes of his stomach. "Leave me alone. Stay out of my life and stop spying on me and looking at me like that. I won't fuck you, *ever*." I punctuated each word with another shove against the wall of his chest. When I tried to cut around him to make my escape, my feet got tangled in his. We fell to the floor and he landed so hard on top of me that I lost my breath.

No, not this again. Not Cowskull and struggling and sickening force and fear twisting in my stomach. I kicked at him and beat on his shoulders. He was talking, trying to calm me, but I didn't hear anything. I needed him off me. "I hate you. I hate you," I shrieked, finally managing to squirm from under him.

I shot to my feet, shouldered my bag and raced out the dressing room door. I ran down the hall and he trailed after me, step for step. I wasn't running from him, not really. I was running from myself, from daddy and all the scary things he did to me. The backstage was empty, the studios dark, and I felt like a little girl again, one step ahead of the devil.

"Leave me alone!" I screamed over my shoulder.

"Ashleigh, stop."

"Go away! Go!" I was rapidly falling apart. He reached for my arm.

"Please—I'm worried about you. You're distraught."

"Because of you. You brought everything back," I yelled, turning to glare at him. "With your rose and your kisses, and your spying and your questions." I swung my bag at him. "I don't want you around me. I want you to leave me alone!"

He ducked back, holding out his hands. "I'll leave you alone, I swear. I'm only worried now about how you're getting home."

"I'll take her home."

We both turned at the sound of the deep, accent-tinged voice. Rubio stood in the hallway behind us, a towel slung over his shoulder. "You go," he said to Liam. He looked at me, his expression strangely cloaked. "You, wait in the studio."

Rubio frightened me almost as much as Liam, standing there in the hallway in ragged sweats, a mere human rather than a god. They both terrified me, but at the moment Rubio seemed the lesser risk. I turned and took off, hugging my bag against me. I could hear them talking in low, sharp voices as I hurried toward the lighted room at the end of the corridor.

I stopped inside the door of the studio, trying to calm my thoughts as well as my racing heart. I felt attacked, ambushed. Liam knew too much about me, too many shameful secrets. He said he wanted to help me, but didn't he realize he was ripping open old scars?

After a few minutes I heard the door to the street slam, heard Rubio's steps echoing down the hall as he returned. We hadn't been face-to-face since our dance debacle and the party afterward. I waited for a sneer, for derision, but none came. He held out a hand that didn't quite touch me, and studied me with his dark eyes.

"You okay?"

I nodded, flushing under his gaze. In the dim light he looked uncharacteristically somber. He stared at me a moment longer, then crossed the room to pick up his bag.

"Where you live at?" he asked.

He really intended to take me home? I gawked as he slung his bag over his shoulder and returned to me. "Hey, girl. You know how to talk?" He snapped his fingers in front of my face. "Where you live? It's late."

"I—I can get home myself," I finally managed. "I'm only four blocks from here. Is he gone?"

Rubio made a face. "He's gone for now. Come. We walk and talk."

"You don't have to—"

"I said come!" He gestured imperiously toward the door.

From his belligerent stance, he wasn't taking no for an answer. We made our way down the corridor toward the stage door and out onto the pavement. It was late, almost midnight, and not many people were around. How bizarre, to walk down a quiet London street shoulder to shoulder with my idol. Well, former idol. He'd said we would walk and talk, so I assumed contractual silence wasn't required.

"Uh, thank you," I said. "Thanks for breaking things up back there."

"Don't thank me," he snapped in reply. "How you get mixed up with him? He is not a good person."

"I thought he was your friend."

"He is." Rubio guided me out of the way of a passing group as we stopped to wait for a light. "That doesn't mean he's a good guy for someone like you. You like hard sex? Without love? That's all he can offer."

I dug in my bag for my jacket, feeling lost and a bit annoyed. Fernando Rubio hadn't bothered to look down his nose at me in weeks, and now he was lecturing me for seeing his friend?

"I don't want him to offer me anything," I said.

The light changed and Rubio stalked into the street, pulling me with him. "You aren't even in the lifestyle," he said. "Liam does sex and

BDSM, and that's all. He is not, how do you say…relationship material. He only plays with certain kind of women."

"What kind of women?" I asked, even though I knew.

"Slutty women," Rubio said. "Masochist women. Usually crazy women." He made the universal cuckoo sign, pointing to his temple. "He gives them so much good sex, it messes with their minds. He is an expert at this. He upset you tonight and I think he probably enjoyed this. You sleeping with him?"

"No!"

"Then why is he always at the theater looking for you?" He gave me a dire look. "You know how many women he had sex with last week? At least five. Every night, new woman. He wants to have sex with you and when he does, you won't know what hit you. He will sex you into oblivion and then he'll leave you when he gets bored."

"Isn't that what all guys do?" I asked a little testily. "Isn't that what you do at those parties? Have sex with whoever you want, all the time?"

"Yes, with girls who are into that. Slutty girls. Sometimes we share women. Sometimes we have sex with three or four women together, orgies. We play and go home, happy girls, happy partners. Just fun and sex."

I blushed, remembering Rubio naked, wielding a whip. "Why are you telling me this?" I asked.

"Because you are not a slut. You are not an orgy girl."

"How do you know?"

He gave an exaggerated snort. "I think by this point in my life I can recognize who is down with things. Listen, girl. You seem nice. Normal. Liam Wilder is not normal. He is…how do you say? Playboy. Player. He is rough and does a lot of sex. Many partners."

I could imagine Liam being like that, as much as it repulsed me. I'd sensed his dangerous, sexy edge from the start. Hell, I'd personally experienced it. He'd held me down in my apartment…controlled me…excited me, at least until I bailed out of the whole thing.

"And listen," Rubio added. "He does not have girlfriends. In five years I've known him, not one girlfriend."

"I never said I wanted to be his girlfriend. I was trying to get away from him. I've been avoiding him ever since that…that party you took me to."

He turned his collar up against a cold gust of wind. "That stupid party. I don't know why you went when you are not even kinky."

My irritation bloomed into outright anger. "I went because you dragged me there. You dragged me into the limo by my arm."

He wasn't even listening to me. He shook his head, his face taut with disapproval. "So many sexier girls already in BDSM lifestyle. I don't know why he chose you to mess around with."

"Don't worry about it," I said with a frown. "I can handle myself."

"Yes, you handled yourself great tonight. So much shrieking. I try to rehearse, but—" He launched into a mocking imitation of my meltdown.

"What were you rehearsing?" I asked, interrupting him. "So late at night, all alone?"

"Nothing." He waved a hand. "I choreograph something for the summer tour. But..." He shrugged. "I don't know if it will come together."

"I didn't know you did choreography."

"I don't. Forget it. Where is your place? You said four blocks."

"It's right up there." I pointed at the door of my building. "I can walk from here."

We both stopped on the corner. The Great Rubio scuffed at the pavement and looked awkward. "Don't tell anyone about the choreography."

Hmm. A weapon to use against him, if I wanted to. "I won't tell," I said, "as long as you promise to never call anyone else a whale."

His eyes went wide. "I didn't call you a whale. I only thought it to myself."

"No, you said it. I heard you."

He pouted, glaring at me. "Well, you felt like a whale. Heavier than a whale. Like lifting two whales, one in each hand."

"Okay. I'm telling everyone tomorrow morning about your choreography."

We faced one another with arms crossed over our chests, then his arch look relaxed into a smile. He laughed—not the maniacal laughter from the party, but light, bemused laughter that almost sounded friendly. "You keep your mouth shut, girl, whoever you are."

"Ashleigh."

"Ash-*lee*. Okay." We stared at each other a long moment before he turned his shoulder away. "Okay. Go home and sleep. Ash-lee, yes? I try to remember this time, your name. I'm not making any promises."

I nodded, understanding him completely. The contract still applied, but this once, he'd let things slide. He'd saved me and warned me, educated me about Liam Wilder, but from now on, I was on my own. If Liam was bad enough for someone like Rubio to warn me against...

I let myself into my building, wondering how Liam had ferreted out the truth about my dad. A wild guess? An assumption? Or more in-depth investigative work? *I want to help you, if there's anything I can do.* Could he help me? The main thing Rubio had stressed to me was something I already knew. Liam was powerfully talented in the arena of sex.

Maybe he could help me.

No. No, that was ridiculous. There was absolutely no way I was spending any more time around Liam Wilder. I wasn't *that* desperate. Not yet anyway.

Or maybe I was.

Chapter Six:
Crazy

He gives them so much good sex, it messes with their minds. He is an expert at this.

I couldn't stop thinking of Rubio's words, couldn't stop thinking crazy, unreasonable thoughts about me and Liam, and how he might...help me.

For me, emotion and sex had been tangled up in negativity for so long that I put all of it away. I did without it, but I wasn't really happy like that. I didn't want to be asexual and frigid. I wanted to have a healthy sex life and a close relationship with someone of the opposite sex. All my life I'd told myself that one day I would take some action to fix my issues, but every time I got close to a guy everything went haywire and I ran away.

But what if...what if I went to work on my sex issues independently of a relationship? With someone, perhaps, who wasn't into relationships in the first place, and who happened to be really, *really* good at sex?

What if Liam could use his BDSM skills and sexual prowess to turn my issues around?

It was a warped idea, but if I got what I wanted out of it, what did it matter? God, I wanted sex. I wanted to be able to make out with a guy without sweating and waiting for the inevitable panic attack. I was tired of being lonely and afraid of my own body, and tired of maintaining control. After so many years of anxiety, this felt like now-or-never time. I was ready to submit to a power greater than myself.

But I didn't know where that power lived. I wished I'd paid attention that day in the limo. I wished I was a super-security-agency-level info-hacker like Liam so I could find his address off the web. I found the location of his company's business offices, but I didn't want to waltz into his place of work uninvited, or linger outside like a stalker, slowly losing my nerve.

Rubio knew where Liam lived.

Did I dare approach Rubio for Liam's address? I couldn't do it during class hours or work hours, or backstage during performances—that pesky contract thing. I would have to catch him alone again and hope he'd condescend to talk to me. It took days of lurking before I stumbled across him in a little-used rehearsal room, long past work hours. I peered through a crack in the blinds to be sure he was alone, and then I kept watching, just a few moments, out of curiosity.

Whatever he was working on, it was expressive and slightly wild. I watched him move through steps, his long, muscular legs eating up the floor. It was a miracle, the way he moved. When people talked about things like "God-given talent," this was what they meant. You didn't get to his level by work. You either had it within you when you were born, or you didn't.

Fernando Rubio did.

I'd never had a chance to watch him rehearse like this, privately, with his own creative energy. He looked tortured, driven… I wondered what life was like for the Rubios of the world, who had to numb their artistic genius down into the required structure of commercial production. If his tormented choreography was any indication, it was hard.

When he paused and went to the wall to write down some notes, I slipped in the door, coughing softly so I didn't scare him. I was breaking every company rule right now. Interrupting a rehearsal, talking to Rubio, looking him right in his shocked, angry eyes.

"What you doing here, stupid girl?" he snapped. "This is a closed rehearsal."

Rules or no, I was tired of him verbally abusing me. "Please don't call me stupid again. If you do, I'll report it to Mr. Thibault."

"Ha, he doesn't care. What he do, fire me?"

"Then I'll report you to the police for assaulting me at that party."

His eyebrows rose, practically to his hairline. "Assaulting? Whut? You—" He snapped his mouth shut like I was too unreasonable to respond to, but I could see color rising in his cheeks. "I was only playing. Not assault. Learn the difference."

"I know the difference. Stop calling me stupid, okay?"

"I'll stop calling you stupid when you stop ruining my rehearsals."

"I didn't ruin your rehearsal. I have a quick question and then I'll go."

"A quick question?" He looked aghast. "What I look like? Information kiosk? You're a stupider girl than I gave you credit for."

"You can do hard time for assault. I'm almost sure of it."

It was hard not to cringe from his black stare, but I knew if I did I'd never gain his respect. He finally made an annoyed sound and turned away. "What you want, then? You have more trouble with Liam? You want another walk home?" He waved a hand at me. "Call a cab. I'm busy."

I looked around the dim rehearsal space. "Busy doing what?"

"I told you. Dance for the spring showcase, maybe. It's none of your business."

"I thought it looked amazing."

He glared at me with such vitriol that I took a step back.

"I need Liam's address," I said before I lost total control of the situation. "I need to go see him and I don't want to call first, because I don't want him to tell me...to tell me no."

Rubio's eyes narrowed. "No to what?"

It's none of your business. I wanted to throw his words back in his face but I needed his help. "Please, just tell me where he lives."

He turned away and snatched his phone off the top of the piano in the corner. "I don't know the house number. He lives in Regents Park, near Cambridge and Chester Gate."

"What are you doing?"

He put the phone to his ear. "Calling Liam to warn him a crazy woman is coming."

I ran across the room and yanked the cell from his fingers. He stared down at his empty hand and then back at me in disbelief. "Did you just take my phone?"

"Will you listen to me first?"

"Sure," he snapped. "Then I'll call him after you leave."

"I'm not going now anyway. I'm not going yet."

He crossed his arms over his chest, his lips pursed in a tight line. "Tell me what you want with him."

"I want to ask him to help me with something."

"What?"

"I can't tell you." When his face darkened I added, "You wouldn't understand. It's complicated."

"If you go see him, it will get more complicated. I told you what he's like." He stepped away from me, executed a few *tendus* and a perfect pirouette. "If you go to him, you'll end up getting fucked, literally and figuratively. Maybe that excites you." He flipped up into a handstand and looked at me upside-down. "I'm getting tight. Go away. I won't call." His leather ballet shoes smacked the floor as he catapulted back to his feet. "I don't get any warning when you show up. You're just there, poof. Now he can have the same horrible experience."

I was beginning to understand that Rubio only had one comfort zone. Nasty. I handed back his phone. "You said Cambridge and Chester Gate?"

"Yes. Big white house. You know when you see it."

"Thank you," I said, heading for the door.

"Hey! Ash-lee." I turned to him. He gazed back at me, one hand braced on his hip. "Be careful. He is stronger than you are. He can make you do things you don't want to do."

"I'm kind of counting on that," I said under my breath as I left.

* * * * *

I didn't go right away. Once I knew where he lived, the whole scheme started to scare me. I reconsidered, I waffled.

Then the week of Christmas arrived, and all my friends made plans with boyfriends and lovers and families. I had none of those things. When people asked about my holiday plans I lied and said a friend was coming to visit me from out of town. We were free by mid-afternoon Christmas Eve, and I had nowhere to go and no one to spend the holidays with. I hadn't even planned any kind of special meal.

Before Liam, this would have been okay with me. I'd been content to slumber away my life like Sleeping Beauty while the world went on around me, while people lived and laughed and loved. But sleeping wasn't doing it for me anymore. I couldn't sleep, I couldn't dream. I didn't want to live like this. I tore the curtains off my bed in a fit of rage around seven that evening. I'd had enough.

I showered, dressed in my one pair of decent jeans and my nicest pale pink cashmere sweater, teased and styled my hair, and even put on makeup. I was going to go see Liam, *now*, even though it was Christmas Eve, because I had to. I had to move forward because I couldn't stay any longer where I was.

It was easy to find his house. I directed the cab to the intersection of Cambridge and Chester Gate and immediately located the white edifice I remembered. I paid the driver and stood outside, marshalling my resolve. The house was quiet. No parties. Would he be home? At a friend's house? At church? I couldn't picture Liam in church, even on Christmas Eve. He might be inside his big house entertaining a woman. Two women. Three. How many women did a man like Liam need to feel satisfied? Orgies full of women, from what Rubio told me.

He needs a hell of a lot more woman than you.

I silenced the voice in my head and took stock of my situation. The cab was gone. I could call another one to pick me up, or I could do what I'd come here to do, which was ask Liam to fix all the broken things about me.

Like Mr. Thibault told me backstage, I just had to get through it. I marched to the door and rang the bell. It seemed like an eternity before it opened, an eternity to fight with myself and not run away. It wasn't Liam who opened the door, though. An elderly, dark-haired man stared out at me. "Can I help you?" he asked with a clipped accent.

Could this be the wrong house? I looked down the block but I'd been one hundred percent sure this was the one. "Does Liam Wilder live here?"

"May I know your name?"

"Ashleigh Keaton."

"Miss Keaton." His face lit up in a smile. "Won't you come in?" He shook my hand and practically pulled me inside. For someone so frail in stature there was amazing power in his grip. "Please make yourself at home in the living room while I inform Mr. Wilder that you are here."

I picked a couch and sat down, but it reminded me too much of the last time I was here, so I stood again. He turned up the dim lights and palmed a phone, tapping out a message on the screen.

"What can I get for you, Miss Keaton, while we wait for Mr. Wilder to arrive?"

"He's not here?"

"Not just yet," he said in a soothing voice. "But he will not want to miss you. Would you like a drink?" he asked, heading into the open kitchen.

"He doesn't have to come home from wherever he is. I'll—I'll come back another time."

"Water? A cocktail? Some hot tea?" He played around with a fancy-looking tea press. "It is a perfect night for tea." He gestured to one of the stools lining the counter. "Please, come and join me. We will chat while we wait."

He was being too nice for me to refuse, so I crossed and sat on one of the leather-topped bar stools. Within moments the scents of cinnamon, orange, and vanilla wafted to my nose. He opened a cabinet and took out saucers and tea cups with a maroon toile design.

"Do you live here with Liam?" I asked. "You're a friend of his?"

"Ah, yes. I live here. I am a friend but I have worked for Mr. Wilder too, many years."

"What do you do? Cook?" I only asked because the tea smelled so delicious.

"Cook, yes. Sometimes. I do many things. Are you hungry? Would you like some Christmas Eve goodies?"

He started piling homemade cookies on a plate before I could say no. He told me what kind they were as he arranged them. Macadamia, mint cream, Russian teacakes. I remembered putting homemade cookies out for Santa as a child. I was so young when I stopped believing in stuff like that. When the tea was done, he gave me a full cup along with some sugar and cream that he produced from the massive refrigerator.

I looked over my shoulder toward the foyer. "Please tell me you didn't call him away from a party or something. A date."

The man's expression didn't change. "He will not mind being called away." He stirred his own cup of tea, meeting my eyes. "He has been waiting for you."

Liam, waiting for me? He must have had me confused with some other girl. It would be so embarrassing when Liam showed up and found me sitting here in his house, at his kitchen counter. I had to find some way out of here before then. Maybe I could make up a story about leaving the oven on at home…

"What are you afraid of?" the man asked, his eyes far too keen. "Not Mr. Wilder?"

In that assessing look, I understood that this man *worked* for Liam, as a security-agent-bodyguard person, not a housekeeper or cook. His short stature and elderly appearance was a foil, a disguise.

"I'm not afraid," I said, feeling a blush burn across my cheeks. "I'm nervous. Embarrassed. I shouldn't have come here tonight. Not on Christmas Eve."

"Ah, but you should have come. This is a great gift for him. He's been worried about you."

"He talked to you about me?"

"Not too much." His voice took on a mild lilt. "You have difficulties?"

Something about his easy manner encouraged me to confide. "I need Liam to help me with something. Something important."

"Ah, Liam likes to help. He will be happy to help you, Miss Keaton. And I am also at your service, if there is anything I can do. My name is Mem. It is short for something that would be very hard for you to pronounce."

"Mem," I repeated. "You don't have to call me Miss Keaton. You can call me Ashleigh."

His smile widened. "Thank you for this honor. I hope we will be friends."

* * * * *

I was having dinner at my father and stepmom's place when I got the first text from Mem.

Little Ishi is here.

I grimaced, hiding the phone on my knee under the table. It had been a week since I saw her backstage, a week since Rubio flew to her rescue. A week of berating myself for making stupid choices. *Send her away*, I typed.

Three minutes later: *I am feeding her cookies. She is too thin.*

Mem texted exactly the way he spoke. I applied the capslock.

SEND HER AWAY

Then, for good measure, *IF SHE'S THERE WHEN I GET BACK, YOU'RE FIRED*

I knew she'd be there when I got back. Mem wasn't usually so oblivious. Rubio was right, it wasn't okay for me to play around with her. Rubio realized that, and he wasn't even aware of her deeper issues, the harrowing abuse in her past. She was too vulnerable, too fragile and emotional with too much at stake.

Is she gone yet? I texted pointlessly. No reply.

"Is everything okay?" my stepmom asked.

I sighed and flipped the phone over in my hand. "I'm sorry. I have to go."

My father looked at me over his glasses. "Work related?"

"No...a friend. A personal issue."

My dad was good about not pushing me to talk, even though he stared at me a little too long with his incisive hazel eyes.

"I wouldn't leave," I finally said, "except that I need to handle this."

"Mem is there, isn't he?"

In other words, *this isn't just some girl, or Mem would take care of it for you.* Sometimes I hated my father's acuity.

My stepmom jumped up in the tense silence and patted my shoulder. "I'll wrap up your dinner for you to take home."

"You don't have to."

She waved a hand, taking my plate and sailing into the kitchen.

"Is everything okay?" my father asked once she was gone—and this time I knew he expected a real answer. I scratched my chin, searching for the vaguest possible explanation. "I met a dancer, a friend of Rubio's. She's a very interesting person, but she might be in some danger." *From me.*

"She's in the market for security?"

"No, not yet. But I'm going to try to convince her she should be." All this double talk wouldn't fool my dad any more than it fooled Mem when I tried to hide stuff.

He leaned forward on his elbows. "Strange of her to turn up at this hour on Christmas Eve."

"She's...slightly strange," I admitted. "And I don't think she has any family in town. I'm sure she doesn't." *Yes, I've run checks on her family. No, I don't want to tell you why.*

"Is this the one who lives in Wyoming?"

"She's from Wyoming, yes. How do you know about that?"

"You used company assets to investigate her."

"It's a private matter. It's my company, right?"

72

"Yes. It's half your company," my dad replied in an acerbic tone. He started eating again. "I won't pry. But if she's really in danger—"

"I thought she might need help. I wanted more information." I clamped my mouth shut before he could analyze the tension in my voice.

"So you don't think the security threat is immediate?" my father asked after a moment.

"I don't know. I need to see her."

"Well, good luck," he said as my stepmom breezed back in with a tote full of take-away.

I smiled at the stack of plastic containers. "You know, I have food at my house."

"I packed a little extra for Mem, and some chocolate cheesecake," she said, handing it to me. "I know it's your favorite."

I stood to give her a hug and a kiss. "Sorry I have to run, Abby." I didn't call her mom, but my father's wife was a much-appreciated presence in my life. "Dinner was delicious, as always. I hope you both have a great holiday."

"And I hope your friend comes around," said my dad. "Safety isn't something to mess around with."

Ha. No one on earth knew that better than me.

Chapter Seven:
Please

Mem's phone buzzed on the dining room table. He looked up from our Monopoly game to glance at the screen. "It is *Ishi*. Mr. Wilder. He will arrive any moment now."

It was a good thing, because I was losing my nerve as steadily as I was losing the game. I counted out a stack of hundreds to Mem's outstretched hand. "What was that name you called him? Itchy?"

"*Ishi*." He placed the money in a neat stack in front of him. "A slip. Forgive me. He does not like when I call him that."

"Why? What does it mean?"

He thought a moment before he rolled to take his turn. "Literally, *ishi* means 'human' or 'person.' In another sense it means someone with no name. With no people. No home."

I looked around the chandelier-lit dining room. "Liam has a home."

Mem inclined his head at me. "Literally—yes, he has a home. But in another sense, he does not. When you know him better, you will understand."

If I ever knew him better. I wanted to know him better since Rubio had planted ideas in my head. But now that I'd gotten up the courage to come here, I worried it was a mistake.

"You are *ishi* too," Mem said, interrupting my fretting. "I sensed this right away. You are not like your people, are you?"

"My people? You mean my family?"

"Yes."

I shook my head, handing over more money. "No, we're not close."

"Do they ever come to see you dance?"

"London's a long way from Wyoming."

In a change of pace, Mem landed on one of my dinky properties and had to pay me. "It is a sad thing, to lose the home from which you come."

"It's not sad, believe me."

We both looked up as Liam appeared at the dining room door, wearing jeans and an obnoxious reindeer-emblazoned sweater.

"Monopoly?" he asked, staring at Mem. His voice sounded mild but his expression wasn't.

Mem inclined his head in that formal way he had. "Ashleigh has come to ask for your help. In the meantime, we were enjoying a board game."

I glanced at my aged opponent. "I'm not enjoying it as much as you, since you're beating me to death."

Liam almost smiled. Almost. "Mem's a board game shark. Never play him for money, trust me. Well..." He spread his arms. "It's Christmas Eve, Ashleigh. What are you doing here?"

Mem pushed back his chair. "I'll make some more tea."

"No," we both said at the same time, but he'd already scooted through the door.

Liam sat across from me and started cleaning up the Monopoly game. I helped until our fingers got tangled together, then I stopped and let him do it, my hands clasped in my lap.

"I told Mem not to call you. The thing is— I just— I had a bad day and—"

"Okay," he said, cutting me off. "You're here."

"But you want me to go."

"I do and I don't." He tapped his fingers hard on the tabletop. "Rubio did both of us a favor the other night. Especially you."

"I know what you must think, after—"

"You don't know what I think, I promise you." He stacked the money and tucked it in the box with the other pieces of the board game. I handed him the lid and watched him put it on. That done, he pushed it aside and propped his arms on the table.

I took a deep breath. "Listen, I'm sorry I flipped out the other night at the theater. I'm sorry."

"Please stop apologizing. Why are you here? Spit it out."

I picked at the corner of the box, choosing my words carefully. "So...that night...Rubio and I had a talk while he walked me home. We talked about you."

"Okay," he said. "And?"

"It gave me an idea that I can't stop thinking about. He said..."

I fell silent as Mem returned with fresh tea and a tray of sugar, cream, and milk.

"Thank you, Jeeves," Liam muttered. "Leave it and get out."

The old man did as he was told, setting the tray down next to the Monopoly box and disappearing out the door. Neither of us made a move to touch the fragrant, steaming cups.

"He's really nice," I commented in the silence.

"He's the most irritating human on the planet." Liam ground his palms into his eye sockets and then leaned forward and fixed me with his gaze. "Why are you here?" he asked, emphasizing each word.

"So...in the course of our conversation, Rubio told me you're really good at having sex. Like really, really good."

His lips tightened in annoyance. "He said that, did he?"

"He said that you knew how to sex women into oblivion."

"If there's an actual point to this, I'd love to hear it."

"I just started thinking... With my issues...and your skills..." His gaze sharpened but he didn't speak. "I was thinking maybe..." I gave a choked little laugh. "So, this will sound really weird, but I thought maybe since you were so good at sex and I'm so bad at it, you might be able to fix my problems. You know. Fix...me."

He stared into my eyes a long moment, then made a soft sound. "Oh, Ashleigh."

I didn't know what to make of that quietly spoken *Oh, Ashleigh*. It wasn't angry but it wasn't kind either. I pressed my hands together and brought them to my mouth like I was praying. I wasn't praying, just trying to think of what to say.

"You were right about me," I admitted. "You guessed right. My father made my childhood a living hell. I won't go into the hows and whys but it started when I was nine. He abused me for five years, until I

76

could get away from him. Until I got good enough at ballet to make it into a school in New York."

He opened his mouth as if to ask a question. I held up a hand. "Please don't. Please don't ask me to tell you any more about it. I've had therapy, I've had counseling. It's taken care of the worst of it. The only thing I still can't handle is sex. Even there it's...it's weird. I can think about sex, and I can get turned on, but there's a certain point where..." I rubbed my forehead and then looked up at him. "There's this point where these memories crash down on me, and I try to ignore them but I can't. I react and I freak out. It's gotten to where I don't even want to try. I'm so tired of going through the trauma of it all, and driving away people I've come to care for. It's painful, falling in love over and over, then having intimacy issues blow everything up. But you said...you talked about no strings attached. Rubio said you have a lot of partners."

"Yes, but——"

"And that you're really good in bed."

"Yes, but——"

"And I started thinking about your lifestyle stuff and the way dominants control submissives and tell them what to do." I said the rest in a rush, because he looked like he wanted to interrupt me again. "So I was thinking you could help me with my sex issues using all those skills of yours, and your dominant thing. You could...maybe...force me do the things I'm uncomfortable with, until I got more comfortable."

He made a face like I was insane. "I couldn't force you to do anything. It doesn't work that way. That's just...so appallingly wrong."

"I don't mean *force* me. Just control me a little, in a dominant way. Give me some parameters to operate inside." I made a boxy little motion with my hands. "Since you like that stuff anyway, you know? And I liked it too, the things you showed me. I liked when you held me down and... Well." I gave him a pleading look. "I thought maybe you could help ease me past my...my sexual hang-ups."

"Sexual hang-ups?" He stared at me, his head tilted to the side. "Listen, I don't want to hurt your feelings. I think you're being very brave right now to ask me to do this, but Ashleigh, sexual hang-ups isn't the word for what you have. You're struggling with deep trust issues and emotional scars."

"No, it's not that bad——"

"Ashleigh."

"I worked through all that in counseling. Honestly, it's just a physical thing with me now." I waved my hands around, trying to explain. "A physical trigger or something."

He gave me a skeptical look and I felt the beginnings of panic. He thought I was crazy, and he wasn't going to help me. "Just because I melted down that one time—"

"Two times. You might call this a third time, showing up on my doorstep Christmas Eve."

I stared at his awful red sweater. The prancing reindeer seemed to taunt me. He wasn't going for my scheme at all, not even to sleep with me. I had to get out of here with some shred of my self-esteem intact. I stood to go but he clamped his fingers around my wrist.

"If you storm out of here, that makes four meltdowns. Sit." He didn't put me back in the chair. He sat me on his lap and pressed my head against the curve of his shoulder. His arms came around me loosely, cradling me. All the emotion inside me welled up like a geyser and spouted through my eyes.

"Your sweater is ugly," I said through tears. "I hate it."

He glanced down at the kitschy design. "My stepmom bought it for me years ago."

"I don't hate it," I bawled, burying my face in my hands. "I don't know why I said that."

His fingers eased into my nape, kneading through knots of tension. "I know why. You're melting down again."

Yes, that seemed pretty obvious to us both. I turned my face against his neck and cried for at least five minutes, babbling on about my wrecked life and how badly I needed his help.

"I just want to be normal," I cried. "I need someone to help me. Someone with skills. Someone I can trust. I want to have a guy on top of me without panicking and losing my sanity. I know you can help me. Why won't you help me?"

He didn't say anything, only leaned forward now and again to take a sip of tea. I could feel each swallow against my cheek.

"Okay?" he asked when I finally petered out.

I slumped against him. "I'm sorry for unloading all this on you. None of it's your fault. I'm sorry you had to leave your dinner for this, or your party, or whatever."

"It wasn't a party. Just my dad and his wife." His fingertips played over my arm in a slow, repetitive motion. "I was upset at first, when

Mem texted me. I'd been trying to leave you alone—the way you asked me to—but I'm glad now you came and I'm glad you shared your thoughts with me." He sat me up and put his cup on the table. "When I saw you at the theater, I didn't mean to upset you. I only wanted to offer help. Although I never considered helping in the way you're suggesting. I was thinking more about whether you still went home. If he still bothered you. If you were dependent on him for anything. I would have fixed that if you were. I don't want him having any leverage over you."

"I've cut all ties with my parents. We haven't talked in years. I'll never be in the same room with him or look at him again, or ask him for anything. I promised myself that."

A flash of something vicious entered his expression. "Good. He's a fucking animal. I investigated him to make sure he wasn't victimizing anyone else. I'm sorry if you find that weird or stalkerish."

"Was there anyone else?" I asked.

"No." He seemed about to say something further but then he didn't. Instead, he handed me my cup of tea. It was cold now but it soothed the catch in my throat. When I'd gulped down a sip or two, Liam lifted me off his lap and stood. "I want some cookies. Let's go in the kitchen."

Cookies. Great. Was he still considering what I'd suggested, or were we moving on to cookies because it was out of the question? I went with him into the adjoining room, trying to gauge his thoughts from his expression.

"Did you go to Cowskull?" I asked as he walked around the counter. "Did you actually go there?"

"No. I wanted to be here, in case..." His voice drifted off as he shoved a cookie in his mouth. He put some more on a plate and brought them over to me. "I sent someone to check things out in a way that wouldn't make your father suspicious." He shook his head as he returned to pour tea into our cups. "Don't ask. The point is, it's just him and your mother at home. No young relatives, no underage help. No vulnerable neighbor kids."

"The neighbors are miles away. You must have really looked into things."

"Our investigators are thorough."

I took a sip of the tea and burned my tongue. "So..." I blew out, cooling off my mouth. "Regarding what I suggested earlier..."

"I'm thinking about it, okay? Give me a minute." He sat beside me at the counter and leaned over his cup. His sweater was tragic but he looked so serious and handsome. He would be so easy to fall in love with, if he was that type.

"I only want you to help me," I said. "Not be my boyfriend or anything. I want you to…" I swallowed hard. "I want you to help me do the things I'm too afraid to do. And I won't hold you to anything, *anything* at all afterward. I promise I won't."

Each time I spoke I had a feeling from his expression that I was saying the wrong things. I shut my mouth and stared at his profile.

"He's a sick man now," he said quietly. "Your father. He looks awful. I have pictures."

I shook my head. I didn't want to see them. No.

"He's dying." Liam pursed his lips. "Melanoma. I didn't want to tell you. I don't want you to feel sorry for him, or feel like you have to go to him."

I thought over the repercussions of this news. A world without my father in it… This was a good thing, but still a shock. "I wouldn't have gone to him, even if I knew," I said to Liam. "I hate him too much. I'll hate him forever."

"I'm afraid if we do this thing you're suggesting, you'll feel that way about me someday."

My palms felt clammy against the slick countertop. I wiped them on my knees. My father was dying. Cancer. What had Liam just said? That I'd hate him for trying to help? I couldn't imagine it. "I won't. I won't ever feel that way about you, I swear to God."

He took my hands in his and squeezed them. "I have to help you, Ash. I can't say no to what you're asking, but I'm afraid I'll hurt you in this process. I won't mean to, but I will."

"You can't hurt me as much as he did," I whispered, shaking my head. "It's not possible."

"I hope you're right." He looked at me with the full force of his amber gaze. "I want to go slow and careful with this, okay? We'll need to talk things out before we do anything. Make plans."

Oh, please. Please let this work for me. My father was dying. What better time to come alive again? "I'm okay with planning," I said. "Yes. Whenever you want. Tonight?"

"If you like. If you don't feel tired."

I shook my head. I didn't feel tired at all. I felt energized and hopeful, and anxious to begin. Thank God, he was going to do it.

His fingers traced the tops of mine. "I'm still not convinced it's a good idea to bring power exchange into the equation. I mean, the power differential between you and your father worked against you before."

I stared at his hand. I didn't understand how we *couldn't* bring it into the equation. He was so dominant in everything. "The thing is, when you did it with me at my place, even that little bit…" I could feel myself flushing with the embarrassment of this confession. "It turned me on more than I'd ever been turned on in my life."

He studied me a long moment. "Okay. If it gets you hot, we'll use it. I'll do whatever I can to help you overcome your issues. But not tonight. Tonight, we'll just talk." He stood and held out his hand. "Ready, Freddy?"

I was so, so ready. I took a deep breath, reached out, and twined my fingers through his.

Chapter Eight:
Plans

She held my hand like I had all the answers, like she trusted me implicitly. Some part of me was aroused by that trust. Another part of me felt like the wolf leading Red Riding Hood into the forest.

I'd never in a thousand years expected her to come seeking my assistance, not after what happened the last time we were together. At some point she'd apparently rethought matters, resulting in this humble request for help. It proved to me how desperate she was—and made it impossible to refuse her.

And I believed I could help Ashleigh Keaton enjoy sex again. I could dominate the fuck out of her if that's what she wanted. I'd fantasized for weeks about taking her to bed and fixing her issues with my legendary sexual prowess. But that was fantasy. It all proceeded according to my imagination, which was lurid at best. Pornographic at worst. As I led her up the stairs, I felt an overpowering desire to control her, to subjugate her. I wanted to pull her hair and spank her ass until it was covered in red handprints. I wanted to torment her until she shuddered with delight, until she cried out and begged for mercy.

But that wasn't the "fixing" she was asking for. I had to focus my attention on her sexual issues, not my over-the-top fantasies of fucking her. I had to use the D/s to make her more comfortable with sex, not to torment her. Oh God—she was turning me into one of those white-knight BDSM guys. Pretty soon I'd be wearing a goatee, carrying around a fur lined paddle and handcuffs with hearts embossed on them. Rubio would never stop mocking me. Hell, I'd never stop mocking myself.

It's for Ashleigh. Do it for Ashleigh, just this once.

I walked her past my bedroom to the largest guest suite, which was decorated in a shade of blue-gray that matched her eyes. The Ashleigh room. From now on, that's what it would be to me. I guided her inside and shut the door. She let go of my hand and looked around.

It was a big room for a bedroom, nearly as large as my master bedroom. There was a seating area by the window with a table and chairs, and a full bathroom to the right. The bed was king-size with a heavy iron frame, a tall spindled headboard and a slightly shorter footboard. A normal person would find the imposing black structure stylish. I found it convenient for BDSM games. I brought girls here when I felt like scening outside the play room. I never, ever let girls in my own bedroom and especially my bed.

Not even this girl.

She looked pretty today in a pink pullover and jeans, her black hair falling in waves past her shoulders. Her hands were clasped nervously in front of her. If she knew half the fantasies running through my mind she would already be down the stairs and out the door.

"Are we going to start right now?" she asked. "With the submission stuff?"

"No. Yes." I pointed to one of the upholstered chairs by the window. "We're going to start, but we're going to start by talking."

She sat down and I joined her. "This is a really beautiful room," she said. "Everything in your house is so beautiful."

She was the most beautiful thing in my house at the moment. I wanted to take all her clothes off and tie her to the fucking bed. *No. Not appropriate at this time.* "Thanks," I said instead. "I'm glad you like this room and I hope you'll feel comfortable here. It's a private, quiet place for us to work together. Ideally, this will be a D/s space. I'll control in here, and you'll submit."

She stared at the bed, and I knew she was thinking the same thing I was thinking. *When does the sex start?*

I cleared my throat, determined to keep the discussion rolling. "There will be times you won't feel comfortable in here," I said. "That's where the submission comes in. I'd like you to do your best to obey me in this room, even if it's difficult. I'll need you to be brave and trust me as much as you can."

She opened her mouth and closed it. "I... Well... Sure. I...I trust you. I don't think you'd do anything to hurt me."

"Of course I wouldn't." I reached across the table and took her hands. "But if you ever feel confused or scared, it's okay to let me know. D/s isn't about toughing out the bad stuff. It's about people enjoying themselves and doing things to please each other. In our case, I'm going to use the D/s to try to move you past your fears."

"And what will I do for you? What will you get out of it?"

He shrugged. "I like to help people and I like to push women's boundaries. In your case, I'll get to do both."

She absorbed this with the slightest twitch of her fingers. "I'll try to do whatever you ask. Whatever it takes. I want to get better."

"I want you to get better too." I drew in a breath and stared down at our intertwined hands. "I can't guarantee your issues will be worked out in a week or two."

"So, how long do you think...?"

"I don't know. We'll see how things go. It's possible this won't work at all and you'll have to seek professional help."

"I've sought professional help," she said with an edge of desperation.

"I know you have. But I've never attempted anything like this and I'm assuming you haven't either. As much as I want to help you, I could just as easily fuck you up worse."

We both fell silent a moment. I didn't want to fuck her up. I leaned closer to catch her gaze. "Listen, Ash. Submission can feel threatening to the uninitiated. It can feel like something you *have* to do. I need you to remember, if things start to feel too difficult, that you always have two options. You can hold tough and stick it out, or you can leave this room and go downstairs to the living room. The living room will be our neutral zone. Our safeword, so to speak. I don't ever want you to feel trapped or forced. I don't want you to feel pressured to do something you don't want to do."

She looked at me sideways. "But—"

"I know. You're afraid you won't want to do anything. But if I do my job right, you will. If we're patient and we work hard, you'll figure out how to enjoy sex again. I have faith in you."

"And I have faith in you," she said soberly. "I can never explain to you how much I appreciate this."

I opened my arms to her. "Come here and hug me before I lose my mind."

She pushed back her chair and came to me, and I embraced her, this scared, vulnerable woman who'd insinuated herself into my life. I didn't normally let people so close. Sexually, I did, but not emotionally. I wondered why I was doing it now.

"I think everything's going to go fine," I said against her ear. "I know you want to get better. Get 'fixed,' as you say…but there are a few things we need to discuss."

I released her and crossed to the bureau, and opened the top drawer. I kept paper and pens in there for naughty subbies to write lines. *I will not be a bad girl. I will not be a bad girl.* I grabbed a couple sheets and a pen and returned to the table. I set them down and looked over at Ashleigh, perched nervously on the edge of her seat.

I spoke with a casual, forthright inflection. "I want to remember everything we talk about, so I'm going to take notes. No one is ever going to see them, okay?"

She blinked at me, once, twice. "Okay," she said, but she didn't completely sound okay.

"Come here, please. These aren't the kind of questions I can ask you across a table."

She'd been suspicious before. Now she knew what was coming—and she was going to balk. She was a second from bailing. I could see it in her face. "Don't, Ash," I said. "Don't overreact. I just need to know what your triggers are before we start. Please power through this so I don't inadvertently hurt you. I'll keep it short. Just the basic things I need to know."

The basic things. Such a stupid way to refer to what she'd endured. I only meant I wouldn't goad her for explicit details. I didn't think I could deal with hearing them.

"Do we have to do this now?" she asked. "I'm kind of tired."

"Nice try." I looked at my watch. "You stay at the theater later than this, and I doubt you go straight to bed when you get home." I gave her my displeased-dominant look. It was a doozy. "You just lied to my face.

If you were a sub of mine, in a scene, I'd punish you. The punishments for lying are the worst."

She paled. "I'm sorry I lied. I just don't want to."

I waited, watching her.

"But...okay. I'm supposed to obey you in this room." She came to me and buried her face against my shoulder. "I already suck at this."

I pulled her into my lap and wrapped an arm around her. "Just don't lie to me, baby. Tell me the truth. *'I don't want to. I'm afraid. I'm uncomfortable.'* It's uncomfortable for me too. I wish we could skip this part, but I can't help you without knowing what you've been through."

She nestled her cheek against my chest. "I know," she said. "But I haven't talked about this in a while."

I held her tight and asked the first question as matter-of-factly as I could. "Did he hit you or abuse you in any way other than sexually?"

She paused a moment. "No."

"Didn't hit you with anything? A belt, a paddle? A whip?"

"No. He hit me a few times with his hand."

"A spanking? On your bottom?"

"On my face. Sometimes on the side of my head when I...fought him."

Fucker. Fucker, fucker, fucker.

No trigger implements, I wrote. *Watch hands around her face.*

"You're doing great, Ash," I said. "Next question. Where did he assault you? Always in your bed? On the floor? Bathroom? Any other place?"

"Just my bed. In my bedroom. He locked the door."

Bed only, I wrote. *Don't lock door.*

"Did he restrain you in any way? Cuffs, rope? Duct tape?"

She shook her head. "He just..." Her voice was so quiet. "He held me down with his body weight."

Restraints okay, I wrote. But this explained why she'd gone so crazy the two times I'd laid on top of her.

"How often?" I asked next.

She sighed. "Once or twice a week. Sometimes more. Sometimes he stayed away and I thought he'd stopped forever and then he'd come back."

Fucker. "Was he always on top?" I asked. "Any other positions?"

"Sometimes he did it other ways," she said. "No matter how he did it, it always felt...smothering. He never let me move or talk or say anything. If I did, he got angry and hit me. If I was still he just did what he had to do and left."

I closed my eyes as she related all this to me. I could see it so clearly. I didn't want to but I did. Little, petite Ashleigh and her fat fuck of a father, pressing her down in the mattress and forcing his worthless prick inside her.

"Did it hurt?" I asked, my voice strained. "Did he hurt you when he...entered you?"

It mattered because I was pretty big, and I didn't want to remind her of him. I wanted him to be hung like a piss ant. She shook her head against my chest. "It always hurt."

It always hurt, I wrote.

I rubbed her back and pressed my chin against the top of her head. "Hang in there, baby. I know this sucks for you." As difficult as this was for me, it had to be a thousand times worse for her. I gritted my teeth and asked the next question. "Did he only assault you vaginally? Did he ever make you go down on him?"

"No."

"Anal sex?"

"No. Sometimes he groped me there, but..."

Vaginal only, I wrote. "Did he use contraceptives?"

"No. Well, he pulled out a lot, I guess. Sometimes..." Her voice trailed off. "He came on me. I can't stand that. The smell."

"It's good that he never got you pregnant. Or did he?"

"I didn't have my period. Not until I was fourteen."

Until she'd left home. I shuddered. I couldn't help it. *No facials*, I scrawled, and underlined it twice. *No cum play.*

"Will you use condoms?" she asked, going tense in my arms.

"Of course I will. We'll take tests too, just to be safe. I usually use condoms so it's no big deal." I gave her a squeeze. "Okay, we're almost done. Did he talk to you when he was assaulting you?"

She trembled against my chest. "He called me a bad girl. Please don't call me a bad girl."

"I won't." *Don't call her a bad girl*, I wrote on the paper. *Ever*. I underlined that three times. "What about other names? Anything else bother you? Baby, honey, sweetcheeks? Honeymuffin? Twinkletoes?"

She giggled the way I hoped she would, and shook her head. "He never talked to me. He never said anything."

"He had a dick the size of a pinhead, didn't he?" I asked bitterly. "Literally, the tiniest dick on earth."

She shrugged her small, tired shoulders. "I don't know. I couldn't really judge."

Of course she couldn't. Motherfucking fuck. "Is there anything else he did to you that I should know about?" I asked. "You can tell me anything. I don't want to hurt you later because I'm not aware."

There was a long silence and I realized she was crying. I held her against me while I folded up the paper and shoved it into my pocket. I didn't think I'd forget anything she'd told me, not for the rest of my life. "I'm so sorry," I said. "I'm sorry for all the things you went through. Someone should have helped you. Your teachers. Your mom. Why didn't you tell them? Did he threaten you?"

"My mom knew."

I thought I must have misheard her. "What?"

She took a long, slow breath. "My mom knew. In the beginning she told me to 'honor my father,' that it said so in the Bible. Later she said it was my fault, that the devil was inside me tempting my father. She said if I told anyone what was going on, she'd say I was mentally ill or using drugs. That she'd yank me out of dance and have me sent to juvenile detention. She said I would get raped there every day."

Bitch. Bitch, bitch, bitch, fucker, bitch.

"She didn't...she didn't want...she wouldn't..." Ashleigh pulled away from me and swiped at her tears. "She liked my father's money, I guess, but she didn't want to sleep with him. So..."

"So she kept quiet while he came to you."

"Yeah. I felt pretty trapped. There was only one way I could think of to get away from them. I had to win a scholarship to an out-of-town ballet school, and I did." Her face was awful, driven.

"Who helped you?" I asked. "A teacher? Your dance teacher?"

"Yes. Miss Melanie. She helped me apply to a company school in New York, and helped set up the audition. My parents didn't want me to go, but Miss Melanie wouldn't take no for an answer. She flew me there herself when they refused."

I had a sickening thought. "Do you still dance to get away from them? Do you enjoy it at all?" It horrified me to think she still danced from that survival compulsion. "They can't touch you now, you know. You could quit tomorrow. Do whatever you want. If you needed money, I'd give you money to go back to school. Whatever."

She shook her head. "I like it, most of the time. I don't want to quit. But someday, in a few years, I might like to stop, get married. Have a normal life. And to do that..." She gave me a hopeful look. "I need to get fixed."

I ran a finger down the side of her cheek, brushing away tears. How many of them had she cried as she soldiered through her hellish life? "I'm going to fix you," I said. "Are you off tomorrow?"

"I'm off every Monday and Tuesday," she said. "But tomorrow's Christmas."

"It's as good a day to start as any. As long as you're clear, it's a good day for me. Every Monday we'll work on things, you and me, until you're better. Okay?"

It was the best I could do at that moment. What I really wanted to do was fly to Cowskull and choke the last of Joe Keaton's miserable life from his lungs. Then I'd move on to Doreen. What was an appropriate punishment for a mother who'd sentenced her daughter to sexual abuse from the age of nine until she could escape her own family? I squeezed Ashleigh's shoulders.

"Do you mind sleeping here tonight?" I asked. "I don't want to send you home alone after the brutal conversation we just had."

She looked surprised. "I don't have any pajamas. Or a toothbrush."

"All the toiletries you need are in the bathroom, and I'll bring you one of my shirts."

I waited on the bed for her to settle in, to make sure she wasn't on the verge of a nervous breakdown. I lent her a shirt even though one of Mem's would have fit her better. I wanted it to be mine, even if it hung off one shoulder and reached almost to her knees. I patted the bed beside me. "Come here."

She crawled onto the covers and settled next to me. "Thanks for lending me your shirt."

I eyed the gaping neckline. "It fits great."

She laughed and yanked the collar up a little. After her tears earlier, that laughter was the most beautiful sound in the world. "Merry Christmas, Liam," she said, staring at my chest. I was still wearing the goddamned deer sweater.

I put my hand over the garish design. "Merry Christmas to you too. When you wake up, go downstairs. Mem will get you anything you need. Coffee. Tea. Breakfast." I touched her cheek. "What about tonight? Do you need some curtains to hang up around the bed? Some blankets?"

She gave a half-smile. "Are you kidding?"

"Yes."

She sobered, tracing a finger along a seam of the comforter. "I tore all my curtains down tonight. The ones on the bed you gave me. One of them ripped."

"Why did you do that?"

"Because I was tired of being scared. I was tired of being scared of you. I'm glad I came over."

I took her hand. It looked so small next to mine. "Thanks for hanging in there this evening. I know it was uncomfortable for you."

"I'm sorry I lied. I won't do it again."

"I know."

She stared down at our hands. "If I was your sub, what would you have done to me for lying? If we were, you know, in a scene?"

"Do you really want to know? It might scare you."

"I really want to know."

I took a deep breath. "Since it was a first offense, and I kind of understood why you did it, I would have been somewhat lenient. I would have tied you to this bed on your stomach, wrists and ankles, and..." I looked into her curious eyes and stood up, and crossed to a long, low bureau on the far side of the room. I opened the middle drawer and sorted through until I found what I wanted. I carried it back to the bed and handed it to her. "I would have used this strap, probably. It's not the heaviest one I have, but it hurts. I would have given you twenty good strokes with it. Enough to make an impression."

She stared at it, blinking, turning it over in her hands. "Will you... Will you show me what one would have felt like? One stroke?"

I narrowed my eyes. "Show you? Right now?"

"I'm curious."

Even as she said it, her voice quavered a little. "I don't know, Ash." I took it away from her. Bad, bad idea to bring out a toy tonight. She looked scared, yes—but she also clearly wanted to know how it felt. And I wanted to use it on her. "Like I said, it really hurts."

She stared back at me, biting her lip. I wasn't made of iron.

"Okay. Lay on your stomach." I got up from the bed to walk around to her side. By the time I got there she was on her tummy, her arms clenched beneath her. "I don't accept that position," I said. "It's defensive. If I was punishing you, I'd make you open yourself up to it." *Because you're mine.* The words came from nowhere, echoing in my

90

head. She looked up at me in question, still scared, still curious. I laid the strap beside her and took her arms in a gentle but firm grip. I spread them to either side of her, then I made her open her legs—not as much as I would have for a real punishment, but enough to feel an acute loss of control.

"Are you sure you want this?" I said. "We can stop now."

"No. I want to see. I deserve it anyway for lying."

I sat down beside her. "Already topping from the bottom, are we?"

"What does that mean?"

I stroked her hair, only to keep myself from molesting her more alluring body parts. She lay so my shirt covered her panties, but the outline of her ass was temptingly obvious. "It means that, as the dominant, I should decide what you deserve, and I should decide when, where, and how to punish you. That's how it's supposed to work."

"I shouldn't have asked you to do this, should I?"

"It's a little early in the game for rules and punishments. But if you really want to know what it feels like…"

I stood and picked up the strap. She wanted to feel one hard stroke. Okay, I'd give her one. "You can't move or turn," I warned. "I'm going to put a hand on your back to keep you still."

She made some strained sound of agreement. I noticed her hands creeping in again. "Arms out," I said. "Over your head and still."

She obeyed, her entire body vibrating with tension. I could feel it under my palm. I drew my other arm back and landed a solid whack across her ass cheeks. It wasn't that hard. I wasn't going to deal a full blow to a newbie submissive who wasn't even warmed up, but I wanted it to be hard enough to impress her. It left a mark, although it would be gone by morning.

She didn't make a sound.

"Well, that's one," I said. "What do you think? Could you take twenty?"

She turned to look at me, rubbing the place I'd strapped her. My cock was instantly hard as hell. I walked away from her to put the strap away, and also to put distance between us. "It still burns," she said when I got back. "It tingles."

"After twenty good ones, your ass would be on fire. You'd have trouble sitting down for a while."

"But that's the point, isn't it? To remind me of the bad thing I did?"

I gave her a look. "You're learning a lot tonight. But right now, you're supposed to be heading off to dreamland." *And I need to go somewhere and masturbate. Furiously.* I leaned down and kissed her on the forehead. "Is your butt okay, brave and curious one?"

She gave a soft laugh. "Yes, it's okay."

"Then go to bed. Santa won't come until you're sleeping." I walked over to the wall to turn the lights out, and watched in the darkness as she crawled under the sheets. "If you need anything, come get me across the hall. I'll leave my door partway open."

"You can sleep here if you want," she said. "It wouldn't bother me."

"I prefer to sleep in my own bed," I said as kindly as I could. It still sounded like a rebuff. "Believe me, you'll be more comfortable here. I'm impossible to sleep with."

Or rather, I didn't trust myself to sleep next to her. That was the long and short of it. "Good night, Ashleigh," I said, forcing myself to turn around and leave her lying there, tingling butt and everything. "Sleep tight."

Chapter Nine:
First Session

I woke up in Liam's bed. I vaguely remembered him carrying me there after my third bawling nightmare. I assured him they weren't nightmares about him, or what he'd done to me with his strap. They were nightmares about my father. Liam had soothed me and held me, and told me that it would never happen again. My waking brain knew that. My sleeping brain sometimes forgot.

In a way it had been a relief to talk about my past to Liam, to have it out in the open, but his questions brought up a lot of buried memories. Liam laid beside me now, one arm around me and the other thrown over his head, muscular even in sleep. His chest was an expanse of bronze, smooth skin bunched into tight abdominals at his waist. His eyelids twitched every so often. Dark circles shadowed his eyes.

I watched him for a while, studying the sculpted planes of his face. This handsome, charismatic man was going to try to heal me. Eventually, I guessed, we were going to have sex. I knew I was in good hands with him, that he would be careful. I believed he could help me. But oh, I felt guilty for keeping him up half the night.

I slid from beneath his arm and used my dancer's grace to slither off the bed without jostling him. I tiptoed to the door and back across the hall to the guest room with Liam's shirt billowing around my knees. I brushed my teeth and used the bathroom, and went out into the hall to make my way downstairs…after one last peek into Liam's room. He'd turned over but he was still asleep, half in and half out of the covers. My God, he was a beautiful man—and I was around a lot of beautiful men at the dance studio. He was beyond a beautiful man. He was—

"Ashleigh. Good morning."

I spun to find Mem standing behind me, holding out a fluffy white robe.

"You're like a ninja," I whispered.

He only smiled at me. "I trust you slept well? Come downstairs. Mr. Wilder often sleeps late."

I shrugged into the robe. It dragged the ground but it was warm and comfy. I followed behind him in my bare feet until Mem turned around. "Slippers. I'll get you slippers."

"No, it's all right."

"We have some. He gets more as gifts than he could ever wear."

He drifted soundlessly into Liam's room and came out less than a minute later with a new pair of slippers in a box. They were huge but I wore them like flip-flops, flapping off the back of my heels.

"Coffee or tea?" he asked when we reached the kitchen.

"Water."

"Ah," he said, smiling. "You are a pure one, I remember."

I had no idea what he meant. He clearly honed this mysterious and slightly offbeat image. I sat at the stool I'd sat on the night before. It was a credit to Mem that I didn't feel awkward or embarrassed during this morning-after breakfast. But when he finished setting toast, fruit, and water in front of me, I decided to set the record straight.

"Me and Liam aren't going out or anything. I didn't sleep with him last night."

Mem glanced up at me. "No one sleeps with Mr. Wilder."

I had actually slept with him, but only in a messed-up, crybaby kind of way. The man turned to the refrigerator. "Would you like eggs, bacon? Waffles?"

"Do you have any peanut butter for the toast?"

Peanut butter was promptly delivered on a small plate with a fancy silver knife. I spread it on my bread, looking up at Mem from under my lashes.

"Tell the truth," I said. "You're one of those guys who looks harmless on the outside, but really you know twelve different ways to kill people."

One eyebrow lifted ever so slightly. "Twelve? I know at least thirty ways. Thirty-two, if I apply myself."

I smiled as he puttered around the kitchen, wiping counters, rearranging plates and bowls as if reluctant to leave me alone. "Where are you from, Mem?" I couldn't place his accent or his slightly ethnic look.

"I am from the United States. From the Midwest, like you."

A bit of peanut butter stuck in my throat. I wondered if Mem was the one who'd gone to Cowskull to dig up dirt on me. "You're Native American," I realized.

"Somewhat," he replied. "I have a lot of different blood in me. Like you. Like Mr. Wilder. Ah." He looked up as he spoke his name. "And so he joins us."

"Good morning, Mem. Or afternoon," Liam said, looking at his watch. His gaze found me next, with a directness that made me shiver. I felt struck dumb by the sight of him. I didn't know why. This was our neutral ground, he'd said, but things didn't feel neutral any longer. He was freshly showered, dressed in jeans and a long sleeved dark green tee that hugged his muscles way too much. I looked around for Mem but he'd disappeared again. Ninja.

Liam crossed to me and stroked a finger down my cheek. "Better today?"

I nodded. "Much better. I'm sorry I wrecked your sleep."

"I'm sorry I wrecked yours. You seemed like you calmed down at the end. I didn't snore all night, did I?"

"If you did, I didn't notice."

Liam went into the kitchen and started making an omelet with all kinds of extra stuff. Mushrooms, peppers, cheese, and pieces of bacon. I watched him, chewing on my toast.

"How come Mem doesn't make your breakfast?"

Liam chuckled. "Sometimes he does. I think he's more concerned with giving us privacy at the moment." He looked up at me. "He's my most trusted friend, Ashleigh. He'll never talk about what goes on here, but he knows pretty much everything."

"He knows about me? About why I came here last night?"

"No."

"Was he the one who went to Cowskull?"

Liam sighed. "Don't worry about that, okay? Your privacy is assured. As for Mem…" He flipped his omelet and shrugged. "He can be very insightful. Don't let it bother you."

"When I came here last night, he said I was…I don't remember. Itchy? Icky?"

"*Ishi?*"

"Yeah."

His mouth tensed as he nudged the omelet onto a plate. "Mem says a lot of weird stuff like that. Take it with a grain of salt."

He called you Ishi too. Why don't you have a home, Liam? I didn't say it. He didn't look like he wanted to discuss it further.

"So, did Santa come?" he asked a little too brightly. He craned his head to look at the far corner of the living room. Last night, in the dim light, I hadn't even noticed the tree. It was a real tree, albeit sparsely decorated. I sensed Mem's involvement. "Damn," Liam said. "Nothing. I was too naughty again."

I laughed as he brought his plate and a cup of coffee around the counter to join me. He slid into the seat beside me with a broad smile. This was my cue to joke with him and be cute but I had nothing. I took a sip of water. "I think Santa only comes for kids."

"I think you're probably right. Anyway," he said, gesturing around, "I already have everything I need. If I don't have something, I buy it." He looked at me. "Do you buy presents for yourself?"

"No. But on Christmas, sometimes, I let myself eat bad foods."

"Bad foods? What is that? What's a bad food?"

"Chocolate. Cookies. Ice cream."

He flashed me a conspiratorial grin. "I have all three of those here, and more. What do you want? Ice cream?" He shoveled in another bite of omelet. "I have, like, eight flavors in the freezer right now."

"Ice cream for breakfast? That's bad behavior *and* bad food," I said. *Bad behavior.* That called to mind a whole slew of other thoughts. Heat bloomed on my cheeks and I looked away from him.

Liam had hit me with a strap last night.

Not only that, but he'd touched my legs and made me open them, and spread my arms out at my sides. I was so hot afterward, so wet. So confused. The sting of the strap had been nothing compared to the throbbing ache in my pelvis, all because he'd hurt me and made me lay a specific way. When I looked up he was staring back at me.

"We don't have to start today unless you want to," he said. "If you want to go home and think things over a little more first…"

"I want to start today."

There, that was blunt enough. He smiled his casual, everything's-great smile and nodded. "Okay. I'm looking forward to it. Maybe after a little ice cream."

I wasn't exactly looking forward to it. It was more like my *Sleeping Beauty* performance, hoping to survive it without fucking up too bad.

* * * * *

Up in the room, he took a chair from the table and dragged it to the middle of the floor.

"Sit."

He meant me. I flopped over in my slippers with the oversize robe still bunched around me. This didn't feel very sexy. I sat in the chair and as soon as I did, he sprawled on the bed. He leaned back against the pillows and waited for me to meet his gaze.

"We're going to start by talking about personal boundaries. Mental and physical."

Hm, that wasn't where I'd expected us to start, but it didn't matter. I put on my listening face.

"So, you're over there," he said. "I'm here. There's space between us. How do you feel?"

"I feel okay."

"More specific."

"Um…"

"No umms," he said a little sharply. "Think and then talk."

"Well, now that you seem irritated, I feel nervous."

"Okay. And what's your reaction to that? Do you want to come closer to me?"

I told the truth. "No, not really."

"So distance, physical boundaries, can help us to relax. To feel safer." He vaulted off the bed and came to stand directly behind me. "How do you feel now?"

I couldn't see him. I couldn't see his expression or what he was going to do to me. "I feel a lot less relaxed."

He moved around to stand in front of me. "I'm all up inside your boundaries now, aren't I?"

I nodded, looking up at all six and a half feet of him.

He reached to touch my cheek, a soft, caressing slide of his fingertips. "You're doing great, Ash. You're listening. You're focusing. Good job." He dropped his hand. "So, when I was praising you and stroking you, it was a lot more pleasant to have me in your boundaries, wasn't it?"

I touched my cheek where he'd touched it, then flinched as he crouched down in front of me.

"You have these boundaries around you all the time," he said. "We all do, especially when it comes to our bodies and sex. Yours are probably thicker than most because, from a very young age, you learned not to trust. But when you trust someone...even if you don't trust someone...you can choose to let those boundaries down. What you experience and what you feel doesn't come from other people. It comes from you."

He waited a moment, until I nodded at him. He put his hands on my thighs. I instantly tensed.

"I crossed your boundaries when I did this," he said. "Now you decide if it's okay or not. But don't base it on other experiences. Am I hurting you?"

"No."

He slid them up a couple inches. "How about now?"

"No," I forced out, wondering when he was going to stop.

"Take your robe off, baby."

I stood up and he helped me. He slung it over the foot of the bed and had me kick off the slippers too. I felt a little chilly without the warmth of the robe. He nodded back at the chair and I sat down in his long, baggy tee shirt. He put his hands back on my thighs. "Feel different?" he asked.

"Yes, definitely different."

He nudged my legs apart and knelt between them, his front pressed to mine.

"I'm so far inside your boundaries now, I can feel your heart beating," he said.

I didn't answer, just stared into his gold-amber eyes.

"You have to try to think a new way, Ash. For so long, you've thrown up boundaries around anything related to sex. You've associated physical intimacy with something bad. Something you didn't want. But you have to teach yourself that's not the case." He moved even closer, put his arms around me and rested his head against mine. "Does this feel good or bad?"

"Good," I said automatically, but it didn't. It felt scary, threatening. "Bad," I said, amending my answer. I wasn't supposed to lie.

"Okay." He didn't sound angry or disappointed. "Bad in what way?"

"It feels bad because I don't know what you're going to do next."

"You think I might do something scary? Something you don't like?"

I hesitated. "Maybe. I don't know."

He was quiet a moment. "Do you really not know?"

I pressed my cheek against his. "I don't think you'll hurt me."

"You're right." He pulled back from me. "Do you want me? Am I attractive to you? Desirable?"

I stared into his intent gaze. "I— I—"

"I'm not asking if you want me to fuck you this minute. I'm not asking if you want me to hold you down and stick my cock in you. I'm asking if I please you. If you want me. If your body feels that you want me."

My breath stole out through my lips. I clenched the inside of my thighs, remembering his hands and his violent kisses. Remembering the strap. "Yes. I always feel like I want you." I flushed, but he went on very matter-of-factly.

"So you want me, and you're not afraid I'll hurt you. This is a great thing between two people." His hand moved on my waist, up and down in a soothing, steady motion. "There are a lot of names for it. Chemistry. Craving. Attraction. Lust. None of it has anything to do with pain or fear. Right?"

I shuddered a little. "Then why am I afraid?"

"Exactly." He eased away from me. "Let's try something else. I'm going back over to the bed."

He left me and I relaxed a bit, but I felt the loss of him too. He sat on the edge of the bed, leaning back on his arms. "I want you to take the shirt off and come over here."

I opened my mouth to demur, to remind him I wasn't wearing anything underneath but panties. His raised finger stopped me cold. "We talked about obedience yesterday. Do you remember?" His low voice contained a warning note.

"But I—"

"Ashleigh."

"But—"

"If you keep talking back over a little thing like this, I'll punish you."

I hugged my arms around my waist. "You're not letting me speak."

"Because speaking isn't required."

"This isn't fair."

"Power exchange is rarely fair. That's kind of the point. Are you finished?"

This was the dominance I'd wanted, the dominance I'd asked for. I could submit or I could leave. I didn't want to leave, but I didn't want to take the shirt off either. I felt safe in his shirt. *There will be times you won't feel comfortable in here...*

"I'll repeat it one more time. Take your shirt off," he said clearly and slowly, "and come over here to me."

My shoulders tensed as I reached for the hem and pulled his tee over my head. For a few moments I held it in front of me, and then I dropped it on the chair. I felt cold, naked. Frozen. When I looked at Liam I expected him to be groping me visually, but his eyes were still trained on mine. I scratched my cheek, balled my hands into fists, and made myself walk over to him. It was only once I was there, standing in front of him, that he dropped his gaze in a cursory inspection of my body. I wanted to shrink into myself. I was so skinny. Very small boobs. My butt was okay but I was wearing ugly cotton panties.

"How do you feel now?" he asked.

"Horrible."

"Why?"

I bit the inside of my lip. I didn't know why. Because I'd made him angry, and I felt too vulnerable. This was what he was supposed to be helping me with!

"I know this is hard," he said. "I'm making you operate outside the boundaries you're comfortable with." He took off his tee shirt, revealing the muscular chest I remembered from gawking at him in bed. He'd seemed harmless then, in sleep. He seemed less harmless now.

"Okay," he said. "We're both naked from the waist up. Look at us." He smiled, tracing a finger over my hip. "Pretty hot."

I took in his broad brown chest, his dark nipples and masculine dusting of chest hair. By contrast I had a skinny, pasty chest, pink nipples and no chest hair. One of us was hot, anyway.

"Come here," he said in little more than a whisper. "Let's do some touching."

He drew me against his chest. I stood between his legs and leaned into the heat and scent of him. It was a relief not to be exposed. He ran fingers over my back, smoothed them down my spine while I held on to his shoulders and stared at the wall. He felt so warm and solid. His muscles moved against my skin and I felt my nipples draw up tight. He leaned back to look at my face.

"You're beautiful, Ash. In case you didn't know that."

I didn't know the correct response to compliments in this little game we played. "Thank you for calling me beautiful," I said, taking a stab.

"I'm not calling you beautiful. You are beautiful."

I didn't really believe him. I deflected. "You're beautiful too."

He drew back and traced a hand down the center of my chest. "You want me to touch you." He nodded at my taut nipples. "Your body does, anyway. Your body doesn't care about boundaries. Only your mind."

I froze. Was that true? Of course it was. I knew all along my hang-ups were mental, but I never considered that my body could work outside of that. If I could just turn off my mind...

"But you need your mind to have really good sex," he said, dashing my sudden inspiration. "Without your mind it's just physical, without meaning or excitement. So turn off the boundaries in your mind and let me touch you. Let yourself feel whatever you want to feel."

With those words he slid his fingers to the side and brushed them over one of my hardened nipples. There was an instant, potent flash of pleasure. "No fear," he murmured. "This feels good."

Oh, yes, it felt amazingly good. My palms slid over his shoulders as he touched my nipple again, then the other one. Each time there was a strong, bright sensation of something delicious. *Chemistry. Craving. Attraction.*

Lust.

Next I knew, I was gripping him by the neck and he was leaning closer to take the tips of my breasts in his mouth. That was a whole new sensation, warm and wet and tingling. Guys had done this to me before but I'd found it vaguely off-putting. I hadn't wanted them to do it. Now I didn't want Liam to stop.

One of his arms held me trapped as he suckled my left breast. The other hand trailed over my hip and then up to my right breast. His fingers closed on the tight nipple and pinched it. The mix of pain and pleasure caught me off guard. The moan that came out of my mouth shocked me, as did the unconscious thrusting of my hips. I pushed away from him.

"Okay." He took my hand to stop my retreat. "It's okay." His lips were half open, his eyes burning with the same building passion I felt. "It's okay to enjoy it. It feels different, doesn't it? To enjoy it?"

I nodded, speechless. Breathless. I looked down at his jeans, at the massive hard-on outlined there, and took another step back.

"All I wanted to teach you today," he said, "is to be aware of your boundaries, and your own power to let them up and down. I want you to be aware of your mind's role when it comes to sex. Or in your case, your mind's interference."

I was aware of that now, one hundred percent. I wanted him to touch me again, to kiss my breasts and hurt them with his fingers, but my mind wasn't ready for the sexual part of me to be in charge. But…I had a sexual part of me. It wasn't gone. The idea of that filled me with hope.

"Are you okay?" he asked.

"Yes, I'm okay." I swallowed hard as he squeezed my hand. "I have a lot to think about."

He took my other hand too, watching me for a few moments. "It's good to have things to think about. I'm also going to give you homework."

My eyes widened. He reached out to brush his fingertips across my still-hard nipples. "I want you to touch these the way I touched them, at least once every day. I want you to do it while you're lying in bed, and I want you to concentrate on enjoying it. Nothing else. No shame. No fear of what comes before or after. Can you do that?"

There was only one correct answer in this room. "Yes, Liam."

"But I don't want you to touch anything else," he added. "Only your nipples. Only right here." He traced around the edges, then back to the middle of the tight peaks. "No other part of your beautiful little body." Before my eyes, his gaze went seductive and smoky. "I want you to save the rest for me. Do you understand?"

I could barely draw breath. I nodded, trying hard not to thrust my breasts against his palm.

He left my aching nipples alone and reached down to catch my fingers. "Your other homework is to get screened for STDs. I will too. It's a pain, but you should ask every partner to be tested. No exceptions."

"Okay. I know." Awkward. Embarrassing. But necessary, I supposed. "I think there's a clinic the dancers use."

"Good. So that will be all squared away." He scratched the side of his neck and looked very directly at me. "There's one more thing we need to discuss before you go. Do you know what that is?"

I thought I knew. I was afraid to say it. His steady gaze pried out the words. "I—I did something wrong."

"What did you do wrong?"

"I argued with you when you told me to take my shirt off."

"And I specifically warned you what would happen, didn't I? If you kept arguing?"

"Yeah."

"Why don't you try a 'Yes, Sir?'" he suggested with an edge to his voice.

I shivered. He was amazingly good at this dominance thing. "Yes, Sir. I'm sorry."

"Okay. We improve through practice. And punishment, of course. That's what it's for, to teach you. You understand that?"

This was madness. *You asked for this, Ashleigh.* I felt scared and turned on in equal measure. "Yes...Sir. I understand."

"Okay. We'll keep it simple today." He stepped away from the bed and I found myself, a moment later, bent over the edge of it, right where he'd been sitting. "Arms out to the side. Don't move them."

Nervous pangs fluttered in my middle. *You asked for this, you crazy person, so suck it up and take it.* He nudged my legs apart a little more with his foot.

"Plant your feet and brace yourself. I prefer my submissives to be still," he said. My breath accelerated to a thousand miles an hour. I heard the clink of his belt buckle and the swish of him pulling it from his jeans. "Five warm ups and five harder ones. You're new at this, but you need to feel what a punishment means."

Oh my God.

I felt his hand on my back, the whisper of leather across the fabric of my panties. It felt smooth and cold. Then... *Whap!* It felt a lot harder than I thought a warm up would be. I barely had time to suck in air before another blow fell, and another. It stung like hell but it wasn't unbearable. The instant of contact was the hardest part. No, the hardest part was waiting for the next stroke to fall. *Whap!* One last warm up. Oww. It was a little harder than the others.

"Look at me."

I turned at the command in his voice. Was he checking to see if I was all right? I wasn't totally sure I was. For one thing, my pussy had grown astoundingly wet since he'd made me bend over, so wet I was afraid it would show through the gusset of my panties. *Please, please, don't make me pull them down.* "These are going to be harder," he said. "Keep your hands where they are and don't move."

"Yes, Sir." The "Sir" came out automatically this time, a reaction to his stern voice.

WHAP!

I cried out in shock. Way, way harder than I expected. Not like the warm ups. Not comfortable at all. Right on the heels of that surprise, the next stroke fell. I knew this was supposed to hurt, to teach me a lesson, but...*God.* My ass burned like fire and there were three more to go. *WHAP!* I wondered wildly if Mem could hear this all the way downstairs. I felt humiliated but I felt excited and turned on too. *WHAP!* Okay, less turned on now. I squeezed my legs together, wanting to turn away, wanting to jump up and run away from him.

"Spread them," he said. "One more to go."

I huffed out a breath and made myself resume the proper position. I expected the last one to be the worst one and I wasn't disappointed. He held me down with one hand and snapped a hard crack right against the middle of my ass cheeks. With the pain I'd already suffered, it brought tears to my eyes.

Then he touched me.

He ran a palm over both my ass cheeks and tugged up the edges of my panties. I looked over my shoulder to find him studying my skin. Assessing the damage? The act seemed more intimate than a kiss. He flung the belt down on the bed and lifted me, and then he did kiss me. I was hyper aware of a thousand sensations as his lips moved over mine...my throbbing ass, the wetness between my legs, his firm grip on my elbow, my bare skin against his. My tears had disappeared. The world disappeared, replaced by his demanding touch and his sexy male scent.

Just as suddenly he broke away from me. The savage look in his eyes was brought under rigid control. "Congratulations," he said, stroking a finger down my cheek. "You took that very well. Although that's not exactly how it's supposed to end."

I searched his face. "How is it supposed to end?"

A muscle twitched in his jaw as he poked a finger toward the far wall. "Corner time. Ten minutes." He reached for his belt and started threading it back through his jeans. "No rubbing your ass cheeks either," he said as I reached back to soothe the sting. "I'll let you know when you can leave."

Chapter Ten:
Liam's Girl

Liam drove me home a short time later. It seemed like I'd spent hours in that bedroom but it had barely been an hour. I got home just after two in the afternoon. My pajamas were on the floor where I'd shed them, and the curtains to my bed were still crumpled in a ball. I felt like I'd changed into a completely different person since I'd ripped them down last night. I still wasn't the person I wanted to be, but I didn't think I was as messed up as I'd been before.

I crawled into my new, curtain-less bed with a book, but thoughts of the past twenty-four hours kept intruding into my head. My father was dying. Cancer. Melanoma. Meanwhile, Liam had taken charge of my skittish sexuality, at least in that room. He'd given lots of orders, dominated me, and I'd submitted. He'd made me take off my clothes and he'd touched me…and I'd gotten turned on by it. Then he'd spanked me with his belt, and God help me, that had turned me on more than anything else.

When the phone rang flashing Liam's name, I jumped on it. "Hello?"

"Hi, Ash. It's me. I'm not going to call you every day to bother you. I'm just checking to be sure you're okay."

"Yes, I'm okay."

"We had some intense moments together and I thought everything went great. But sometimes after people have an emotional session, especially newbies, they experience a drop. A blue, depressed feeling."

I hunkered over the phone, cradling it to my ear. "I'm not depressed, but…"

"But?"

"I'm sort of confused. About what happened at the end."

"The kiss? Listen, Ashleigh—"

"No," I interrupted. "The part before, when you used your belt on me. I know it was supposed to hurt, and it did hurt and I did feel punished, but…"

"You liked it too."

I swallowed hard. "Yes. Does that make me a bad submissive?"

"No." I heard his chuckle carry over the line. "That makes you a masochist. Did you do your homework yet?"

My cheeks got really hot. "No. Not yet."

"Do you have clothespins at your place?"

I stared across my apartment to the bathroom, where I'd clipped up about twenty pairs of leotards and shoes. "I have a few."

"You only need two. Sometime after you touch your nipples, after you make yourself feel good and excited, I think you should try clamping them with clothespins." His voice dropped lower. "Fair warning. It'll hurt. But if you're a masochist, you might enjoy it."

Oh my God. "Do I… Do I have to do that?"

"I want you to try it, yes. It doesn't have to be tonight. Whenever you feel brave enough. Start with one. If you can't stand it, take it off. All I ask is that you try it and see how it feels."

"Or…?"

He tsked. "Or you'll be punished for not doing your homework, and I'll do it to you on Monday anyway when we meet. Be brave, Ash. Break down boundaries." His voice went soft and warm like a caress at the last part.

"Okay, I'll try."

"Just be careful. If a belt spanking turns you on, nipple clamps probably will too. Remember what I said about touching other parts of yourself."

"Oh… I…"

"You do remember what I said, don't you?"

It was pretty much all I'd thought about. "You said to save it for you."

"Mm-hm," he drawled, and then his voice turned brusque. "Okay. Just wanted to check in. If you need me or if you have any questions, call me. Otherwise I'll see you Monday afternoon."

"Yes, Liam. Thank you."

I'd almost busted out with the *Yes, Sir* over the phone. We were supposed to be equals outside the bedroom but now that I'd experienced his dominant side in action, I could only seem to think of him as *Sir*. Later, as I was doing my "homework" in the dark, by the light of my flickering LED candle, I thought he might as well be lying next to me in my bed. His bed. The bed he'd given me.

I was embarrassed at first and I only fondled myself through the sheer lace of my bra. The second night I pulled the cups down and touched my nipples the way he had, with that same light, lingering touch. I tried to focus on what he'd taught me. No boundaries. No fear or shame. I tried to enjoy it and I did kind of enjoy it, but only when I thought about him at the same time. The third night I made myself go into the bathroom and get a couple of the clothespins. I closed them on my fingertips and it didn't seem so bad, but as soon as I brought one close to my nipple I lost my nerve and threw them on the side table.

Was I really a masochist? In class, in rehearsals, I could hardly bear to think of Liam and the hurty things he'd done to me. I stammered through my visit to the clinic, wishing he was with me but knowing I'd be mortified if he was. I had a new, weird, hyperaware feeling about my breasts and my ass, all the time. I felt my nipples while I was dancing. Not felt them with my fingers, but felt them trapped against my leotard, or brushed by my wrist when I folded my arms over my chest. I felt his hands on my ass in my daydreams, or his belt. Every so often I touched my nipples during the day, just because it reminded me of him. Just because it felt pleasurable. Because it made me feel brave and sexual.

This was all very alarming to me.

* * * * *

"Ash-lee. *Ashhh-lee.*"

I stopped mid-bang, crouched over in the dressing room. I could have sworn I heard Rubio calling me.

"Ash-lee?"

I spun to look at the door. Rubio *was* calling me. He darted a look around the room.

"Anybody in here?"

"I'm here."

He made an impatient wave. "No, I mean, anyone else? I need to talk to you."

The Great Rubio needed to talk to *me?*

He looked past me and gawked at my pile of shoes. "Geez, girl. You have enough to last all season. Obsess much?"

"I want to be prepared." He was ninety-nine percent of the reason I did this. He still hissed "*Asshole!*" in my nightmares from time to time.

"You stay here too late," he said. "You look like hell. Raccoon eyes. When you ever sleep?"

I squeezed a toe shoe in my palm. "The same time you sleep. At night."

He narrowed his eyes. He was in practice sweats—and he was sweaty. "Hey, I need your help. You busy? Can you help me a minute?"

I stared at Fernando Rubio. He was *asking me for help.*

"Sure, I can help you," I said, trying to sound casual about it. "What do you need?"

"I'm working on steps. I need someone to mark steps with me. You're the only one here, so come help me." He scowled at my pile of shoes. "If you have any pointe shoes that don't sound like hammers, this would be good. Bring them. Come."

I got to my feet and sorted through my shoes, picking a good pair and dumping the rest into the bin under my carrel. My mind raced in excited shock. Yes, Rubio was mean and rude but I still admired him as an artist—and he wanted me to mark steps with him. He was inviting me into his private creative process.

I had to run to catch up with him in the hall. He led me to the same rehearsal room he'd been in the night me and Liam argued. "You warmed up?" he asked. "Go on. Warm up first."

I did a few stretches while he paced back and forth, talking through combinations under his breath. At some point I guess he figured I'd warmed up enough because he grabbed my hand and dragged me to the center of the floor. He turned me to face the mirror and described a series of steps in garbled counts and a smattering of Portuguese. "Okay. You do it?"

I tried my best to execute what he wanted. He stopped me halfway though and changed the steps, partnering and coaching me at the same time. This back-and-forth went on for about twenty minutes, but at the end of it he'd developed a pretty cool sequence. "Stay," he said. "Remember the steps in case I forget."

He ran over to his book to diagram the combination. I moved through the steps again without him, marking them in my mind. He had a unique talent for choreography. The steps felt energizing, and I enjoyed the flow and sweep of them. When he had everything down I said, "You're good at this. Have you choreographed before?"

He wore the funniest expression, like he was trying to think of something nasty to say but couldn't. He shrugged and half-smiled. "Never like this."

"I think it's good when dancers choreograph. The steps feel more organic. Natural."

He stared a minute, then crossed to me. "What you think of this?"

He showed me another, more intricate combination. I mostly liked it. I told him the parts that tripped me up or didn't flow right. For another fifteen minutes or so he bounced ideas off me and had me try them out. I don't know when I stopped feeling self-conscious and started to enjoy dancing with him, but for whole long minutes I wasn't worried about being judged or measuring up to his expectations. I was collaborating as his dance partner. I was living in his world.

"What's this ballet about?" I asked as he spun me and caught me in the crook of his arm. He released me with a frown.

"I don't know what it's about. Why it has to be about something? Why it can't just be movement? Dancing?"

"It can be," I said, trying to regain our earlier camaraderie. "That's what Balanchine did, right? Just dancing?"

If anything, his glare deepened. "I am not Balanchine. I do my own thing."

I shrugged, doing some *passés* to stay warm. "Well, I think it's good. Even if it's not about anything. What kind of music are you going to use?"

"I am still considering." He pursed his lips. "Or rather, I am still fighting with Yves. I have some ideas."

"He doesn't agree with your ideas?"

"Not yet," he said. "You want to listen?"

He went to the audio station in the back and put on a track that sounded very evocative and lyrical, with faint, thrumming guitar strains and crying violins. For the choreography, his choice was perfect. I started doing the steps to the music because they fit, and he joined me a moment later. We watched ourselves in the mirrored wall, dancing all out, even improvising a few steps at the end. After the music stopped, after he went back to switch off the track, I kept moving, lost in his vision.

"You go to see Liam?"

His question jolted me. I turned and dropped off pointe. "Did he tell you I did?"

"He didn't tell me nothing. Did you go?"

I poked the tip of my shoe into the floor. "Maybe."

He snickered. "That means yes. You sleep with him? You play BDSM with him?" The lurid gleam in his eye took me right back to that night he'd groped me and lifted me in the air.

I gave him a quelling look. "Why should I tell you when you won't even tell me what your ballet is about?"

"I gave you his address, you remember? I introduced you to him."

"And?" I went to the barre and stretched out my arms. "What we're doing together is none of your business."

"Ah. So you are doing something together."

He smirked at me. I'd been having such a good time dancing with him, I'd almost forgotten what a jackass he could be. "Do you need any more help?" I asked. "It's getting late."

"Yes, getting late." He frowned and waved at me. "We're done. Enough."

"I mean, I can stay if you want—"

"No. Go. Is late, Raccoon Eyes. Go home to sleep."

I started for the door, then turned back to him. "Thanks for letting me work with you tonight. I don't know if you think about stuff like this, but you've always been an inspiration to me. You're the whole reason I auditioned to join this company, because of your talent and your expertise. You're an inspiration to a lot of people, and..." He looked away from me, over at the wall. Apparently I was boring him. "Anyway, no matter what your ballet is about, it's really beautiful and a pleasure to dance. So thanks for letting me help with it tonight."

I turned to leave, embarrassed by my fawning soliloquy, but his voice stopped me.

"Hey! Ash-lee." He jogged over to meet me by the door. "I meant to tell you, your shoes. Much better." He did this awkward little wink and thumbs up. "And maybe...if you stay late again and I need help... If you're around, maybe you come help me again? Is easier to think of the steps if there is someone to try them."

Was The Great Rubio really standing in front of me, tapping me as a practice partner? Or was this some bizarre fantasy world? I tore my eyes from the definition of his chest and forced them to his face. "Sure. Of course. I'll help you anytime, Mr. Rubio. Like I said, I'm a huge believer in your art."

He wrinkled his nose. "My art, heh? Why you call me Mr. Rubio?"

"It's in my contract."

He threw back his head and laughed. "It is not."

"Yes, it is."

"Call me Ruby if you want, like Liam." He waved a hand. "If we're all going to be friends. Anyway, Ash-lee. You go. I got more work to do. If I need you again, I'll come find you with your shoes."

"Or you could call," I said. "Liam has my number. Or, I could give it to you. We could set up, you know...times to work."

"Hm." That was it, just "hm," and he walked away from me, lost again in his dance.

* * * * *

The days ticked by, Wednesday, Thursday, Friday, with no word from Ashleigh. I was okay with this. I preferred it that way. If she'd glommed onto me and called me constantly, I would have called the whole thing off. What we were doing was really intense, and really intimate by default. I didn't want her to get the wrong idea—that we were going to start dating, become a couple, get married. My lifestyle wasn't set up for that kind of commitment, especially to someone with problems like hers.

Then why are you thinking about her all the time?

It wasn't so much that I was thinking about her, just that I couldn't get into the idea of hanging out with other women. I'd become too focused on our little sex training program to work my usual game. I ignored the backlog of sexts on my phone, even though it was my habit to flirt just for the fun of it, and maybe hook up a few times a week with an especially persistent slut. I should have been hooking up every night. I had a lot of built-up sexual energy and I didn't want to unleash it on Ashleigh.

Not yet.

Ruby came over on Saturday to hang out and use my gym, which was another poking reminder of her presence in my life. He handed me an envelope just inside the door.

"Your invite to the New Year's Gala."

"Thanks."

"You coming?"

"I might."

He smirked at me. "Your girl will be there."

I headed toward the gym. "I don't know what girl you're talking about."

Ruby let it lie until we were well into our workout, until I was sweating through a series of bench-presses with his ugly face looming over the bar.

"She told me, you know."

"Are you going to spot me, Rube, or are we going to girl-talk?"

"She told me she came to see you."

"I think Lousha left some makeup upstairs. Maybe we could do each other's eyes. Talk about getting our periods."

Ruby chuckled and pushed down on the bar until I hissed at him to stop. "I know you like Ash-lee," he taunted. "You never went to see so much ballet."

I ignored him and readjusted my grip, pressing against his opposing force.

"Aw, come on," he said, pulling a pout. "You talk to me about the other girls. You tell me everything."

"You work with this one."

"Ah. You 'respect' this one. *Maniero*," he drawled in Portuguese.

"You're getting on my nerves." I frowned and powered through another few reps. "If I didn't know any better, I'd guess that *you* were interested in her."

Ruby shrugged. "I practiced with her. She helped me, a few nights ago."

I rattled the barbell into the uprights and sat up. "You practiced what with her? Where?"

"This ballet I'm working on. She's the only one there so late. Still banging her shoes, but less hard now." He gave me a speculative look.

"You sleep with her, yes? She has that…" He wiggled his fingers around his head. "That fuck-my-face look."

"Stop. I'm not going to tell you anything."

"Maybe I find out myself, now that you've brought her into the lifestyle."

"She wouldn't touch you with a ten foot pole."

"No?" His demonic features twisted into a grin. "She told me I'm her inspiration. She admires me."

I leaned on my knees and faced him as he went to work with a couple of dumbbells. "What do you want me to say? 'Don't touch her, you dirty bastard?' 'Hey, no, she's mine?' I know you're not interested in her. She's not your type. If you're curious about how she plays or how she fucks, I don't know. I don't know how she fucks yet. I haven't fucked her, okay? We haven't scened yet, not really. She's new to the lifestyle stuff."

Ruby dropped the weights and rolled his shoulders. "You haven't fucked her? What do you like about her then?"

"Her body." That was something he'd understand.

"I know a lot of girls with bodies like that," he scoffed. "Not sexy. No boobs. No fat to grab on to."

"I like her face too. She's pretty."

Ruby pursed his lips and ignored me, picking up the weights again. He was more of a drama queen than any of the women I hung out with. I got on the treadmill and tuned him out, settling in for a long run.

"You think she dance good?" he asked a few minutes later. "Ashlee?"

"You're the dancer. You tell me. You think she dance good?" I parroted his words, nailing the accent.

His brows drew together. "She dances different," he finally said. He put down the weights and started pulling poses in the mirror. "She dances like, uh…" He made a motion, a gripping gesture at his center. "She dances like something eating at her. Like she have sharks circling under her in a tank."

It was something I normally would have laughed at, especially with his grasping illustration, but I knew too well what fueled that intensity.

"You should help her out," I said. "Help her get ahead in the company. Put in a word."

"You could put in a word better than me. You give so much money to City Ballet. Go to Yves, tell him to promote her to soloist. He'll do anything for a price."

I thought about it, biting my lip. "She would hate that, if I bought her a promotion. She can do it on her own. She has the talent."

"Pfft. She has a lot to learn. She pay her dues, like everyone else."

"Did you pay your dues? It's been easy for you."

"Yeah, because I'm special. For her, it's work. For most dancers, work."

"But you can work with her. You can practice with her." I was getting winded, but I kept pushing. "What if you used her in that ballet you're working on? Like, officially cast her as your partner in the spring showcase? It would be great visibility for her."

"Ugh." He waved a hand. "I don't even know if I'm doing it. I don't know."

That was my cue to tell him that of course he had to do it, and of course everyone would be devastated if he didn't. Instead I said, "I'll pay you to put her in your ballet."

He narrowed his eyes. "What?"

"I'll pay you, what…what's your price for a ballet sponsor? A thousand pounds?"

He made a face like I was insulting him.

"Ten thousand pounds, then. Any more and you're just being a bitch, because you're going to do the ballet anyway. We both know you are."

He still pretended to balk. "I was going to ask Heather to do it."

"Heather is jaded and plastic. Plus you look shitty together."

"Suzanne then."

"You're an asshole. Thirty thousand pounds. And you can't tell Ashleigh."

"Can't tell her she's in it?"

"Can't tell her about the money. That I paid you to cast her."

Ruby did a few standing jumps and went up onto his hands, something he frequently did when he was thinking something over. "You know," he said, looking at me from upside-down, "it's only a short piece. Twenty-five thousand, okay? I buy a new car, maybe."

"You don't drive."

"I can learn. How hard can it be?" He was doing inverse pushups now. Show off.

"Stop fucking around and stand up like a normal person."

He did a back flip and came to his feet. "Li-am, how is this different from you paying Yves?"

"Because Yves wouldn't have agreed to it." I pumped up the pace on the treadmill. "You know, you could do it for free. Cause you're my friend. You could not be an asshole for once."

He snorted. "Is much more lucrative to be an asshole. Hey, I can't dance forever. I need money for my retirement! You write me a check, and I'll talk to her in a few weeks, when she proves she can do it."

"She can do it. If you don't cast her, you have to give my money back."

"Maybe. Minus a deposit."

Before I could come up with a retort, my phone buzzed. Well, what was twenty-five thousand? Nothing to me, and possibly a whole new future for Ashleigh. I shut off the treadmill and checked the message.

I'm not sure I'm a masochist...

I laughed to myself, angling the phone away from Ruby. I typed, *How long did you manage to leave them on?*

About .5 seconds. It HURT.

I sprawled on the weight bench while Rubio fired up the treadmill. *We'll experiment more at some point*, I texted. *I bet you could take it longer than that.*

"Who you texting?" Ruby asked, working into a long, fast stride.

"None of your fucking business."

"Ash-leeee," he sneered in a high-pitched voice. "*Li-am loves Ash-lee, Li-am loves Ash-lee*," he sing-songed in time with the rhythm of his feet.

I'll try, Sir, she texted back a few seconds later.

My groin tightened. I dropped the phone and slung my arm over my eyes, picturing Ashleigh's serious, pretty face, and her body just waiting for me to awaken it. *I'll try, Sir.* She'd used the "Sir" just to get me hot.

I'll try too, Ash, I thought. *For as long as I have to. You deserve to be free of your fears.*

I rested there on the bench and thought wildly lascivious thoughts about her. Ruby and his schoolyard chanting ceased to exist.

116

Chapter Eleven:
Second Session

I was mentally prepared—mostly—to see Liam on New Year's Day, which was our next appointed meeting. I was not prepared to see him New Year's Eve at the City Ballet fundraising gala, dressed in a kickass tuxedo with a black bow tie, and his hair all sexy and tousled.

He was hot in jeans and a sweater, hotter in a suit, but he was devastating in a tux. He stood out in the crowd, so at ease as he talked and laughed with the other guests at his table. I could see the businessman in him, the capable leader. At first I thought the pretty woman on his left was his date, and I felt unreasonably jealous, but then she held hands with the guy on the other side of her and I breathed an equally unreasonable sigh of relief. Liam wasn't my boyfriend. I didn't want him to be. Or...let's be honest...it wasn't realistic for him to be my boyfriend. I still felt jealous when other women approached him—and they did, in droves.

As for myself, I stole glances at him from behind columns and stuck to the fringes of the room. I didn't know how to relate to him in this very public, very non-sexual setting, especially since I'd been fantasizing non-stop about his deep voice and masterful dom thing, and the way he'd bruised my ass with his belt. I'd also been groping my nipples the entire past week at his instruction. I wasn't ready to come face-to-face with him, especially when I was in my dancer-fundraiser-leotard outfit and he was in that tux.

For a while it was easy to lurk around and gawk because the lights were low. The company presented a couple hours of special ballet snippets from the season's repertoire, none of which I was in, but then the lights came up and I was rolled out onto the floor with the other underlings to smile and hock autographed programs and pointe shoes.

I kept one eye on Liam while I smiled and interacted with the guests around me. At some point I lost him and I thought maybe he'd gone home. Yves gave a rousing and obsequious speech and Rubio spoke too, working the room like an expert. He knew how to smile and be nice when he needed to, and I saw him give more than one rich old lady an inappropriately deep kiss. Around eleven-thirty they started passing out noisemakers and hats, and the large screens on either side of the stage were tuned to a cable New Year's Eve show that everyone was too drunk to watch. I soldiered on with my fundraising duties. The drunker people got, the more likely they were to shell out a hundred bucks for a worn-out pair of shoes.

Then someone touched my elbow and I knew without looking that it was him.

I turned as he pressed his cheek to mine. "Fancy meeting you here," he murmured. I could tell from his teasing tone he knew I'd been hiding from him all night. I stepped back and drank in the sight of him.

"It's good to see you, Liam. I didn't know you'd be here."

"Yves roped me in. What are you doing?"

I glanced down at the basket on my arm. "Selling autographed ballet shoes."

He poked at the pile of dingy satin and ribbon. "They're used. That's disgusting."

"Not to the wealthy foot fetishists of the world. Would you like to buy a pair?"

He lowered his voice and gave me a smoky look. "Are any of yours in there?"

"Ashleigh Keaton shoes aren't a big money maker."

"Someday they will be." He picked a shoe off the top and flung it down again. "Jesus. That one's still sweaty."

"The sweaty ones cost extra," I said in all seriousness. "They're fresher." His gaze flew to mine but I couldn't hold back the grin.

"You little fucker. I almost believed you." He grabbed my arm. "Put that down and come with me."

I looked around but no one was paying attention to us. He hustled me to the side of the auditorium and into the shadows near the stage door. "Where are we going?" I asked.

"I don't know. To a closet somewhere."

I tugged against him, gripping my basket. "I can't leave. I'm supposed to sell shoes."

"I'll buy the whole fucking basket of shoes, okay? Just…quit selling those. It's creepy. Put that down." We fought for a minute over the basket but he managed to strip it from me. He put it down next to the wall. "You can come back for it later. I need a minute with you. Alone."

Just a minute? He seemed really keyed up, and I was adrenalized just to be close to him. From the beginning, I'd felt that way. He pulled me into the first room we came to, a cramped, obsolete sound room.

"Speaking of creepy," I whispered, "I think someone died in here."

"No one died in here. Someone probably got groped in here a few times." His hands opened on my throat and he kissed me, pressing me against the wall. "I've missed you, Ash," he said in between ravishing my mouth. "How are you?"

I struggled for breath. "I'm— I'm— I don't—"

He kissed me again, his black tie standing out against the white of his shirt in the dim room. I touched his neck, his cheek. There were no other bare spots to touch. His fingers roved over my pale pink leotard with its short, diaphanous skirt. "I could see the outline of your ass in this leotard," he whispered with ferocious craving. "I've wanted to grab it all night." He did then, firm and hard, and kneaded it in his palm. "Your body is ridiculous."

I probably should have said "Thank you" or something similar but I was losing my ability to speak. His hands were all over me but they didn't feel smothering or scary. They felt wonderful. I was turning all liquid inside, growing hot and wet. He cupped my breasts and then he yanked down the bodice of my leotard and ran his thumbs across both my nipples.

My breath stuttered in my throat. "You're—you're t—touching my boundaries."

"Yes, I am. They feel beautiful." He nuzzled his face against my neck. "You're coming tomorrow?"

I gasped as his fingernail flicked one of my nipples. "Yes, Sir."

119

"What time?"

"Noon."

"What happens if you're late?"

I could feel the heat of his lips against mine. "Punishment," I whispered.

He brushed my hair back and feathered kisses across my brow. "Don't be late. We have so many fun things to do."

"N-No. I won't be late."

He gave me one last, mesmerizing kiss. "Happy New Year, Ashleigh."

I could hear everyone out in the auditorium exclaim as the clock struck twelve. It was the very last thing on my mind.

* * * * *

She rang the doorbell promptly at twelve. Which was fine. If I wanted to punish her I could find a thousand reasons to do it that were more creative than *"Naughty girl, you're late."* Honestly, I wasn't out to punish her. I was trying to fix her, even if my motives were more and more a mystery to me.

Ashleigh had dolled herself up in a plum-colored knit dress, dark lipstick, and a braided, intricate updo that must have taken her forever to create. Mem fluttered over it, running his fingers all over her head—he was really into braids. I touched her cheek and told her she looked pretty. She looked stunning, but that carefully arranged hair would have to come tumbling down.

We were getting naked today. Together. Happy New Year.

It was part of the plan, the process. I'd already seen her down to her panties, of course, and in a variety of tight-fitting leotards and costumes. I didn't know how she'd feel about being completely naked, though.

I led her upstairs and sat her on the edge of the bed, then I sat behind her so she was between my legs. I took her hair down, lock by lock, braid by braid, while we talked about safe, uncomplicated things, like our STD screenings and how much clothespins hurt. We joked a little about sweaty, used toe shoes and touched on New Year's resolutions. We both agreed they were stupid. By that point her hair was unraveled and unbraided, and she seemed relaxed enough for us to move on.

I turned her to face me. "This afternoon I'd like to talk about consent. Give and take, negotiation and reading signals. Let's start the conversation with a question. If I do something to you in this room and you want me to stop, are you allowed to stop me?"

"No. I'm supposed to obey you. No matter what."

I sighed. "That is...the wrong answer."

"I meant no. No, Sir."

I gave her a warning glance. "You're not lying to me now, are you?"

"Yes. No! I don't know." She twisted her hands in her lap. "Now I'm confused. I forget what you asked me."

"Don't freak out. Think back to what I told you last week. Can you stop me if I'm doing something you don't like? If I start doing something you're not okay with?"

I saw when she hit on the answer. "Yes," she said. "I can leave the room."

"Right. You can walk out the door. Even if you're the submissive in a scene, you have power. You're consenting to be here."

"But you're the one in charge, right?" She looked confused again. "I mean, you're the dominant."

I stroked my hand up and down her arm to soothe her. "That doesn't mean you can't leave. I'd be unhappy about it, and I'd stop playing with you if I thought you were manipulating the system. But I wouldn't ever grab you by the arms and force you to stay once you've told me you want out of here. Even if you're tied up...if you tell me you're done and you don't want any more, I'd have to untie you and let you go. Otherwise I no longer have your consent."

I reached for her hands and squeezed them between us. This was the touchier part.

"Ashleigh, what your father did to you as a child...there was no consent involved. You weren't allowed to say no, you weren't allowed to leave the room. I think some part of you remembers that feeling of powerlessness. When someone like me, who means you no harm at all, climbs on top of you intending to give you pleasure, that feeling overtakes you and you turn into that scared little kid. You feel trapped and disgusted, because that's what sex was to you for so long." She held my gaze, even when her eyes started filling with tears. "That's what I think, anyway," I finished gently. "And I hope your dad burns in hell when he dies."

121

She stared at my chest, then back at me. "I think you're right. About that feeling. I do feel that way. I feel…" She let go of my hands as she searched for words. "Frantic. Like something really bad is about to happen, even when I want it very much."

"So, our next step is to help you realize that you don't have to feel frantic, or trapped, or disgusted. You have the power to stop things whenever you want, no questions asked, no matter how intense things are. No matter if I'm on top of you, if my dick's inside you, no matter if I'm going to come five seconds down the line. It doesn't matter. You can stop me. You can stop anyone you're having sex with." I waited, studying her face. The sheen of tears was gone, through some well-honed method of control. "Does that make sense to you?" I asked. "About consent?"

"Yes, it makes sense. At least in my head. We talked about all this in counseling, but whenever I get to that moment…"

That was her problem, that moment and her conditioned response to it. It wasn't something I could fix through conversation. I think she realized that too. I stroked the skirt of her pretty purple dress and squeezed her leg. "What I would like to do now is lie down with you on the bed. Both of us are going to be naked, but I don't want you to feel weird or nervous. I don't want us to make any plans about what we're going to do. I just want you to remember that you have control."

She pulled a lock of hair over her shoulder and worried it between her fingers, but she didn't say no. She didn't start undressing either. "Why don't I go first?" I said, unbuckling my belt.

She watched me undress with bashful curiosity. It aroused me a lot more than I thought it would, especially when she was trying so hard not to look at my cock and ended up looking anyway. It was all I needed to start going stiff. Before I finished she was twisting around to reach her zipper. It was always easier to get naked when someone else was naked. I helped her pull the dress over her head and then buried my face in her soft, floral-scented hair. I could feel her trembling against me as I reached behind her to unhook her lace bra. She inched down her panties, blushing but wonderfully obedient. No arguments today.

Oh, Jesus. It was hard to stay in control standing so close to her beautiful naked body. I suppressed a groan as I guided her to the bed and eased down next to her. We lay on top of the covers, propped against a pile of pillows.

"Comfortable?" I asked, even though I was not at all comfortable.

She shifted a little. I couldn't blame her. My cock was reaching monster-size proportions against her leg. "It's gonna get hard," I said, readjusting it so it wasn't flat-out poking her. "I don't want you to stress about it. It's natural, and most men have control over their sexual impulses."

"Well…what do I—? Do you want me to—?"

I put an arm around her, drawing her closer. "You don't have to do anything about my hard-on. I just want you to relax and lie here with me, and talk with me about some stuff. Because the nakedness"—I waved a hand over our bare, intertwined bodies—"does not mean anything. Not if we don't want it to. It doesn't compel you to do anything at all. Got it?"

She stared at my dick. "It's getting bigger."

"I'm aware," I said, palming my balls. "It's because I think you're hot. You can touch it if you want." I stopped her when she reached for me automatically. "It's not a command. You can touch me *if you want to*." Not the sexiest chat up ever, but I didn't want her to feel pressured or threatened. That was the whole point of this exercise—to teach her that she had control.

After a few moments she reached out to stroke a hand down my extremely stiff length. It was hard not to react, not to grab her hand and make her stroke me harder, faster. She circled the head with her fingers. "That feels good," I said in a soft, encouraging tone. "You're really making me feel good. I could stroke you too, stroke your clit for instance, and make you feel good. Know why I'm not?"

Her hand stopped moving. "No, I don't know."

"Because I'm not sure yet about your signals. I'd probably start with something like this first." I brushed my fingers across her hip, tracing the delicate curve. "I'd wait for some signal that you were warming up. That you wanted more touching. Movements or sounds, or words. You could ask me to touch you, as long as you asked really nice."

She laughed a little, her fingers curving around my cock. "What does that mean, 'ask really nice?'"

"You can't throw orders at me," I said, grinning. "I'm a dominant, I don't like orders. But you could probably figure out a sweet, deferential way to ask for what you wanted, if you wanted it bad enough."

She gave me a look that made my cock buck in her hand. She dropped it like it was on fire and then I laughed along with her. "See what you do to me?"

With my other hand, I traced the graceful slope of her shoulder. She continued to play with my cock, stroking, touching, making lazy forays into my thatch of pubic hair. "That feels so great," I sighed. I moved my arm a little so I could reach to caress one of her breasts. I started lightly at first, just a tease of sensation. She pressed her face into my neck when I raked over her nipple with my thumb. "You like that. I remember." I nuzzled the side of her head and toyed with her until she forgot all about my cock. Her body tensed against mine.

"Maybe… Please… Can you touch me…?"

"I'm already touching you," I said, giving her nipple a quick pinch. "You'll have to be more specific."

"Can you touch me…please…between my legs?"

"You want me to touch your pussy?"

She trembled against me, but I was ninety-nine percent sure it was from pleasure, not fear. "I— Yes, please."

"Tell me then, very pretty. I adore begging. *'Please, Liam, will you touch my pussy?'*"

"Please, Liam, will you touch my pussy?" she whispered.

"Show me where. Show me with your body where you want to be touched."

She looked up at me, confusion clouding her gaze. "What do you mean?"

"Show me. Spread your legs. Turn toward me. Open for me and show me that you want me to touch you. Be responsive so I can read you."

She let out a long, slow breath and shifted against me. I moved my hand down her waist, across her thigh. I wanted to feel her wet heat so bad but I couldn't grab her the way I wanted to. I couldn't grope her and thrust three or four fingers up there so she moaned and fought me. No. Those were the other girls. This was Ashleigh, who was looking a little more scared now.

"Jesus, baby." I slid my fingers over slick, bare skin to part her pussy lips. "You have no idea how much you excite me. You're shaved bare. It's so pretty."

"We…we have to be bare," she stammered. "For dance."

"Well, I like it. Your pussy is beautiful. So soft and wet."

She made a stifled moan of a sound as I found the hood of her clit and massaged beneath it, to her thrusting little pearl. "*Ohh,*" she said. Her whole body arched off the bed.

"I wish I had some clothespins to put on your nipples," I whispered. "And on your clit. I think you'd like that even more."

"They hurt," she sighed.

"Like this?"

I pinched one of her nipples—hard—at the same time I manipulated her slippery button. Her mouth fell open and I pinched it harder. She pressed her body against mine, seeking the roughness at the same time she tried to push my fingers away.

"No," I said. "Let me."

I pinched the other nipple just as hard, caught up in her sweet stuttering breaths. I almost kissed her, but then I didn't. This was power exchange, not romance. *No strings attached.* I held her close and stroked over her clit again. "I can tell you enjoy that, baby. Do you want me to make you come?"

I almost said "Do you want Daddy to make you come?" because I was with a lot of girls who got off on that, but I'd retained just enough sanity to catch myself. "Let me make you come," I whispered. "I can tell you're close."

She opened her legs a little more, thrusting her hips against my side. It was criminal that this sensual, responsive woman had gone so many years without the pleasures of sex. I hoped she didn't stop me or ask me to do something else to her because I really, really wanted to bring her to orgasm right here, right now. I could feel her draw up tighter, hear her breathing intensify the closer she got.

"Please," she said. "Please, try now."

"Try what?"

"Sex. Please, I want you inside me. Please, Liam."

Damn her for the begging. It was a weak spot with me. "Are you sure?" I rasped. My cock was aching, about to explode.

"Yes, please."

Her eyes were closed. I studied her. Worried a little. "Look at me. Eye contact." She opened her eyes but she wasn't really looking at me. When I pressed deeper between her folds to finger her pussy, I could see I was losing her.

"Tell me to stop if you don't want it. Just tell me."

"Don't stop. Please! Please just make me. Make me do it!"

It was like a bucket of ice water. I sat up on the bed beside her, shaking my head. She looked about to shatter.

"Why are you stopping?" she cried. "Just make me."

"No. You know I'm not going to do that. I'm never going to force you, I told you that from the beginning."

She burst into tears. I rubbed her back and then I pulled her to me and hugged her. "I know," I said against her ear. "I know you're angry, I know you're frustrated. I know you want me to keep going, to force you to do it, but I can't. If I'm trying to help you, honey—" She pushed away from me but I held her tight. "Look at me. If I'm trying to help you, why would I do exactly what your father did to you? I'm trying to give your sense of safety back, not make things worse."

"You don't understand," she cried. "I just need to— I just need to get past it. Then I think everything will seem better."

"Oh, you think that? I think everything will seem worse. Because then Liam Wilder is Daddy with a different face."

She struggled away from me, ran to the corner and started to dress. "I have to go. I can't do this."

"It's okay if you have to go."

"Yes," she said over her shoulder. "Consent, right? Great. But you're not helping me." She flailed behind her, trying to reach the zipper of her dress. I pulled on my jeans and crossed to her, but she batted my hand away. "Leave me alone."

"Let me help you," I said.

She slid away despite my best efforts and yelled at me from across the room. "I don't need your help. All of this is stupid and pointless. Stupid games that mean nothing!"

"Games?" My temper flared. "I'm doing what you asked. You *asked* me to help you, sweet pea. Remember that?"

"I asked you to help because I thought you'd actually help me."

"I'm trying to do the responsible thing, trying to protect you."

"And I have no say in anything? Oh, that's right, because I'm the fucking submissive in this—this—ridiculous farce!"

Ridiculous farce? Oh, even better. "You wanted the D/s," I reminded her. "You practically begged for it."

"Because I thought you'd know what you were doing, but you don't. You're too wishy-washy. Too soft."

The longer she stood there screaming insults at me, the more I questioned what the fuck I'd ever hoped to accomplish in these sessions. What on earth made me think I was qualified to help her?

"Fine. Go," I said with a dismissive wave. "Let's not waste any more of each other's time."

"Get out of my way then. You're blocking the door."

I gave a mocking bow and moved to the side, resisting the urge to grab her and hold her down and make her take all her words back. I let her go without trailing along after her, because the whole purpose of my "consent talk" was to teach her that leaving was okay. Mem would have heard the yelling from downstairs. He'd intercept her, calm her down and see her back to her place.

As for me, I didn't know my next step. I knew this process wouldn't be a cakewalk, but I didn't think it would get so wretched by the second session. I felt protective toward her, too protective, too involved, and I hated that feeling. I could run a company providing services for thousands of clients, but I couldn't bear to feel connected to this one tormented girl. I could play with dozens of "crazy" partners and feel nothing, but playing with Ashleigh...

I sat at the table and stared into space, steeling myself against hurt feelings. *No strings attached.* That was the only way I'd survive this. I wasn't going after her. I couldn't force her to return for another session, any more than I could force myself between her legs.

I heard a quiet knock at the door. I wished it was Ash, but no, it was Mem's signature tap. I looked over my shoulder at him.

"Not now," I said. "Some other time."

He ignored me, entering and sliding into the chair across the table. "Travis has left to take *Little Ishi* home."

"That's not her name. Stop calling her that."

He said nothing, only stared at me with great forbearance.

I steepled my fingers and leaned my forehead against them. "Okay, give it to me. I'm ready for my lecture. Say whatever you need to say, whatever will get you fucking gone."

"I only wonder what you are doing to her in this room."

"What I'm doing doesn't concern you. It doesn't concern anyone but Ashleigh and me."

He inclined his head in slow agreement. "I do not wish to pry. But just now, when she left, she was very upset."

"Was she? I hadn't noticed."

Mem smiled patiently at my bitter joke. I hated when he looked at me like that, like I was the world's biggest, stupidest asshole. "We had a fight, okay?" I said, hiding my agitation in a casual shrug. "People fight. They have arguments. Me and her..." My voice trailed off, because I was about to lie to him. "We aren't anything alike. We probably won't be hanging out much anymore."

He absorbed my lies with a thoughtful, probing expression. "You know," he said quietly, "the world won't end when you open your heart to someone. Nothing catastrophic will happen."

He was treading too close to a line he wasn't allowed to cross. "That doesn't apply here," I said. "This has nothing to do with my heart."

"What about her heart?"

"What about it?"

"Are you being careful with it?"

Mem and his fucking questions. "I told her the deal from the beginning—I don't want anything to do with her heart."

"Ah, the familiar refrain. No hearts, no love. No feelings." He heaved a sigh, tilting his head at me. "You must let go of your past, *Ishi*. Too many years now, you've been punishing yourself, and now you're punishing her."

"Jesus Christ," I groaned, burying my head in my hands. "How many fucking times do I have to say it? I'm trying to *help her*."

"If you truly wish to help her, you must first make peace with what happened to you. Just as the storm must crash before the flowers bloom—"

"Mem, no." I ground my fists into my eyeballs. "No storms, no flowers. Stop. This isn't about me, not in the slightest. She has issues, okay? She came to me for her issues, to help her with her issues, but they're *her* issues. That's all this is about."

"She is not the only one who has issues, my son."

"I'm not your son. I'm nobody's son, as you well fucking know." I was finished with this conversation and his goddamn interfering ways. "Get out. Just get out and fucking leave me alone. And if she comes back, tell her... Tell her..."

"Tell her what?" Mem asked, rising to stand behind his chair.

Yes, tell her what, Liam? That this is starting to feel too risky? That she hurt your pride? That you're a fucking loser who's afraid of falling in love with her?

"Tell her I'm finished playing games," I said roughly. "She'll know what I mean."

Chapter Twelve:
Drama

I didn't want to visit Liam Wilder any more. I decided our thing was weird and inappropriate, and unlikely to work anyway. I busied myself doing other things, whatever it took to keep my mind off the idea of going back again. By the second week of January I'd prepped enough pointe shoes to last me until summer, so many pointe shoes that the costume department cut off my supply.

I took up knitting instead. Dancers loved legwarmers. I made about twenty pairs of the fuckers, until people started looking at me funny. Now I'd moved onto working crossword puzzles late into the night, backstage in the dressing room, because otherwise I'd be in my apartment staring up at the branches of his bed.

If I didn't stay busy I'd run back to Liam and beg his forgiveness, beg for another chance, another wrenching session in his pale blue room, and I didn't know if I could survive it. Still, some part of me wanted him to come get me, storm over to my place and drag me from my bed of branches. I wanted him to keep helping me—because he had been helping me—but it was so painful to do things his way. Too painful. I couldn't hack it.

I wanted him to force me but he wouldn't. I thought if he could just force me through my first experience, I'd realize it wasn't so bad and I'd be cured. What good was a dominant who didn't force you to do the stuff you didn't want to do?

At least there was Rubio and our times in the studio. He saved me from myself, from the shoes and crosswords and leg warmers, even if he was a holy terror to work with. My phone buzzed and I looked down. After three weeks I still hoped for Liam's name, but it was always Rubio.

Ashlee. Cum practice.

I shoved the crossword puzzle into the top drawer of my carrel and grabbed my bag. When I got to the rehearsal room I flung it in a corner. "If you don't stop spelling 'come' like that I'm going to stop helping you. I'm serious. It's not funny anymore."

He stretched out at the barre. "I think it's funny."

"It's not funny, it's gross. And my name is spelled Ash-leigh. L-E-I-G-H."

"That is a stupid way to spell Ash-lee. I spell it how I like."

I groaned and dragged my hands down my face. He stared at me with a frown. "Why you so grumpy, girl?"

I started warming up, trying to remember that this was the dream of a lifetime. I was working with Fernando Rubio. A few short months ago I couldn't even look him in the face. If he wanted to text me to "cum" just to annoy me, what did it matter? I moved to join him at the barre, muttering an apology.

"I'm sorry, okay? I have a lot on my mind."

"Oh. I thought maybe you on your period."

"I'm not on my period."

"Here, I'll help," he said when I started stretching. He stood in front of me and pressed back on my leg to offer resistance. Dancers did this kind of stuff but Ruby always enjoyed it a little too much. Today he gave up any pretense of doing it with platonic intent and pressed his crotch against my front until my leg was curled over his shoulder. If we were naked, we'd be having sex.

"What are you doing?" I asked, although it was pretty obvious.

"Grinding my cock on you."

"Why?"

He stepped back, pouting, and gestured for my other leg. "I thought you and Liam are not exclusive. Not a couple."

"We're not. That doesn't mean I want you sexually harassing me."

"Not sexual harassment," he said petulantly. "Stretching."

"Oh, I see."

130

He pressed back on my leg just enough to loosen it up. He might be a pervert, but he was an excellent stretch partner. He backed away and I brought my leg down to place it beside his on the floor. We stood like that a moment and then he tapped me with his heel.

"Hey, girl. You want to do this ballet? Do with me for the spring showcase, and the summer tour?"

"Sure. I said I'll help as long as you need me."

"No, I mean, do it. For shows."

I stared at him. "What?"

"I mean, perform it. Do the ballet. With me onstage. People clap at the end, etcetera."

I scrutinized his expression to see if he was teasing me but he wasn't. He made a face and shrugged. "I mean, you already know it. You dance it good enough, I guess."

I looked down at his flexing, perfect feet and let out the breath I hadn't realized I was holding. "God, wow. I—I don't know."

He ducked down to catch my gaze. "What the hell you mean, you don't know?"

"I mean, I don't know." The invisible Ashleigh was freaking out, running for cover. I started grasping for excuses. "It's hard to dance with you because you're so...so talented and flawless. When we danced *Sleeping Beauty*...remember? You were angry with me."

"I was angry at your shoes, not you. I didn't even know you then."

"You called me a whale. Everyone judged me."

He scoffed. "No one judged you. No one even noticed you."

"Exactly. If I'm going to go unnoticed I'd just as soon do it from the back of the corps. The stakes are a lot less high."

He shook his head at me. "Sad. This is sad. Low stakes. This is what you want? Instead, why don't you try to beat me? Dance better than me?"

I rolled my eyes and turned back to the barre. "Dance better than you. Right. Because that's so easy."

"No, it's not easy. It's hard, very hard. Something to strive for. Something to expire to."

"I think you mean 'aspire,'" I said, although expire was probably more accurate.

"Whatever." He stood behind me, frowning at me in the mirror. "You disappoint me, Ash-lee. This is a chance for you to do something

131

amazing. Something to make everybody say 'oh look, there she is. Look at her. Where she been hiding?'"

I spun on him, shaking my head. "I don't want that. That's the last thing in the world I want."

He looked like he would have happily kicked me square in the stomach. "Whut? Why you dance then? Why you practice your technique, why you spend hours at the barre if you don't want to be looked at?"

"I don't know. Because I have to. Because I don't know what else to do."

He rolled his eyes and flipped backward into a handstand. "You stupid, stupid girl." He flipped back to his feet, then over again onto his hands. "Liam would want you to do it. He won't believe it when I tell him you refused."

"Don't tell him." I didn't want Liam to know I was still cowardly chickenshit. "It's none of his business anyway."

"I'm telling him." He took to his feet and crossed for his phone. "I'm texting him right now." He turned around and snapped a photo. "I'm going to attach a picture of you. Total loser."

"Just—" I let out my breath in a miserable huff. "Don't text him, okay? Give me some time to think about it."

"Time?" His face contorted in disgust. "You don't need time. Fernando Rubio asks you to dance in the spring showcase. On worldwide summer tour. There is one answer, and you give it immediately. Yes, yes, *yes!*"

"Okay, yes," I yelled. "Fine. I'll do it." I crossed my arms over my chest and glared at him. "Just don't tell Liam I didn't want to."

"Why?" His angry face transformed to a lurid smirk. "He would spank you, huh? Whip your ballerina bottom?"

No. He would know that I'm a hopeless case after all. When I didn't answer he took that as confirmation and got a completely filthy look on his face. "What would he do to you for punishment? Tell me. Something awful? Degrading?"

"No."

"I already told him we practiced this together. He'll be glad you got this role." He grinned at me. "Rubio and Ash-lee, partners. I want to rub my cock on you again."

I sidestepped his approach. "No, thank you."

"When are you coming to play downstairs at Liam's with all us other pervs? I'd like to play with you."

I raised my eyebrows. "That is not likely to happen. But I'll let you know."

"Not likely, why?" He was looking at me too closely now. "What happened? Liam hurt you? Scare you out of the lifestyle? I told you. Didn't I warn you?"

"Jesus, Ruby." I looked away from him but he yanked my chin back over again.

"What he do to you?"

"Nothing! We just— Our thing didn't work out. You understand that, right? When people don't click together? I don't think I'm really good at…" I waved a hand. "You know, all that stuff you guys do."

"Aw, girl." He stroked my face, and I had a sense that he could be a dangerously seductive lover. "Maybe you just need a different person to top you."

I laughed so I wouldn't start crying. "Let me guess. You?"

"Why you laugh? I'm good at it."

"I'm sure you are," I said, pushing his hand away from my face.

"What? You're not attracted to me? You think I don't make good sex?"

"Oh, I'm sure you make good sex. I just don't… I don't even think of you in that way." This seemed to befuddle him. "I'm not available," I finally said. "It's a long story and it will bore you to hear it."

"You still like Liam."

I sighed. "I said it was a long story, so no. It's not as simple as that."

"I'm looking right at you and I see you still like him and you're sad."

Rubio had a way of laying it on the line that I really hated. "Can we get on with it?" I said, gesturing to the floor.

"Sex, you and me?"

"No!"

"Oh, practice. But listen, Ash-lee. If you still like him, go see him. You talk. In lifestyle things, there has to be adjustment sometimes. Cooling off period and then you move on and things are better because you have…" He stared at the ceiling, trying to think of the word. "Grown a little. People grow together. It takes time. You and me, we are friends now, and remember? You used to hate me."

"No, you used to hate *me*," I reminded him. "And you're not really my friend."

"Whut?" He clutched his heart. "How can you say that? I am your friend. We're doing this ballet together, no? A partnership. But I get top billing," he added with a wink.

"What's it even called, this ballet?"

He shrugged. "I don't have a name yet. It will come to me. Things take time." He wagged a finger at me, my mercurial Brazilian idol. "You're so impatient, Ash-lee. Too impatient. Don't you realize this?"

I hated that he was right. Yes, I was too impatient, especially when it came to fixing my broken sexuality. I looked at him and sighed.

* * * * *

The following Monday, at noon, I climbed the steps to Liam's house. The more I thought about Ruby's words, the guiltier I felt. I'd been impatient and rude to Liam, who was only trying to help me. I'd expected miracles and gotten angry when he couldn't provide them. I'd expected him to do things to me that he wasn't comfortable with. More than anyone on earth, I should have known how wrong that was.

When I rang the doorbell, Liam opened the door instead of Mem. I hadn't expected that. I'd thought Mem would ease me inside and help bolster my courage before I had to face him. Liam didn't ask me in but he didn't shut the door on me either, only stood there wearing an expression I couldn't parse. It was a cold day and he had on a chunky fisherman's sweater I wanted to cuddle up against. I was in a blouse, cardigan, and miniskirt, shivering down to my boots. I pulled my coat closer around me.

"I'm sorry," I said when he made no move to invite me in. "I came to tell you I'm sorry. I got scared and…and impatient. I was trying to give orders. Trying to top you, when you're supposed to be the one in charge."

He blinked, his lips tightening a little. "I accept your apology."

The winter sun was blinding. "Can I come in?"

He looked at his watch, then back at me. "It's noon on Monday. Are you here because you want to start up again?"

I didn't have an answer for that, because I wasn't sure what I wanted. He said something rude under his breath and pulled me inside. Mem drifted by to take my coat but Liam didn't offer me a seat. I picked at the trim on my cardigan while we stood in his foyer looking at each other.

"If you want to start up again…you and me and your sex thing," he said, "I'd advise you to think about it, honestly."

I hated the way he called it my "sex thing." I hated the way this moment felt. "I have been thinking about it," I said. "I— I don't know what to think, or how to make up for what I did, but I want to make up for it." I stared at the patterns in his marble tile. "Maybe you could punish me."

"For what? For exercising your right not to consent? That would be pretty stupid, considering that was the whole point of the session." He crossed his arms over his chest and glared at me. "Although I'd enjoy tearing up your ass. I'm not going to deny it."

It was difficult for me, being so emotionally raw and open, but I let him see everything, all the angst in my heart. "I'm sorry, Liam. I know you were trying so hard, doing everything so carefully. All you wanted was to help me. Even when I was yelling at you, I realized that, but I couldn't stop my mouth."

"You freaked out, like you always do when you're confronted with sex. I understood all of that. I'm not angry because you left, Ashleigh. I'm angry because you didn't come back. If you're not going to do the work— If you're just going to leave me hanging—"

Mem rattled some plates in the kitchen. Liam turned to him with a violent look. "This is a private conversation."

"I am not listening, *Ishi*. Just hoping to see some harmony. Will you not invite her to sit? It is very bad luck to argue in front of a door."

Liam inclined his head to me, his gestures stiff with annoyance. "Would you like to sit down?"

"If you want me to go—"

"If I wanted you to go, I would ask you to go. Please, come and sit down with me."

His words were polite, but his voice was strained. I sat on the couch closest to the door and he sat beside me. Mem appeared a second later. "Can I get either of you—"

"Mem. Enough."

The old man nodded and went upstairs. Liam turned to me with that same blank, equivocal look he'd worn at the door. "Here's the thing. I didn't realize when we started how emotionally invested I would get in your situation. How invested I would get in you. So when you left, and you didn't call, and you didn't come by, I felt torn up about it—and I don't need the drama. I'm not sure I want to be around you anymore."

Wow. Harsh. I looked down at my hands in my lap. "Why didn't you call if you wanted me to come back? Why didn't you—"

"Make you come back? Here we go again. I can't make you do anything. I don't want to do the same things he did to you. I don't feel like I can trust you and I'm not sure I can fix you. I'm wondering if all of this was a mistake."

His quiet, calm words felt like a thousand stab wounds. "I'll try harder, I promise. I'm here now. I'm here because I want to get better. You were helping me feel better. If you drop me now—"

"I'm not dropping you. You dropped me first. And I quote: 'All of this is stupid and pointless. Stupid games that mean nothing.'"

I put my head in my hands, letting out my breath in a long, slow exhalation. If Liam pushed me away now, I wasn't sure I'd survive it. I looked up into his hard amber gaze.

"Please take me back," I begged. "I'll do anything. Please give me one more chance. I know you can help me. Don't give up on me yet. I mean, I know I was the one who gave up, but— But I won't this time. I won't."

"Why would you want another chance, if it's just stupid games?"

I'd really hurt him. He was *really* hurt. "I'm sorry I threw all your wonderful things back in your face. I wish I could go back and not do that." I took his hand, his big, rough hand, pressing it against my cheek. "When I'm with you, I feel like I'm getting better. I feel excited and turned on and...and...I want to be with you."

He held his hand slack against my jaw. "Guess what, Twinkletoes? A lot of women want to be with me, and they're a lot easier to deal with than you."

Oh, wow. He could be a cold fucking bastard when he wanted to. This was what Rubio had tried to warn me about. I stood up, narrowing my eyes. "Did you just call me Twinkletoes?"

"Yes." He took in my pugilistic stance. "Are you going to bitch me out again? Storm off?"

"I think I will storm off, if you're going to be such a prick."

He jabbed a finger at the door. "Be my guest."

Of all the ways I could have left his house after this ill-conceived visit, storming out was definitely the most satisfying. I stalked toward the door in full flounce, but my dramatic exit was ruined when I slipped halfway across his glossy marble floor and fell on my face. Ow, that floor was hard. He made a sound and vaulted up off the couch.

"Jesus, Ashleigh. Such balletic grace."

Tears gathered in my eyes. Not tears of pain, because I'd fallen plenty of times in my dance career. It was more tears of wanting to fade into the floor and die. "Don't," I said, pushing his hand when he reached for me. "Don't touch me."

"Let me help you."

"I wanted you to help me," I yelled. "You said no. You told me to leave!"

"I never told you to leave. That was your decision."

"Because you called me Twinkletoes," I bawled from the floor at his feet.

"Jesus," he said under his breath. "You're killing me." A moment later he held out his hand again. "Get up. Let's attempt to talk together like two fucking adults."

I hated him and I loved him. Apparently I couldn't even navigate a marble floor without his help. "I'm sorry," I sniffled, as he led me back to the sofa. "I'm really stressed out."

"Did you hurt anything when you fell?"

I shook my head. The only thing hurting was my shredded pride. Even if I'd managed to leave without the pratfall I would have been back again in a week. I knew that, and I was sure he knew it too. He went to get me some tissues and then sat heavily beside me, bracing his hands on his knees. "There have to be more rules this time. If we start up again."

I nodded. "I know. I need rules."

"Like, if you leave, you have to come back. You have to call me and talk to me within twenty-four hours. And no more..." He shook his head and grimaced. "No more emotional meltdowns. We're going to stay on task. I don't want girlfriend drama. I don't want all these tears and big scenes."

"No, I agree. No more drama. I don't want that either." But the word *tears* brought an old conversation to mind. *He upset you tonight and I think he probably enjoyed this.*

I stared at Liam, wiping my hands over my face.

"What? What is it?"

"Nothing." I straightened my shoulders. "I'm done crying. It seems like you always make me cry. It's like you enjoy it or something," I pretended to joke.

I watched his face for some reaction to my comment, watched for some sign he was getting off on all this upheaval. Getting off on breaking me down. I'd willingly sought out the services of a player and manipulator, so if he was, I couldn't really fault him for it. I tried to read him but his expression was carefully blank.

"I think I need a week," I said, shrugging off my misgivings. "A week to get ready, to get myself in the right frame of mind. Is that okay?"

"Sure, it's okay. Next Monday?"

I nodded. By Monday I'd be back with my emotional armor. Our thing was just supposed to be about sex, and I'd make it about sex, come hell or high water. I didn't want the emotional bullshit either, just a functioning sex life. Thanks to Liam, I was halfway there.

"Oh, you know what?" I said as he was helping me into my coat.

"What?"

"Rubio cast me in this ballet he's working on. It's kind of a big deal. It's for the spring showcase and also the summer tour. I've been helping him practice, and I guess he figured, since I already knew the steps…"

"*Or* he figured you're totally underrated as a dancer and decided it's time for the world to see what you've got. If you got the part, I'm sure you deserved it. I didn't even know he was working on a ballet."

I gave him a sideways look. "He never said anything to you about it? That I was practicing with him?"

Liam shook his head in a slow, fake kind of way. "No. He never said anything."

I wondered why he was lying when I wasn't allowed to. I wondered when I'd stopped trusting Liam Wilder. I thought maybe I'd never trusted him in the first place.

Because trust had always been a really touchy issue for me.

Chapter Thirteen: Progress

It had to become about the sex.

For me to survive handling her, for her to survive dealing with me, it had to become about hardcore, focused, balls-to-the-wall sex. I knew I didn't want to get any closer to her emotionally, and I knew she was impatient to ride a cock that wasn't attached to a soul-crushing rapist. We'd talked about boundaries and consent. Check. She had the tools, I told myself. It was time to up the game.

The *stupid* game, as she called it. It didn't feel like a game to me. It felt like hell.

I wasn't sleeping with other women. I couldn't, and when I scened with them at the parties my performances were lackluster at best. Women still wanted to play with me, still came on to me, but my heart wasn't in it. Ruby poked at me and mocked me, but none of that mattered.

All that mattered was Ashleigh and sex.

The first session back we focused on exploring each other's erogenous zones. I turned off the lights and blindfolded her, exhorting her to feel her way through the exercise rather than worry about what she could see. I lay beside her in the guest bed and touched every part of her, and encouraged her to touch every part of me. I stroked, I explored. I ate out her pussy like a starving man and then gritted my teeth while she tentatively licked my cock.

The next session rolled around near Valentine's Day. I used toys on her. Vibrators, ruthlessly. I made her climax over and over for a good hour, until she was too limp and exhausted to struggle any more, then I lubed up a small anal plug and worked it into her ass. She was scared and nervous, but once it was in, I could tell the feeling turned her on. Kinky. So kinky. I told her I wouldn't take it out until she sucked me to orgasm, and that got her even more worked up. We discovered in the course of these sessions that foreplay-type activities didn't bother her, since she didn't have any experience with them in her abusive past.

The session after that, I helped her explore some of her masochistic fantasies. I took her down to the play room and showed her how it felt to be tied down to the various tables. I let her try out whipping racks and spreader bars. I gave her little smacks with all the various implements so she could experience the differences between them. Even though she got extremely turned on, she never begged me to fuck her the way she had during the second session. We were going at my careful and deliberate pace; she seemed to understand that now.

After we left the play room I took her upstairs. I had an aching hard-on that needed attention. I made her stand against the wall with her back to me, so I could look at the collage of marks I'd made on her ass with paddle, crop, tawse, and whip, among other things.

"Okay, Ashleigh?" I asked her.

"Yes, I'm okay," she said, shivering when I traced over a welt on the back of her thigh.

"Does it still hurt?"

"A little."

"But you liked it." That was obvious in the way she responded to my touch. My ultimate goal was for her to find pleasure—and only pleasure—with her future sexual partners. I tried not to think about whether one of those future partners would be me.

"When it comes to impact play," I said, pinching another pinked-up welt, "you need to remember the things we talked about earlier. About what you do if your partner is pushing your boundaries. About your power of consent."

She turned to me with a sardonic tilt of her lips. "You've told me about that, like, a hundred times by now. Maybe a thousand."

I narrowed my eyes at her flippant tone. "Maybe so. But it's important. Especially for you."

"I know that, and I appreciate your consent speeches, but I liked pretty much everything you did to me today. Sir," she added, finally noticing my darkening gaze.

"The 'Sir' at the end doesn't negate all the snark that came before it."

"I'm sorry."

"Are you really sorry?"

"I'm just saying, we've been over consent a bunch of times."

I grabbed a handful of her hair and tilted her head back. "What about respecting your dominant? Have we been over that a bunch of times?" My gaze strayed down to her tightening nipples. "I'm willing to concede you're still learning about the concept of submission, but you're fully aware you were being mouthy just now." I put a hand on her shoulder. "Down."

She sank to her knees, her back stiff as a ramrod.

"Let's put that mouth to better use," I said. "I'll punish you for the attitude later."

In some sense, I loved the attitude. More attitude meant more assertiveness meant more presence in her experience. More presence meant more control and hopefully more comfort in sexual encounters. I still got to punish her for being mouthy. Rules were rules.

"Open," I said. "I'm going to tell you exactly what to do and I want you to do it. No mouth."

"I can't use my mouth?"

"You know what I mean. Watch the smartass remarks, little girl. Bratting is not part of our dynamic."

"Bratting?"

"Acting like a brat," I said. "Like you're doing right now."

"I'm sorry, Sir."

I didn't think she was that sorry. I guided the tip of my cock to her lips. "Suck me, sassypants."

She started with the head, licking skillful circles around the bulging crown. She was still turned on from our trip to the play room, because she was caressing and exploring me with more spirit than usual. My muscles tightened, my groin drawing up in pleasure. "Open wider," I sighed after a few minutes. "Lick me like I'm your favorite flavor of lollipop."

She started to speak but I stopped her.

"If you tell me you don't eat lollipops, it's twenty with the strap right here on the floor."

She grinned against my cock, gazing up at me. I took her face in my hand and shoved my dick into her pretty little mouth. While she did a fair job of sucking my length, she had to do a lot of the work with her hands. I gave distracted instructions—*Faster! Slower! Squeeze the base of my cock!* Meanwhile, I allowed myself to daydream about how I'd punish her for her earlier sassiness. She'd already been whapped with a bunch of implements. I thought I'd spank her with my hand to change things up a little, really wring her out and send her home sore.

"Okay," I sighed. "Try to take me deeper. I know it's hard. Open your throat and take me deep in your mouth." God bless her, she tried. Gagged and teared up a little. I was so thankful that blowjobs weren't a trigger for her. They were the only things keeping me sane during these sessions. "Okay, baby, keep trying. Get it wet. Make it hot."

I was pretty good at this coaching thing, considering most of the women I fucked around with were already vastly experienced. There was something sweet, almost wistful, about developing Ashleigh's oral skills. When I thought about her using them on anyone else, though, I felt a pang of jealousy deep in my gut.

"Jesus Christ, Ash." I sat back on the bed, pulling her with me. She looked up at me, my throbbing cock in her hand.

"Is everything okay?"

"Everything's great. You're just making my legs shaky. That's a good thing."

I put a hand on the side of her head, guiding her, murmuring instructions and encouragements. I wanted to jab my cock all the way to the back of her throat, but hard force was still a trigger for her. I twisted my fingers in her soft black hair instead, picturing it crisscrossed with spurts of my semen. Gross? Yeah, but that's the kind of stuff perverts like me thought about in the middle of a blowjob. She sucked my length in and out, using her tongue and lips as far as she could, and her hands on the rest. I shuddered, my body going tense with peaking arousal.

I took her hand and made her caress my balls, staring down at my fingers over hers. The visual was as powerful as the sensation. "Ash," I managed to groan through the haze in my brain. "I'm going to come soon, and I want you to swallow every fucking drop— Oh God." I grasped for control as her hot mouth worked up and down my length. "I'm coming. Jesus. Holy…Christ."

She wasn't an enthusiastic swallower, but since she hated the smell of cum, she'd decided a while back that swallowing was the easiest way to make it go away. I always rewarded her afterward with a hard, deep kiss. God, I'd needed that nut. I melted down onto the carpet beside her and laid my head in her lap.

"You're good at blowjobs," I said with a sigh.

She touched my hair, stroking her fingers through my tangles. "With other guys, when the sex thing wouldn't work, blowjobs were something I could handle. It was something I could do so they wouldn't have to go home all hot and bothered."

"You know, it wasn't your responsibility to finish them off if you weren't feeling it. I was hard as a fucking diamond that first night when you…" I paused. We hadn't talked about that encounter in a while. "Anyway, I didn't expect anything from you."

She brushed back my hair with a frighteningly familiar tenderness. "That's because you're a good guy. I'm glad I met you. I—I'm feeling so much better these days. I'm so different from the person I was that night."

We gazed at each other, so connected. So close. *Too close.*

I sat up abruptly and moved to kneel in front of her. "Okay, it's your turn to come now. Lie back and open your legs." I frowned at her when she didn't immediately obey. "Did you not hear me? Or do you want more punishment than you're already getting? I know you're into the hurty stuff, my budding masochist, but don't bite off more than you can chew."

She inched her legs apart a tiny bit and I pushed them open the rest of the way. "Don't be self-conscious. You're beautiful." I braced my knees inside hers so her legs couldn't close the slightest bit. "I think it's time to work on letting go a little, and overcoming those inhibitions. So, you're going to touch yourself and make yourself come while I watch you and hold your legs apart."

She gawked at me. "You're going to stare down at me while I jack off?"

"Yes. Until you come." It was delicious, bracing her legs open while she fought to clinch them closed.

"What if I can't come with you watching me?"

"Then you don't close your legs. Which is fine. I can hold them open for days if I have to. My work schedule is pretty flexible. I don't know about yours."

"I can always just leave," she pointed out.

"I'm glad you remember." I pushed her legs even wider and she gave up her fruitless attempts at out-muscling me. She was strong for her size but she was no match for a six-and-a-half-foot man. "Go ahead and start," I said. "Don't be self-conscious. I masturbate all the time." *Especially since I met you.* "And you might as well make yourself feel as good as you can for as long as possible, because once you finish, it's punishment time."

Her lips twisted into a pout. "Now I really can't do it. Not if I'm thinking about that."

I laughed at that huge lie. "While you touch your hot little pussy, I want you to imagine me pulling you over my lap and punishing your ass cheeks while you kick your legs and try to get away. Because that's what's going to happen. I'll even let you close your eyes to imagine it better. Now, start."

She paused and then slid her fingers into the crease of her pussy. Her pert little nipples were hard, but they'd been hard for a while now. She touched and stroked herself, shyly at first. She made little pants and sighs but I could see her lingering self-consciousness. She always had trouble reaching that letting-go point, the point when her body overrode the fears and constraints of her mind. After several minutes I ran my hands up and down her thighs.

"Okay. Stop. Freeze. Wait…" I got up and went to the dresser and got some clamps out of a top drawer. I adjusted them down from scream level to *ooh-baby-make-me-hurt* level. I returned to Ashleigh. "Let's put these on before you go any further. I want you to come with them on."

"What if I can't?"

I sighed heavily. "Do we have to go through this again?" I leaned over and pinched her nipples, preparing the sensitive tips for the bite of the clamp. I don't think she realized that this was her main panic position, that I was over her, on top of her, my dick half hard. I applied the first clamp and she made a little keening sound that made me three-quarters hard. By the time I'd attached the other one I was looming over her with a full-on erection. I sat back and braced her legs open again. "Do it. Come for me. Come for me because it hurts and it makes you feel good. Come because you're ready for me to spank your tight little ass and make you cry."

She swallowed hard and arched her back. The delicate chain between the nipple clamps slid across her chest.

I watched her touch herself, tentatively at first, then more boldly. After a few minutes, she eased down into the naughtiness of it, her hips moving in concert with her fingers. Our eyes met and held. "How does that feel, baby?" I asked. "Does it feel good?"

"Yes," she said, then, "No. The clamps hurt."

"If you want them off, you have to come, don't you? Like a good girl."

"Yes. Yes, Sir, but…it hurts."

Her fingers were working harder now, faster. "How much does it hurt? Tell me. Does your pussy feel full and wet? Does the pain make you hot? Is it an aching, needy throb?"

"Yes," she gasped. "It feels so good. I want to come so badly."

"Come on, baby. I'm not letting you close your legs. Not ever. Not until you come for me. Close your eyes and think about what you have coming to you. This is going to be a long afternoon for poor little Ashleigh." *Don't call her a bad girl. Don't call her a bad girl.* My cock was rock hard in my fist. What little control I had was focused on not plunging into her pussy. "You can come, but that's just going to be the beginning for you. I want you to come for me now. I'm not taking those clamps off until you're gushing against my hand."

"Oh…"

She was almost there, lost in the throes of fantasy and pleasure and pain, a combination I loved myself. I took a risk then… I touched her. I cupped her mons and slipped one finger inside her, up inside the tight wetness I wanted more than life itself. *Make me. Just make me do it.* God, I wanted to, so badly. "Come on," I gasped. "Come for me, so I can give you what you deserve."

She cried out and screwed her eyes shut, arching her chest. I pumped my finger in and out of her spasming pussy, kneeling over her braced on my arms, and I stayed that way through her luscious orgasm. She opened her eyes and stared up at me. I was fully over her, my legs braced over her legs, practically mounting her. She went very still. I stroked her pussy one last time. "So beautiful," I said. "That was so beautiful." I stroked a hand down her face. "Are you afraid?"

She thought a moment and shook her head. "Not right now. No, sir."

My lips spread in a wide smile. "That's progress then. Good girl."

I stared at Liam above me with a kind of wonder. *Good girl.* I loved being his good girl. It was such a relief not to feel like the bad girl anymore. He was over me, naked, and I wasn't freaking out, not in the slightest. I was getting *better*.

I was also getting a spanking.

With silent, stern determination, he rocked back and pulled me across his legs, and smacked my butt with his big slab of a hand. I was so dazed from the afterglow of my orgasm, all I noticed was that it hurt. Then he spanked my ass again and I realized that it *really fucking hurt*. "Oh. Ow!"

I tried to roll away from him but he only caught me and delivered another spank.

"*Owwww*... Please, that's so painful."

"Oh? Not what you fantasized about?"

Oh my God. *Ouch.* He never made punishments feel good. Not only was his hand the size of a tennis racket, but he wasn't letting me catch my breath between smacks. I wailed and bucked off of him, for all the good it did me. When I reached back to block his hand, he trapped it and secured it up between my shoulder blades.

"You earned this punishment by being snarky and sassy to me, didn't you?" he asked.

"Yes, but I didn't realize—" I gasped. "I didn't think—" I went limp over his lap. "I didn't think your hand would hurt this much."

He caressed over my blazing ass, squeezing it like he owned it. "I have big, evil hands, Ash. But we can try a paddle if you like. Paddle punishments are good for curing smart mouths."

He helped me to my feet. I rubbed my bottom, feeling dazed and concerned and weirdly horny for a woman who'd just gotten off a few minutes ago. My breasts ached. Now that I'd come, the nipple clamps turned from sexy to torturous. "Please, can I take off the clamps?" I asked in my most respectful and begging submissive voice.

"*You* never take off the clamps. *I* take them off when I think you've had enough. Bend over the bed. Arms out to the side, legs spread."

I parted them a little on my own, hoping he wouldn't spread them more if I obeyed him promptly. But when he put his hands on me, it wasn't to spread my legs, but to grope through the wetness at my center. I muffled a cry against the bedcover, but I wasn't really protesting. I was trying to understand. Or trying to come to terms with the fact that this powerful, kind of scary man was touching me sexually, almost violently while I was powerless, and I only wanted more.

He left me and went to the dresser, returning with a small paddle. Or maybe it just looked small compared to him. I moaned as he leaned over me and pulled my arms out straighter.

He stepped back. I buried my head in the covers, afraid to look.

"Ready?"

"No, not reall— *Oh God!*" The paddle hurt every bit as much as his hand. I was never, ever, ever being a smartass to him again. I was going to be the poster-child for respectful submissives. "Oh, please," I cried as he whacked me. The sting was a solid burn across my backside, fading away to a throbbing afterglow. My ass was already on fire from the spanking and my nipples hurt worse now that they were pressed against the bed.

"Oh, no more, please," I cried.

"A few more," he said. "To really drive the point home."

"But really...please. Liam... *Owww!*" I squeezed my eyes shut against the spreading pain. "I have really learned my lesson. Absolutely learned it. It's not worth it to smart off to you."

"I'm glad you've realized that. You can smart off to me"— *Crack!*—"just not in this room, when we're doing a session."

"I won't! Ow!"

"Because this is about you getting better. It's serious. It's a matter we both need to approach with respect."

"Yes, Sir," I cried out as two or three smacks fell in succession. *Yes, yes, I'll respect you forever. Just, please, that* really *hurts.*

He paused and rubbed my ass, intensifying the burn. I wanted him to grope me again but at the same time I knew this wasn't sexy time. This was time for Ashleigh to pay the price for real and imagined faults.

"Five more," he said. "I want you to count them."

The last five just about pushed me past my limit, by design, I'm sure. By the time he finished I was bawling onto the pristine blue bedspread, and both my hands were full of scrunched up, sweaty fabric.

He put the paddle away and eased onto the bed next to me. "Come here," he said, his legs tangling with mine. I lay in his arms, a limp, sniffling, ass-aching submissive. He turned me onto my back when I tried to shrink into him.

"Close your eyes," he said.

I did at once, chastened sub that I was. He took off the nipple clamps and tingling discomfort flooded my breasts. I put my hands over my nipples. "Ow."

"Okay," he said, gathering me against him. "The punishment's all done."

"I'm sorry," I whispered into the hollow of his neck. "I'm sorry for being bratty."

He reached down and grabbed a handful of my sore ass cheeks. "Don't be too sorry. I enjoy punishing you. You know that, right?" He eased a gentle fingertip between us to tweak my nipple. "Tender?"

I was, but I deserved it. I didn't know why I'd pulled the attitude with him. I guess because I was falling for him and I wasn't supposed to. My tears had mostly dried up, replaced with a relaxed, wrung-out feeling. I cuddled closer to him, nestling my thigh against his half-erect cock. I loved how careful he was with me. I loved that he didn't pressure me, that he was waiting so patiently for me to be ready.

I knew we were supposed to be focused on my sex issues, on fixing me, but more and more, I fantasized about him in more than a fixing way. I fantasized about him falling in love with me and swearing off his playboy habits. I fantasized about a life with him, about pleasure like this for the rest of my days. If he knew, he'd probably laugh at me. Liam, who slept with four or five women a week, who shared "sluts" with Rubio and participated in orgies at his BDSM parties.

I had to stop daydreaming about impossible things, no matter how much I wanted them. I pressed my nipples against his chest, just to hurt them some more. He drew away from me and propped his head on his hand.

"You know what I think, Ash? I think the BDSM part is the key. I think you're super kinky. I think you'll have more success at sex if you stir a little kink into the mix. The bad news is that being kinky narrows your dating pool quite a bit. Especially if you're looking for relationships and marriage and all that crap." He stroked my tummy. "What do you think?"

I think you're kinky. I think we could get married. "I think... Yes. I think the BDSM part of it really turns me on. I like when you dominate me." I looked down at his hand, then back at him. "I wish I was a better sub. You know, more experienced, like the other girls you're used to."

"I like that you aren't like the other girls. I dreaded having to teach you all the lifestyle stuff but it's been fun playing with you so far."

"So, are we still going to try to have sex?"

He looked over at me in surprise. "Of course we are. That's what we're working toward, right? You seem a lot more comfortable with me now, and a lot more at ease in your body."

"I am."

He thought for a long moment, his fingers trailing over the smattering of hair on his chest. "Why don't we go away next weekend, after your Sunday performance? Go somewhere peaceful and comfortable and spend a couple days naked together? See what develops?"

He meant, *see if we can have sex*. I didn't feel the least bit afraid, not in this moment, with him warm and strong beside me, looking at me with so much affection in his gaze. "I'd like that."

"No pressure," he said. "I don't want you to feel like it has to happen while we're there. This is all to help you, so it's whatever you feel comfortable with."

"What about after?" I asked. "After I'm...better?"

"You mean, will we keep having sex?" He looked away, just for a second, then back at me. He looked so distant I almost flinched. "I guess that's up to you. It's your life, you know? But it's pointless to talk about it now, when we haven't accomplished it even one time."

"Yes. I guess so." I swallowed hard, feeling abandoned even though he was lying right next to me.

"Do you want to stay here tonight?" he asked. "Have some breakfast in the morning before you go?"

I said yes because I could tell he didn't feel like taking me home, but really, I should have gone back to my bed of branches. That was where I belonged, behind the wooded barrier, sleeping. I wished my prince would kiss me, but after a few more moments, he got up and went to sleep in his own room.

Chapter Fourteen:
Now, Please

On Wednesday I was called to Mr. Thibault's office between rehearsal and the evening performance. As soon as I arrived he handed me an embossed envelope with a Cheyenne postmark.

"This arrived at the City Ballet offices addressed to you."

I looked down at the return address. "It's from my old dance teacher."

"How delightful. When you write her back, you can convey the good news—Mr. Rubio has decided to cast you as the female lead in his new ballet."

"He just told you that now?"

Mr. Thibault laughed. "Don't look so nervous. There are merely contracts to sign. A pay raise, although not as much as I'd like to give you."

He gestured to his desk and slid some papers over for me to read and sign. I tried to concentrate on the small print and legal phrases, but my mind was on the letter. I hadn't spoken to Miss Melanie in years, even though I owed her everything. Life circumstances had separated us by an ocean. I hoped she was okay. As soon as I finished signing all the papers, Mr. Thibault drew me into a conversation about Rubio and the ballet, and my ambitions within the company.

Ambitions? Me?

But it was ambitious to dance with Rubio. Now I'd be part of the shark-tank crew, the sharp, scrabbling dancers who were always trying to get ahead, usually by stabbing each other in the back over roles and partnerships.

"I'm not sure what my plans are for next year," I told him honestly. "I wasn't considering trying out for soloist."

He gave me the same look Rubio had given me the day I almost turned down the role. *Whut? Why you dance then?*

"I'll think about it," I said. "Things are kind of crazy now." Yes, because I was apparently going to the country with Liam for the weekend, to a picturesque little cottage he owned a couple hours north of London. I wanted to have sex with him there, but I was afraid it wouldn't work and he'd lose patience with his Fix-Ashleigh initiative. Lately it seemed like he'd been distancing himself and I wasn't sure he wouldn't drop me altogether if I had another meltdown. I accepted that Liam wasn't my boyfriend, that he wasn't anybody's boyfriend, but that didn't mean I didn't fall a little more in love every time we were together.

As soon as I left Mr. Thibault's office, I went to the dressing rooms and hunched over my carrel, ripping open the envelope with Miss Melanie's note.

Dear Ashleigh,

I hope this letter finds you well. I think of you often, gracing the stages of London with your dancing, and I'm so proud of all your accomplishments. You were a very special student and a diligent artist. I knew you would go far.

I'm writing to send love but also to ask you to solve a mystery for me. A couple weeks ago I learned from my bank that both my dancing school and my house mortgages had been paid off by an anonymous donor. When I asked for more information I was told the funds came from London, from "a friend of Ashleigh Keaton." My deepest thanks are due to you for remembering my modest academy, and to your astoundingly generous friend.

I can't explain to you the difference this gift has made in my life. The school has struggled the last few years but now we'll be able to stay open. I'm thinking of changing the name to the Ashleigh Keaton Dance Academy in honor of our most famous graduate. What do you think? Thank you, thank you, dearest Ashleigh. Please let me know the name

and address of your friend so I can thank him or her for their kindness.
You can write to me or email me at the school.

In closing... I only recently learned of your father's illness. From
what I understand he is approaching his final days. Please know you will
be in my thoughts and prayers. I hope you are well and happy where
you're living.

Much love,

Melanie

I held the letter against my face. Miss Melanie, with her short salt-
and-pepper curls, her sharp gaze and her gentle corrections. I never
confided the depth of my problems with my father but she'd sensed my
desperation and been kind enough to help. Then there was Liam Wilder,
who took helping to a whole new level. I didn't need any more reasons to
adore him. I found the school's email online and wrote to my old teacher,
giving her Liam's full name and address. I also begged her not to name
her school after me. I didn't want any part of me back in Wyoming, not
even on the awning of a rural dance academy.

That night, while I was getting ready for *Bayadère*, I noticed looks
from my fellow dancers, and not many smiles. Of course. The word was
out. Me and Rubio were dancing in the spring showcase. If anyone had
asked me, I would have talked it down. *Just a short piece. I don't know*
why he asked me. It doesn't even have a name. But no one asked me,
because no one seemed to want to talk to me. Professional jealousy was a
bitch.

So was romantic jealousy. Why didn't Liam want me? Who else
occupied his time? What was I missing that his other sexual partners
had?

Well, I knew the answer to that question. Mental health.

* * * * *

I assured Ashleigh that our weekend in the country wasn't going to
be about pressure.

I didn't want it to be about pressure, but from the moment I picked
her up at the theater, there was an uneasy tension between us that grew
by the hour. We drove north out of London, had dinner at a quiet
restaurant, and then continued on to my secluded haven, a small, old,
extremely English cottage I'd restored a few years ago from a hollowed-

out shell. It looked prettier in spring and summer, with the blooming trees and wildflowers, but Ashleigh said she loved it.

There wasn't much to see inside. No TV, no rooms except a small bathroom with a shower. She fluttered around the cottage as if looking for a place to land, but there wasn't any place except the bed.

I second-guessed everything as I watched her. Yes, the cottage was rustic and private, but I wondered if I shouldn't have taken her somewhere with more luxury—and more distractions. This cottage was four walls and a bed, a kitchenette and a few paintings on the walls. It must have seemed that I'd only brought her here to fuck her.

Well, I had, right? We were here to fuck. I couldn't draw out this mentoring arrangement much longer, not without becoming hopelessly entangled. I wanted to go back to my former life, where women were just pals and sex was easy and fleeting, and I didn't have to worry about eviscerating someone's damaged soul. I wanted to spend my nights scening with random partners who were objects, not people. Objects were so much easier. Girls like Ashleigh were hard.

I brought in our bags and fired up the wood stove in some effort to settle her. She perched on the edge of the bed while I double-checked the locks and shut the window blinds.

"Are we— Do we follow our rules here?" she asked. "The rules we follow in the guest room?"

I turned back to her, considering. "I don't think this weekend should be about D/s, but I like being in charge of you. I think everything works better between us when I'm in charge."

"When you're around me I feel like you're in charge," she said.

"Someone can be in charge though, and not abusive. I have authority over you but..."

"But I have power too. I know." She didn't say it in a smartass way. She stood and crossed to me, and took my hand. "I don't know how I'm going to thank you for all this, for all the help you've given me. You've changed me. Even if this doesn't end up working..."

I studied her as she skittered away from me again. "Do you think it's not going to work?"

Ashleigh shrugged and stood near the window, peering out through a crack in the blinds. "My dance teacher wrote me. I know that you sent money to her."

"She deserved it. She helped you."

"So what can I do for you?" she asked. "What can I possibly do for you, to thank you?"

"Get better. That's all. Get better and be happier. You deserve a happy life."

"Like yours?"

I slowed on the way across the room. "Well, yes. Like mine. A life where you feel comfortable and content. Where you have all the things you want, the relationships you want, all of that." I was the world's biggest hypocrite and liar, holding my life up as an example of happiness. But we weren't here to fix my issues. We were here to fix hers.

When I reached her I tilted her face to mine in the dim light. "You're so beautiful, Ash. You always have been. If I changed you in some way that makes your life better, that's all I need as thanks."

I stared down at her, at her pale blue-gray eyes and her sensual lips. There was a time I'd thought of her as an object too. If she hadn't been troubled and sad, and damaged due to her childhood, what would our relationship have been like? I would have fucked her that night, I was sure. And since she was mostly vanilla, that probably would have been it. I wouldn't have given her my number, even if the sex was really awesome. I might have noticed her in ballets now and again, remembering our torrid night together. It would have been easy and pleasant. I wouldn't have had to spend the last few weeks fighting with myself, questioning all my life choices. I definitely wouldn't be standing here now, half afraid it would work and half afraid it wouldn't.

If it worked, I would have to start letting her go.

"I don't want to hurt you," I said. I didn't know where the words came from, I just knew I meant them passionately. Maybe, more accurately, I could have said *I love you* because the sentiment was the same. Holy God.

"You won't hurt me." She gave me a tremulous smile. "I feel really ready. You've been a great teacher."

I traced her brow, then cupped her cheek and kissed her parted lips. It was so quiet, so still. No hovering Mem, no parties, no music blasting in the background, no computer, no TV, and for her, no backstage hustle-bustle. She smelled like flowers and baby powder and her hair felt like silk. I'd never brought anyone here to my hideaway because I didn't think they'd appreciate it, but Ashleigh belonged here. If it wasn't so cold I would have taken her outside under the stars and made love to her on the ground, on the earth. *This is what it should be like*, I would have told her. *Beautiful and fearless, tender and affectionate and rough and elemental...*

"Ashleigh," I sighed. "I want you. I want to hold you down and be inside you. I won't hurt you, I swear."

She blinked at me, then stared down at my chest. I owed her a big seduction—she deserved a big seduction—but I felt too raw to work my game on her. That was for other girls. With Ashleigh I wasn't a player, but someone else. A lover. A friend. "Are you ready now?" I asked. My voice sounded strained, almost desperate.

"We should get it out of the way, huh?" She gave me a comic, panicked look that started both of us laughing.

"Yes, let's get it over with," I said, playing along with her. "The sooner the better."

We undressed, layers of clothing coming off until we were skin to skin. I felt pressure, yes, but I also felt an almost painful lust. We'd had weeks of foreplay, lessons on personal boundaries and consent, explorations into the lifestyle. I was achingly hard from wanting her. I nudged her back onto the bed and lay down beside her. She squiggled right against me, into the circle of my arms, seeking protection or encouragement. I drew her close and hugged her tight.

"We can go slow," I said. "We can take our time. All the time you need. We can do it an hour from now. We can do it tomorrow."

"No," she said. "Now. Please. I know I'm ready. I'm not scared."

"You feel a little scared. You're shivering."

"I'm nervous, not scared. It's not the same." She reached between us, taking my cock in her hands, and smiled as she noted its rigid length. "You don't feel scared or nervous. At all."

That touch alone was almost enough to set me off. "I'm not nervous, no. I'm turned on like hell because you're so lovely, so beautiful. I can't wait to be inside you."

"Just don't..." Her confidence seemed to waver for a moment. "Please just...be careful. Don't be too rough."

I won't be like him. Never like him. "Ashleigh, look at me." I held her close, cupped her face and ran my thumb across the satiny texture of her cheek. "Just remember, the fear is all in your head. Don't hang on to those old wounds, those old experiences. Let them go. It's here. It's now. I'm here and I want to make you feel good. Trust me to be careful with you."

"I know. I know you'll be careful." She touched my cock again, cradling it in her hands. "I know I'm ready. I'm just a little nervous now that the moment is here."

"Baby..." I was going to come in a second, if she didn't stop stroking me. She'd gone on the Pill so we didn't have to use a condom, but I almost wished for one, to desensitize me, to help me last a little longer. I worried that as soon as I got inside her I'd go off like a bomb. "Baby, I want to touch you first, make you feel good. Make you feel excited for me."

I knew all the spots that got her hot and wet. I kneaded her ass and pinched her nipples, reveling in her responsiveness. She'd come so far in her ability to enjoy this, to trust me, and I wanted to be worthy of that trust. I ran a hand down her body, from her sculpted shoulder to her beautifully shaped breasts and down to her flat, tight stomach. I parted her pussy lips, finding her clit, moving my hips against hers. *I just want to help you. I just want to help you...*

She was wet, so wet. I grasped my cock and nudged her legs open, settling her onto her back. "Look at me," I said. "Everything will be okay."

Her eyes fixed on mine, wide and intent with feeling. Her fingers dug into my arms but she didn't fight my forward motion. She was breathing fast and hard as I arched my hips against hers and eased into her oh, so slowly. I studied her face, noting every flitting twitch and expression. Every second felt like an hour because I was so afraid of losing her. I was afraid of her calling everything to a halt, jumping up and running away, but she didn't. She smiled at me and moved her fingers down to my hips, pulling me deeper inside her. That pressure of her fingers—it was the most wonderful feeling in the history of the earth.

"Oh, baby, wow." My voice rasped between us in the silence. I could have died from the tightness of her pussy. She said something in reply, *yes* or *oh*. I could barely think to decipher the sounds. I stroked her hair and leaned down to kiss her, intently, then voraciously. As I explored her sweet mouth, my cock found her center, pressing deep. We were fully joined together, my pulsing hardness embedded in her heat.

After so many days, so many hours of effort, we were connected with nothing but trust between us. She stared up at me, and I swear the deeper I thrust inside her, the deeper I fell in love with her.

It was disaster, and bliss.

Liam, Liam, *Liam*... I'd feared panic and terror-filled blindness, but my only thought was Liam. He was above me, around me, pushing into me and it *didn't hurt*.

So this was sex. Making love. It was *wonderful*. It felt like force and yet it felt beautifully tender, like being hugged from the inside. He was big and hard, but not scary. He cradled me in his arms and filled me until there wasn't room for anything else. In, out, deeper and deeper. I wrapped my legs around his, needing him as close as possible, and even when he crushed me a little it felt okay.

I didn't even care about a climax. I was too caught up in this amazing new world where sex wasn't horrible and I didn't feel the urge to run to the bathroom and vomit in revulsion. For the first time in my life, I was enjoying the experience of having a man inside me. That it was Liam—tall, strong, gentle, rough Liam—that made it even better. He drew my hands over my head and held them as he made love to me with infinite care. I tried to explain to him what I was feeling, in gasping, worshipful whispers, but then it all became too much for words. Pleasure took over, a building fullness above and beyond the fullness of his cock stretching me, and when it peaked...

I strained where his hands held me and shuddered as my pussy contracted around his length. He pressed inside me hard and rested his forehead against mine, and I felt so close to him, closer than I'd felt to anyone else in my life. Tears filled my eyes and squeezed from between my lids.

He arched against me and made a noise like he was dying. He released my hands and I clung to him, hiding my face in the soft, flowing curtain of his hair. His arm came around my waist and he lifted me right against him. It felt like dancing—hot, violent dancing. He collapsed on me, heavy and still, his cock twitching inside me. I buried my face against his chest.

"Please don't let go," I whispered.

"I won't." His voice sounded harsh with his own short breath. His fingers moved over my back, a light, soft touch like velvet. After a while, after he pulled away and we were breathing normally again, he bent his head to mine. "Ashleigh, baby. I think it worked."

I grinned and closed my fingers in his hair. "I think so too. I never imagined it could feel like that, that it could feel so good. It was nothing at all like I..." *Like I remembered.* We both filled in the words but I didn't want to say them. I didn't want my father to have any part of this moment, any part of this experience between us. All I wanted to remember was this closeness and my feeling of finally being *normal*. There was nothing wrong with me, and nothing to keep me from doing this again and again with whomever I wanted.

But I only wanted Liam. "Can we do it again?" I asked.

He didn't make me beg. We did it again, and then again. The last time I started to feel sore but I didn't care. I was insatiable, like a sugar-deprived child let loose in a candy store. I was binging on sex, but it was more than that. It was a connection to Liam, something above and beyond lessons and advice.

After the third time, we slept the sleep of the dead, Sleeping Beauty's hundred-year sleep, and woke up still reaching for each other.

Well, this was why we'd come here. Why not fuck and fuck and fuck? We ate and drank right in the bed, only to gain the necessary energy for more sex. The second day, when I started to flinch at each thrust, when my body couldn't keep up with the demands of accommodating his size, he brought out lubricant and we kept going, slipping and sliding together. By Monday afternoon we'd had sex at least ten times, in several creative positions. I loved the way he moved me around, the way he pinched and stroked me, and slapped my ass sometimes, and basically did whatever he liked.

But that was why I'd chosen him to help me in the first place. He knew what he was doing. He hadn't let me down. "Thank you," I said the second day, as we lay resting together. "You fixed me."

He chuckled and pressed his forehead to mine. "And then I think I broke you again."

You didn't break me, Liam. You saved me. He was so talented, this man. He could open locked doors and heal broken women. He was patient and seductive, and oh, so caring. I could have stared into his eyes for hours, but I was afraid he'd see the guilty truth in my gaze. *I'm in love with you, Liam Wilder.* I was head over heels in love with this man. I loved him hard enough to marry him if he asked.

He sobered and ran a hand over my waist, and up to my neck, like he was measuring me. "Beautiful girl," he said. "You'll make someone so happy."

I almost flinched. How could he say such a thing, just as I started planning our fantasy wedding? It hurt me so badly that I blurted out stuff I shouldn't have. "Why not you?" I drew back to look at him. "Why can't I make *you* happy?"

"You do make me happy." He traced across my cheek bones, avoiding my gaze. "But you should meet someone who can make *you* happy. Who'll give you all the things you deserve."

"You make me happy," I persisted, even though his expression wasn't welcoming. It was like he'd heard the words in my head and was arguing against them. I closed my eyes, fighting a wave of tears. He didn't say anything for a long time but I felt the band of his arms around me loosen a little.

I bit my lip, determined not to say anything else, wishing I hadn't said so much to begin with. I sounded pathetic, whining for him to want me. This was Liam, who could have any woman he wanted, whose play room was filled to the hilt with sexy, available sirens every Saturday night.

"I'm sorry," I said. "That was out of line. Forgive me."

"Stop," he said, touching my lips.

"I just... I know. I remember. This was supposed to be no strings attached. I forgot for a minute because I felt so close to you."

He sat up in an abrupt motion. "Jesus. Speaking of remembering..." He took my hand and squeezed it. "I was supposed to check in at the office an hour ago. Maybe you should get some rest."

I swallowed hard. "You're calling in to work?"

He nodded. My close, warm, slippery-sliding Liam wasn't there anymore. This was the Sir side of him, that was focused and businesslike. "It's okay," he said. "You could probably use a nap. Do you need anything? Something to eat or drink?"

"No, I'm fine. Don't worry about me. I forget sometimes that everyone in the world doesn't have Monday off."

"Okay." He moved to go but then turned back and gave me a peck on the lips that felt as cold and impersonal as a handshake. I forced a smile to answer his fake smile, swallowing back the emotion choking my throat.

He dressed and grabbed his phone off the table. I closed my eyes and lay back in the fluffy counterpane, hugging his pillows against me. They smelled like him, the man I wished would fall in love with me. I'd gotten what I asked for, and now I wanted more, which is what he'd warned me would happen. *I can't say no to what you're asking, but I'm afraid I'll hurt you in this process. I won't mean to, but I will.*

Now I'd freaked him out, pressured him for a deeper relationship. I heard him talking on the phone outside, and it sounded business-y, but he could have been setting up his next date. I shut it all out. My feelings, his voice, his scent on the pillows and the memory of his lackluster kiss. I wiped my lips on my hand and forced my eyes closed. At some point, I must have slept, because next I knew Liam was sitting beside me on the bed, nudging me awake.

"Hey," he said. "You've been sleeping a couple hours. How do you feel?"

I nodded through the haze of fading dreams. "I'm fine."

He brushed my hair back when it fell over my eyes. "I'm sorry to do this to you, but something came up at work. A touchy situation, and the office is in an uproar."

Lies. Horrible lies. "If you need to go, we can go," I said, using every ounce of my strength to sound casual. "We accomplished what we came here to do."

"We did," he said, seizing on my words. "And it was amazing. Honestly, Ashleigh, I'm so proud of you. I hope it was all you wanted. I hope you feel..."

"Fixed?" I took his hand to still its nervous motion. "I feel wonderful, Liam. And now I feel well-rested too. But you must be tired."

He shrugged. "I'm used to working through that. I'll be fine. Maybe in a few days, after you have some time to recuperate, we can meet up again."

To have sex? To have dinner? To say our final goodbyes? He didn't specify and I was afraid to ask. I was afraid to press him now when he seemed so desperate to get away from me. Maybe in a few days, with a little space, he'd realize there were things he liked about me, perhaps enough things to...

Oh God, I was back to creating impossible fantasies. I might as well be scrapbooking about Rubio again. Liam had done what I'd asked him to do, at great personal and emotional expense. He'd gone out of his way to help me, and now I had to let go of him the way I'd promised. "I'll get dressed," I said, throwing back the covers. It was cold in the room, and not just because of the weather. "I'll be ready in a minute, if you want to start packing the car."

Chapter Fifteen:
Free and Clear

"Liam. Liam, dear?"

I looked up at the sound of my stepmom's voice. My dinner plate was cooling in front of me. "Yes? I'm sorry. I wasn't listening."

She put the back of her hand to my forehead. "Do you feel all right? Are you getting enough sleep?"

I smiled at her, the best smile I could muster. "Not really, but when do I ever?"

It was Sunday, and tomorrow was Monday, the day Ashleigh would have come over, except that I had messaged her and told her not to come. I told her work was still hectic—and it was. But it always was. She'd messaged back with chipper, depressing acceptance.

That's okay. I understand. :)

She didn't understand, not at all, and I didn't want to explain it to her. She didn't understand the depth of my fear of commitment, my fear of love. The way my stomach turned in knots at the thought of losing her, which is why I couldn't have her in the first place. I didn't want anyone in my life who had the power to reach into my chest and rip out my heart, and she had that power. Therefore, I didn't want her anymore.

But I *wanted* her. Oh God.

I dreamed of her at night, of her body pressing against mine, her urgent little moans and sighs. I told myself I only needed time and distance, and I'd be able to look at her like I looked at other women, as a body to use, as a pretty ornament to decorate my play room on the weekends. Until that time, I had to avoid her. I needed space.

I forced my attention back to my stepmom's cheerful conversation, and then my dad and I talked about work. I could always distract myself with work. I threw myself into the discussion about recent dramas, new hires, and possible expansion.

"By the way," said my father, "how is your dancer friend? The one with the security threat?"

"Oh, my," Abby murmured. "Not Fernando?"

I shook my head and tried to answer in a normal voice. "There was another dancer I met. A woman."

"She had some problems, I seem to remember," my dad said. "Did everything turn out all right?"

I couldn't tell if my father was yanking my chain or making casual conversation. Any mention of Ashleigh and my brain went haywire. I picked apart layers of lasagna.

"Yes, she's fine. Her, uh, issues have been resolved."

"I'm glad to hear it."

"Yes, that's good," my stepmom said. "And how is your friend Fernando? I think I read in a City Ballet article that he's dipping his toes into choreography. That he's working on an original piece?"

"Yes. Ironically, he's doing it with that same dancer who was…having some trouble. But she isn't anymore, so yeah, everything's fine all around."

Except me. I'm not fine. I'm in love and I don't know how to deal with it. I can't fucking sleep at night and I don't know if I can survive seeing her again.

I didn't say that out loud, but my father was studying me with his usual hyper-perception. I avoided his gaze and picked up an asparagus spear, twirling it in front of me. This would pass. All of this would pass. One thing I'd learned through doing BDSM…even the worst pain and agony eventually faded away.

* * * * *

162

Rubio snapped his fingers in my face.

"Where are you, girl? Earth to Ash-lee." He walked over to switch off the rehearsal music, then returned to me, leaning down to peer into my eyes. "You okay? What's wrong?"

"Nothing's wrong."

"Then I need you. Focus." With his accent, "focus" sounded like "fuck us." I hung my head because he was right, I was out of focus. I was dancing in a haze. "Is now March," he reminded me. "We debut this in April. That's next month."

"I know," I said, avoiding his concerned gaze. "I know the steps. I just zoned for a minute."

"Zoned? What is this? I don't like it." He put an arm around my head and pretended to choke me, pulling faces. "You feeling sad? Whut? Other dancers still giving you mean looks?"

"No, that's died down. Everything's fine, Ruby." *Everything but my aching heart.* I forced a smile but I didn't think he was fooled. Over the course of our deepening partnership, he'd developed a disconcerting ability to read my moods.

"Hey," he said. "Why don't you come to the party tomorrow at Liam's? Relax and have fun." He let go of my neck and slid a hand down to my boob. "When I get to see you naked? In chains?"

"You are never going to see that," I said, pushing his paws away.

"You let me whip you? Please? I'll do it so I don't draw blood. I'll just make little marks on your back. Whip kisses."

"You know what? There is zero chance of that happening."

He came to stand behind me, making whipping motions and fake "*whi-pshhh*" sounds.

I talked over him, looking in the mirror. "Hey, does Liam ever say anything to you about me?"

"Say anything? Like what?"

"Just, whatever. Do you guys ever talk about me?"

"Sure," he said. Then, "No, never."

I turned to look at him. "Which it it?"

He stood frozen, his imaginary whip mid-crack. "It's no. No. We never talk about you."

"Does he talk about other girls?"

Rubio made a face. "I'm not going to do this conversation. I don't want to be in your drama. We have to rehearse, yeah?" He gripped my waist, hauling me around in a lift we'd practiced approximately a thousand times. He set me down with his mouth by my ear. "I told you to be careful. I warned you."

I pulled away from him and brushed a hand over my messy bun. "Forget it," I said. "Me and Liam just had some weirdness between us last time we were together."

"He put his cock in your asshole, huh?"

"What? No. It's just... Forget it. It's cool."

His expression brightened. "Hey, you know what, Ash-lee? I thought of the name for the ballet."

"Awesome. What is it?"

"*Waking Kiss*."

"*Naked Kiss*?" I still had trouble with his accent sometimes.

"*Waking Kiss*," he said, laughing. "Like to wake up. I get the idea from *Sleeping Beauty* ballet. You know, that moment when she sleeps in her fancy bed?"

Yes, I knew that moment. I had the fancy bed.

"And the prince comes," said Rubio. "And when I perform, I wonder what she dream of, you know? And in that moment when she wakes, does the world seem new again? People sleep, Ash-lee. They don't feel. They don't understand." He spread his hands. "Nothing. But sometimes someone comes with a kiss. You know, a real kiss or...a word or an inspiration." He looked into my eyes, holding my gaze. "Something new to wake them up from a—a long, lonely sleep. *Waking Kiss*. This ballet is about coming awake again. New beginnings. You think it's a good idea?"

Coming awake again. He was describing me. I'd been doing a dance about my experiences with Liam and I hadn't even known it. "We don't kiss in the ballet," I said, staring past his shoulder.

He shrugged. "We could add a kiss somewhere. Maybe. Why must it be so literal? Sometimes what wakes you is not a kiss. It is a vision or an action. A feeling." He leaned down and stared at me with uncharacteristic gravity. "A person you meet, who changes you some way."

Like Liam Wilder. Memories of his smiles and his warmth flooded me.

"You just don't want to kiss me," I teased. If I didn't tease him I'd start to cry.

"I kiss you, maybe in the first *arabesque*." He grabbed me, silly Rubio again. We did the opening combination, but he added a clumsy, cartoonish kiss halfway through.

"Stop," I said. "Eww. Too much tongue."

At that he grabbed my face and started licking my cheek and ear while I shrieked for mercy. When I tried to dance away from him he caught me and pulled me off balance. We both went stumbling sideways across the studio, howling with laughter. Then we noticed a third person reflected in the mirror.

Liam stood in the door, my memories made real, only he wasn't smiling. Rubio let go of me and took a couple steps away.

"I heard you screaming," Liam said, his eyes fixed on me.

"Heard me screaming from where?"

"Down the hall."

"I didn't know you were here." I looked over at Rubio. He seemed very interested in the floor. "Are you and Ruby headed out together tonight? To party?" I couldn't quite keep the irritation from my voice.

Liam leaned against the door frame. "I didn't come here to see him. I was looking for you. So, is that the new ballet you two were rehearsing? It looks pretty ragged to me."

Rubio grinned at him, but it was a forced grin. "We were only playing around. We have to..." He shrugged and rubbed a hand across his forehead. "I think we add a kiss in somewhere. We were practicing."

"Yes, I saw."

I narrowed my eyes at Liam. "You're not jealous, are you? Of a fake ballet kiss?"

"I'm not jealous."

"Then why are you using that voice?"

He looked at Rubio again and something vicious flitted across his expression, only to be quickly cloaked. "You know what? You two go at it. Have fun." He turned to leave in a huff, like I was the biggest bitch on earth for rehearsing with my partner. He was the one who couldn't make time to see me all last week. I took off after him.

"What the fuck?" I asked. "'*You two go at it.*' Really? What are you insinuating?"

He barely turned to me. "I'm not insinuating anything."

"Me and Rubio are artists. We work together. I never had his slimy lips on me before tonight. Before three minutes ago."

"Hey!" Rubio trailed us down the hall. We all came to a stop outside his dressing room. "I don't have slimy lips," Ruby said, scowling at me. He jabbed a finger at Liam. "And why you care what he thinks, Ash-lee? You're not a couple."

Liam jabbed a finger back at Rubio. "Whether or not we're a couple is none of your fucking business."

"It's my business because she's my friend," he shot back.

"Oh, she's your friend? Really?"

"He's a better friend than you are," I said, interrupting Liam. "He doesn't lie to me."

"When did I lie to you?"

"Several times lately."

"Name one. One lie."

"How about '*ooh, something came up at work. I have to get back.*'"

"You think I made that up? Something did come up at work, a shitload of trouble with one of our government-contracted agents in D.C." He turned to Rubio. "You started all this. You told her I don't have relationships, that I'm a player. You spilled all your warnings in her ears."

"You *are* a player!" Rubio said.

Liam looked back at me. "And you! You judge me based on things he's said about me, most of which probably aren't true."

"No," I said. "I judge you based on the way you act. But I agreed to your terms. That's not the issue here. The issue is that you don't have the right to come in here and give me the mean-disgusted-face because I'm dancing with Rubio. It's not like you caught us fucking in the middle of the floor."

"I don't give a shit," said Liam. "It's your life, your choice. If you want to fuck Ruby in the middle of the floor, then fuck him. Why would I fucking care? God, I'm happy for you. You can even do it at my house if you want, in my play room. It would truly make me happy to see you having a healthy, avid sex life."

"See!" I pointed at him. "That's what I'm talking about. Every time you say something like that, it's not to be nice. It's to push me away."

"I'm not trying to push you away. I'm just saying, if Ruby's what turns you on, go for it."

"Ruby doesn't turn me on. He's selfish and annoying."

"Hey," he protested. "I'm standing right here."

"I know you don't want me," I said to Liam. "I think you came here tonight to catch me with Ruby and cause a big drama. He told me, Liam. You love to mess with women's minds."

"Oh yes," he said, throwing up his hands. "More friendly warnings from Rubio. Shocking. Did it ever occur to you that it helps his agenda to tear me down? Do you think he doesn't want to fuck you once he warns you away from me? And that he won't fuck you over afterward, ten times worse than I ever would?"

"Again, I'm right here," yelled Rubio. He stuck a finger in Liam's face. "Want to talk about agendas? She deserves to know who you really are—"

"Shut the fuck up!"

"And the reason you do this to her! *Jesus Cristo*, it is enough. When you going to be honest? When you going to tell what happened to you, why you behave this way?"

Liam shoved his finger away. "Shut your fucking mouth. You don't know anything about it."

I watched them, lost. "What are you talking about?"

"Do not tell her," Liam said in a voice like death. "For once in your fucking life, don't be a backstabbing asshole."

"What happened?" I pressed. "Something bad? What?"

"Nothing." Liam flicked his fingers. "More character assassination from the most jacked up, hypocritical player on the face of the planet. He wants to sleep with you and he'll say anything to do it. He won't give up until he's found a way between your legs."

"Whatever," Ruby said with a petulant curl of his lip. "Is your problem, Liam. Your stupidity. You can kiss my round Brazilian ass."

"So, why did you cast me in your ballet?" I asked, turning on Rubio. "To piss off Liam? To make him jealous? Is there some weird competitive thing going on between the two of you?"

Rubio laughed, a hard, sharp laugh. Liam glared at him. "Don't."

"You want to know why I cast you?" he said to me.

"Don't," Liam said again. "Don't do it."

I looked between them. "Why are you guys speaking this secret language?"

Rubio turned to me with his satyr smile. "I cast you in my ballet, Ash-lee, cause Liam paid me money to do it. I was going to ask Heather." He rolled his eyes. "I should have asked Heather. All this drama isn't worth the twenty-five."

I turned to Liam. "You paid him twenty-five pounds to put me in his ballet?"

Liam pursed his lips. "Twenty-five thousand."

"Don't be modest," Rubio snarled. "Tell her all of it. You offered me thirty at first."

"I offered you a thousand but you sneered at it, you greedy bastard."

I gawked at Liam. "You paid him all that money to...to cast me?"

He leaned back against the wall and let out a sigh. "Yes, okay? Guilty. I thought you deserved the role and he didn't want to give it to you."

"No, that isn't why." Rubio cut him off in a savage tone. "Tell the truth, you fucking asshole." He turned to me. "He did it to distract you. Because he's going to dump you soon. I don't know. In a week or two, I think. The ballet will keep you busy, fix his guilt."

"That's not why I did it," Liam snapped.

"No? You can't even admit the truth to yourself," he said, poking a finger into Liam's chest.

Liam grabbed it. "I would be more fucking careful if I were you. It's hard to dance with two broken legs."

"You acted all impressed whenever I talked about the ballet." My voice sounded wooden. "You were all like 'wow,' and 'awesome,' when all the time it was you who..." I blinked at him, feeling horribly betrayed. "Why didn't you just tell me the truth? And you?" I said, spinning on Ruby. "You're *both* big fucking liars who play games."

Rubio muttered something under his breath in Portuguese and walked away. I glared at Liam.

"I know we're not together," I said in a very cold voice. "I know that. I don't care if you're going to leave me, because you were never with me to begin with—"

"I was with you," he said. "I went out of my way to help you."

"You're such a generous, kind person." My voice grew edgier by the moment. "That's why I don't understand how you can lie and manipulate me at the same time. I mean, I know you get off on it—"

"Ashleigh—"

"You're probably getting hard in your jeans right now because I'm freaked out and upset—"

"Ashleigh!"

"Rubio told me," I yelled back at him. "He told me you get off on this. That you like to use women, and mess with them. He warned me how easily you get bored. I know that you're playing me, Liam. I would respect it more if you let me in on the whole load of bullshit from the start."

"Do not," he said, holding up a hand. "Do not call our thing bullshit. I didn't spend one moment with you that was bullshit. What kind of monster do you think I am? That I would prey on a damaged, sexually vulnerable woman?"

"I don't know, Liam! I'm just telling you what I see."

"You're looking through the wrong pair of glasses, damn you. You're blind. If you take Rubio's word over mine— You don't know— Jesus. Fuck it," he said. "Go ahead. Go back to your 'friend' Rubio and practice your goddamned ballet some more. I'm finished here. We're finished. Have a nice life."

He turned and walked away from me, then turned back a moment later.

"Oh, and the reason I came here was to tell you that your father died today. This morning. Congratulations, Ashleigh. Now you're free and clear."

I stood and watched him go, stunned into silence. My father died today and I hadn't even known. Somehow I'd imagined I'd feel it, when his evil presence ceased to exist in the world. All the loss I felt was attached to Liam. He wouldn't see me again, not after this. I didn't even think we'd be friends.

"Ash-lee?"

I turned and looked down the hall. Rubio leaned against the door of the studio, watching me with a grimace. "You okay?" he asked.

I stalked back to him, fully intending to bitch-slap his face.

"Don't," he said, backing into the room. "Don't start with me. I am not involved in this."

"Why didn't you tell me about the money?"

"Because he told me not to." He *jeté*'d away from me and then tipped forward into a handstand. "He manipulates. He lies. I told you."

"What were you saying to him, about telling me the truth? What truth?"

"It doesn't matter." He huffed out a breath, pointing his toes at the ceiling. "He's bad for you, okay? I told you. You don't listen."

I stormed across the room. "Stop that. Get off your fucking hands and talk to me." I pushed him and he went tumbling down in a heap, then he grabbed my legs and pulled me down too. He leaned over me, trapping my hands behind me, and kissed me on the mouth. Not a silly, exaggerated kiss this time, but a real kiss, seductive and demanding. For a moment I was too shocked to react to the questing pressure. Ruby was kissing me. Why? His force and his weight panicked me a little.

"What are you doing?" I said against his lips.

He stilled and drew away, sat up and shook his head like he was coming to his senses. "It's ridiculous idea, no? You and me?" Ruby ran a hand through his hair and sprawled back on the floor. "Oh, Ash-lee, Ash-lee. *Ash-lee.* You love Liam. I warned you. He doesn't love anyone." He looked over at me. "I'm sorry, girl. Is very sad."

"Not sad." I sat up, brushing dust off my leotard. "Our relationship ran its course. Not that we ever had a real relationship."

"You keep saying that. You and Liam both. Liars."

"We didn't. We were always going to end things. It was just a little uglier at the end than I expected." Ugly. Miserable. Horrifying. I felt sad, but also strangely free and clear. I didn't want to be with any more guys who made me feel bad.

Rubio leaned up on his elbow, his face lighting with a sudden thought. "Hey, Ash-lee. Come with me to the party tomorrow. To Liam's."

"Why the hell would I go to Liam's after what just happened?"

"To make him jealous," he said, growing more animated with every word. "You go to Liam's to show you don't need him. That you are not at home crying into your pickles. You go with me."

"Crying into my pickles?"

"Maybe he'll see what he's missing and he'll think about how he hurt you." He batted his eyes. "Me, I won't play with you too hard. No whips. Maybe just a pink crop like the glitter kinksters use."

I pushed to my feet as he reached to grope my breasts. "What the hell is a glitter kinkster? Stop touching me." I was about to give a resounding no to his offer, but then I pictured myself going down the stairs to Liam's play room, dressed in tight sexy clothes, looking around the room like those other women, like I was hot and available.

Because I was hot and available.

When I thought about it, it wasn't such a bad suggestion. That was why I'd done all this, so I could find an actual partner to fall in love with, someone who wasn't as guarded and closed off as Liam. His party would be full of kinky prospects and, as a bonus, I could show him that I was over him. "I might go," I said. "But I'm not showing up with you. If I go it will be on my own."

He considered that a moment, then reached out and grasped the tip of my shoe. "I like you. You have quiet shoes now. I think maybe even…without the money…I would have asked you to do the ballet."

"Liar," I said, kicking his hand away. "You would have asked Heather. She has bigger boobs."

"Okay. You're right. But I think you're good in it anyway. I like how you dance." He jumped up and reached out a hand. "Come on. It's late now. I'll walk you home."

Chapter Sixteen:
Play Room

I was sitting at the table in the guest room Saturday night when Mem came to get me.

"*Ishi?*" His knock was sharp, his voice low. "Are you...occupied?"

"No." I'd brought a girl up from the party but I'd sent her down again. Nothing about her measured up, even though she'd dropped to her knees and worshipped my cock like it was gold-plated. I couldn't stay hard.

I'd drunk too much, that was all, and I was tired. I stared down at the dog-eared paper spread out in front of me, the mish-mash of notes I'd scrawled at this table a few months ago with Ashleigh trembling in my arms. *Watch hands around face. Don't lock door. Restraints okay.*

Don't call her a bad girl.

It always hurt.

I had hurt her too, distanced myself and pushed her away. The party went on beneath me, the drumbeats of music reminding me that life went on, that people were having fun and enjoying themselves as they always did, just as I would again. Eventually.

Mem entered and crossed to me. "She's here."

"Who's here?"

He paused. "*Little Ishi*. She is downstairs."

I spread my palms on the cold, slick tabletop. I'd never expected her to come here. She didn't belong in this careless crowd, not yet, not when she was so new to the lifestyle. I hauled myself to my feet. "Why did they let her in? She's downstairs? In the play room?"

He nodded. "She was headed that way."

Oh God, she was headed for the play room. I pushed past Mem with a muttered curse. I didn't know if I was going downstairs to play with her, beg her forgiveness, or throw her into a taxi. If she was with Rubio... Well, if she was with him, it was exactly what I deserved.

I stopped halfway down the stairs and scanned the various play spaces. I saw Rubio first, standing near the back wall, engrossed in a conversation with one of his off-and-on playmates. He wasn't with Ashleigh then. I felt relief even though I had no right to be possessive.

I finally found her lingering near the corner on the left side. She was wearing her representation of sexy, but on her it was a caricature, an ill-fitting skin. Teased hair rather than sleek locks, a tight, low-cut dress that made her look more child than woman. My nerves throbbed with anxiety as she prowled the fringes of the room. I stood back in the shadows and watched, because it wasn't my job to rescue her. Isn't that what I'd snapped at her last night? *We're finished. Have a nice life.* If she wanted to play with someone, I had to allow her to do it.

Except that she didn't know all the rules, only what I'd taught her.

My fingers tightened on the stair rail as a couple guys strolled over to her, the one in leather gear offering her a drink. I knew them. They were safe players, like all the people I invited here, but they didn't know Ashleigh. They didn't know she was inexperienced, that she'd been abused as a child, that she was vulnerable.

I started toward her but I wasn't the only one watching out for her. Rubio got to her first, chatting her away from the guys, greeting her with a kiss and a hug. If his nudity bothered her, she didn't show it. When I got to her side I took her arm.

"What are you doing here?" I asked in a low voice.

"If she wants to be here, who cares?" said Ruby.

I held up a hand to him. "Don't start with me. You know she doesn't belong here. She's not..." *She's not like the other girls.* "She's not experienced enough," I said instead. "If you want to play, Ash, you should come some other time and I can...maybe..."

"Help me?" she provided when I snapped my mouth shut. "You don't have to help me anymore. You don't have to be responsible for me."

I tried to draw her away from Ruby so we could talk privately, but she planted her feet. I frowned at her. "When I said that yesterday—"

"No, Liam. You can't tell me we're finished and then try to prevent me from living my life. This is what you wanted for me. You said that. You told me I could come play at your house. You told me I could fuck Ruby if I wanted to," she said, gesturing at him.

She was right. I'd said all that ridiculous shit to her for some reason. "I meant you could do that kind of stuff when you were more experienced."

"Oh God," said Ruby, throwing up his hands.

"I still care about you a lot," I said, tuning Rubio out. "I always will. It's just— I'm not sure you're ready yet to swim in this pond." I held her gaze, communicating my concern for her well-being. *I'm the only one here who knows, Ash. I want you to be careful. I'm afraid you'll get hurt.*

She twisted her hands in front of her, looking past me to scan the room. "Why don't you play with me, then?" she asked, squaring her shoulders. "If you think I'm not ready, why don't you do some scenes with me? Ease me into the swing of things?"

I stared at her. Why hadn't I foreseen this clusterfuck? I'd helped her overcome her fears. I'd released her and now she was here, and she wanted to play. If I didn't play with her, there were ten or fifteen other guys who'd be happy as hyenas to take her under their wing. Rubio would play with her in a heartbeat. She looked over at him when my silence stretched out too long. "Or you could play with me. You promised me a pink crop."

I narrowed my eyes at him. "You promised her a pink crop?"

He spread his arms. "She wants to play, Li-am. I know she's a beginner. Why don't we all play together? We show her good time, both of us. You rather someone else...?"

No, I wouldn't rather someone else, but both of us? Ruby and I had shared dozens of women in the past, but this was Ashleigh. I scratched my forehead and looked at her, struggling to remain detached. I had no right to possessive feelings or jealousy and she...she looked guardedly interested in Ruby's suggestion.

Okay. Fine. Maybe...both of us. With both of us, I could keep an eye on her and still keep my emotional distance. With both of us, she could see that Rubio wasn't the prince she thought he was. With both of us, I could touch her and fuck her again and not feel like I was losing my mind.

"Sure, both of us," I said, in a voice that didn't quite sound natural. "Three is always a lot of fun. You want to try it, Ash?"

She looked around the play room, at all the other depravity going on, and nodded with a spreading smile. "Okay, I guess so. Why not?"

Why not, indeed? She knew I wouldn't let anything happen to her. Ruby took her hand and led her to an unoccupied bondage rack in the corner and I followed without a word. He nodded me toward the adjacent wall of implements. "Go get stuff. Pink crop, most important thing," he said with a grin.

While I crossed the room, he started undressing her. I had to numb myself from the urge to run over and stop him. I was already half naked and Ruby was fully naked, so why did I want to shield her from everyone's gaze as he pulled her dress up over her head?

He took off her bra next, pausing to kiss and caress her breasts before folding the bra and placing it on top of her dress. I studied her, looking for signs of ambivalence or anxiety, but she seemed okay with what he was doing. After all, they'd become very close "friends." When he reached for her skimpy black panties, I walked over and stopped him. "That's enough for now. This is her first time playing in public."

Ruby frowned like he might argue but then he shrugged and looked down at my hands. All I'd collected in my distraction was a couple of leather cuffs. "You bind her up," he said, rolling his eyes. "I'll get the gear."

He left Ashleigh and me alone together. She cracked a nervous smile and crossed her arms over her breasts. "You're okay with this?" I asked. "You're sure?"

She shrugged. "It's just play, right?"

"You can put your bra back on if you want. A lot of people play in clothes." I turned and gestured around the room, where absolutely no one was playing in clothes. "Maybe not tonight, but…"

By the time I turned back her arms were at her side. "I'm being brave," she said. "I want to do this."

Fuck me. I'd only exhorted her to be brave a hundred times or more over the course of our sessions. "Let me have your hands," I said gruffly. I buckled on the cuffs, leaving her wrists very little room for movement.

"Are *you* okay with this?" she asked, watching me as I worked the clasps. "If you're not comfortable—"

"Honestly, I never expected you to come here. So I don't know how I feel about it. But since you're here and you made a promise to Ruby about the pink crop..."

"That was kind of a joke."

"Was it?" I said with an edge to my voice. "It's not going to seem so funny in a minute or two."

Ruby was back with a strap and a flogger, and yes, a whippy pink riding crop from God knew where. "Arms up," I said to Ashleigh. I clipped the cuffs to the chains on either side of the bondage frame, then stood behind her to test the slack. She'd need a bit of room for writhing around, but not too much. She looked back at me and through all my numbness, my confusion, I felt a powerful surge of desire. I pressed the outline of my rigid cock against her ass. "The safeword is twinkletoes," I said in her ear. "Use it if you need it, because"—I rattled her cuffs—"in this case, you can't walk out the door."

"Yes, Sir," she said in a quavery voice.

Was she scared? She deserved to be scared, but I still reassured her out of habit. "I won't leave you until the end of this scene, I promise. Not until you're unbound."

She took in a deep breath. "Thank you."

I spoke over my shoulder to Ruby. "I'll get her warmed up for you." I caressed down past her waist, her delicate hips and firm bottom and landed a slap to her right ass cheek. Another followed to her left. She clenched her hands in the cuffs but there was no other reaction. I wished now I'd let Rubio strip off her panties because I would have loved to feel her skin against my palm. Instead I stopped between every few smacks and slid my hand beneath the sheer black material.

"I'm waiting," said Ruby in a sing-song sneer. "If you can stop feeling her up for a minute."

"Give me the flogger." He handed it over and I stroked fingers down her back. "Okay, baby?"

"Yes... Yes, Sir."

"All right then. Here we go."

I grasped the chains and stood as still as I could. The first blow fell, a jolting, stinging impact. Liam didn't start out too hard with the flogger, just warmed up my back and shoulders with thuddy strikes. I couldn't tell if I liked it. I felt overstimulated by the noise and activity around me. The music beat in the background as the flogger landed on me in spreading stings, four, five, ten times or more.

In some way the sensation relaxed and loosened me. Then Liam stopped and Rubio stepped closer, caressing his hands over my waist and stomach. He nuzzled his face against my ear, murmuring something in Portuguese as his fingers traced lower to massage the gusset of my panties. Rubio had good dance-partner hands and it felt great, but I wondered what Liam was doing. I didn't want him to be jealous.

But what right did he have to be jealous?

Then Liam appeared at my other side and grabbed my teased-out hair. "What the hell is this mess?" he whispered. "Who are you?"

Before I could answer I felt a biting sting on the outside of my right thigh. I jerked and turned my head to see Ruby with a big smile, an erection, and a pink crop. "Move, Li-am," he said. "You're blocking my strike zone."

"Don't move," I said to Liam, only half-kidding.

"I'll hold her for you," Liam assured Ruby, shooting me a look. He braced a leg in front of me and curved an arm around my waist. "There. Now you can't miss."

Rubio stung my ass cheeks with the crop again, and again. For a cute, pink implement, it hurt like hell. I jerked away at each stroke but thanks to Liam, I couldn't go anywhere and I definitely couldn't run away. "Having fun?" he asked when Ruby took a breather to flick a nearby woman and flirt with her.

Honestly, I *was* having fun. I liked the sting and the feeling of being bound and helpless in the chains. I liked being able to connect with Liam this way, on his terms, in his play room. I hadn't wanted things to stay angry between us.

"I'm having a blast. Are you having fun?" I asked back, smiling to show how much I appreciated this experience. Liam buried his fingers in my hair and tilted my head and kissed me.

I'd wanted him to kiss me, to acknowledge our history and our closeness, but this kiss felt wrong and not close at all. It was a player kiss. He wasn't present in it, not the way he used to be. I wished we were both naked back in his cottage, feeling deeply connected, but that was a onetime thing. I arched my hips against the front of him, only to brush against the cool roughness of his jeans.

"Ouch!" I cried out against his lips as something harder smacked my backside. That would be the strap, and Rubio the maniac wielding it. I gave Liam a pleading look and he reached out to his friend.

"Give it to me. Let me have a go at her."

I almost sagged in relief when Rubio handed it over without an argument. Now his hands were on me again, around my waist as if to help me pirouette, but I wasn't doing any pirouetting right now. Ruby gazed at me with a curious, attentive look. I was staring right back at him when Liam landed the first stroke.

Oh my fucking mother of God!

I spun around to Liam. "Please, no. Ow, that's—" It was much harder than Ruby had hit me. I wanted to reach back and cover myself but my hands were cuffed above my head. Ruby grinned down at me.

"Oh, no, little girl. You must hold the position."

"Help me out, Ruby, will ya?" asked Liam.

"Certainly."

He wrapped his arms more tightly around me. His muscles bunched against my skin as another blow fell and I struggled helplessly, trying to pull away.

"You remember the safeword?" asked Liam.

"Yes, Sir. But..."

Another stinging blow. It wasn't unbearable, but it hurt so much. "Make him stop," I begged Rubio.

"You don't want to stop," he said, his dark eyes glittering. "Let go, Ash-lee. He's trying to help you let go."

"I thought he would—*ow!*— I thought he would hit me softer than you."

He shook his head. "I told you. You don't listen. I told you Liam Wilder plays hard."

My ass was on fire. I was shaking in the cuffs, my arms straining to defend myself, but I was defenseless and Rubio wouldn't let me move an inch. I hopped from toe to toe like that could soothe the pain. "It hurts," I cried. I jerked as Liam hit me again, catching me under both ass cheeks. Adrenaline surged through me as I processed the spreading, aching fire. Ruby's hands slid down and rubbed over my panties, soothing my flaming cheeks. It was such a relief I almost sobbed.

"Is he done?" I asked.

"For the moment," said Ruby. "He's giving you a break."

I felt a second set of hands caressing me. I smelled the scent of Liam, felt the presence of him at my back. I looked over my shoulder and he smiled at me, which gave me the courage I needed. I was a masochist—I wanted this—but I was still kind of scared. What if he pushed me too far? What if I had to use my safeword? Some unseen signal passed between the two men and Ruby's hands tightened on me again. I braced for pain and Liam didn't disappoint me. It was no harder than that one demo stroke he'd given me so long ago, but now the blows came one after the other, two, three, four in a row.

Wasn't I supposed to fall into subspace or something? It wasn't happening, maybe because this was my first real "hard" scene. Even without subspace, I felt turned on, electrified with adrenaline. My pussy felt heavy and throbby. I pressed my face into Rubio's chest. Another stroke, even harder. I loved the thrill of it but *oh God...* If he spanked me that hard again I would have to safeword.

"Okay. One more," said Rubio. I didn't know if he was talking to me or Liam.

"I can't. *I can't!*" I cried out, but the last one landed and I survived it.

I sagged against Rubio's chest. I felt so much relief, it was more like euphoria. A moment later Liam joined us. I turned my face to him but I didn't know what to say. I wanted to thank him for pushing me, for opening me up to this kind of experience. I was enjoying it more than I ever thought possible. I was definitely, for sure, one-hundred-percent kinky. My pussy ached with arousal even as I strained at my bonds, but I needed something more, some respite, some affection from Liam. He sidled up behind me and brushed my hair aside to kiss the back of my neck.

"Please," I said. "Please, Sir."

I said it over and over, until I didn't know if I was calling Liam Sir, or Rubio, or whoever might calm the storm of need inside me. I didn't know whose hands were where anymore. There was one on my ass and another tracing up my side, and another sliding down into the front of my panties, groping and fingering me. I was powerless, but not in the way I was when I was a child. This was a thrilling, erotic powerlessness. Rubio's cock poked against the front of my thigh while Liam's ground against me from behind. I was so keyed up, so horny by that point that I didn't care who put it in me. I just wanted someone touching and holding me, and fucking me until the aching pressure in my middle could break wide.

"Do you want to go upstairs?" It was Liam's quiet voice against my ear. "Do you want to go upstairs with me and Ruby?"

All my breath went out in a rush. I shuddered as his fingers closed on my hard-tipped breasts. "Answer me, baby," he prompted. "Do you want it?"

"Yes," I said. "I want it. Please."

Ruby reached over me, working the cuffs, extricating my hands. They both had frighteningly intent looks on their faces. What had I agreed to? At the moment I didn't care. As soon as my hands were free I reached back to rub my ass but Liam stopped me. "No. Let it hurt. I want you to hurt right now."

He lifted me in his arms so I couldn't do anything but hang on to him. He carried me to a door on the back wall and stepped aside to let Ruby open it, then carried me up two flights of winding, dark stairs. "Servant passages," he explained. "From the old lord-of-the-manor days. They're useful for sneaking naughty, horny girls up into bedrooms."

Liam wasn't even winded when we reached the landing. Someone groped my ass. That must have been Rubio. He opened another door for Liam and we were on the second floor, walking down the hall to the blue-gray room. As soon as Rubio closed the door Liam let me down and I was between their hard, tall bodies again, but this time my wrists weren't cuffed. Liam peeled off my panties while Ruby pressed my hands down to cradle his cock.

"Down on your knees," Liam said. He handed Rubio a condom and Ruby put it on while Liam stripped out of his jeans.

I sank to the floor and opened my mouth when Ruby prodded his cock against it. The condom tasted nasty but I was too worked up by this point to care. Liam held my hair in a firm grip as I licked around the head of Ruby's shaft. He was as big as Liam, but his scent and the sounds he made were totally different. Instead of Liam's growls, Rubio egged me on with musical-sounding Portuguese phrases. I didn't know what any of them meant.

"What a good girl you are," Liam said, massaging my scalp. Ruby stepped back and then Liam pressed his cock into my mouth. I didn't know if this was choreography they practiced regularly or if all this was off the cuff, but it felt so natural, so erotically charged. I wasn't crazy about giving blowjobs but I could have sucked both of them off for hours. There was something about being on your knees, submitting to such physical and sexual dominance. I understood all the women downstairs now, all the sultry slut girls. Was I going to become one of them? Probably not. I didn't have the wardrobe, the personality, or the physical equipment, but this night anyway, I wanted to join the ranks of my sexy sisters and see where I ended up.

After another couple rounds of alternating cocks, Liam lifted me and led me to the bed.

"Bend over," he said. I complied, shivering a little as he nudged my legs open and held down my arms. I was a little scared, but at the same time, I wanted to be fucked so badly.

When I was posed to Liam's satisfaction, Rubio slapped my ass a few times and parted my cheeks. He probed at my asshole while I gripped the smooth comforter. He asked Liam something in a low mutter and Liam said no. I think he'd just asked permission to assfuck me and been denied. *Thank you, Liam.* Instead Ruby eased his cock into my pussy.

Liam sat in front of me, cradling my head in his lap. "Okay?" he asked, brushing my hair back.

I checked in with myself, and yes, I was okay. Wonderfully okay. I gave myself up to the pleasure of Rubio's thick cock parting me. Ruby braced his hands on my hips and moved inside me with the sensual rhythms of a trained dancer. This wasn't like the times I'd fucked Liam. Then, my heart had been as involved as my head. Now, it was just about getting off—and that wasn't a bad thing. When I moaned at an especially deep thrust, Liam shoved his cock into my mouth and then they were both fucking me and grasping at me, making deep male sounds of satisfaction.

Bizarrely, all of it felt completely natural, like a necessary development in the progression of things. Even though they were overpowering me, it was by my choice. My consent, on my terms. This was dirty, horny craziness and I loved every second of it. I pressed back against Rubio, moving my hips, seeking more contact. I didn't think I could come this way, and I really wanted to come.

"Move," said Rubio to Liam. "Let me use the bed."

Liam eased to the side, fisting his cock and pumping it as Ruby turned me onto my back. He parted my legs and came over me, and for a moment I felt panic, but then he slipped inside me smooth as silk, lifting my hips and manipulating me while I clung to his neck.

Oh... He moved right over my pulsing clit and sent it singing into overdrive. *Yes, yes, please. More, more, more.* He hit a spot inside me that set all my limbs shaking. "Please, don't... Please don't stop," I whispered. I felt Liam's hands in my hair again, or maybe they were Ruby's. Ruby rested his cheek against mine and I reached to stroke short dark hair rather than Liam's long waves.

"Oh, God. Please don't stop." I repeated it over and over again, squeezing my eyes shut and arching my body in abandon. I didn't want to know who was who anymore. I didn't care, but I still had some awareness of the different touches, the different sounds. Liam rubbed my shoulder. I knew it was Liam by the size of his hands and his long fingers. He squeezed my nipples as I ground my hips against Ruby's, scrambling to reach the momentous climax building inside me.

"Yes, Ash-lee. Good girl." I opened my eyes from some faraway, sex-enraptured place and felt Rubio's lips whisper down over mine. He kissed me tenderly at first, this complex man who used to be my idol. What was he now? My friend-with-benefits? My dominant? And why was he kissing me so gently?

It didn't last. By steady degrees, his lips commanded mine in a harder, deeper kiss. Liam's fingers still pinched and caressed me, driving me wild to find release. Their soft, lurid encouragements blended together into background noise. Then Liam's voice sharpened.

"Jesus! Enough! Why are you kissing her like that? Like you're in love with her or something?"

Rubio laughed, his trademark wild laugh. I didn't care about the kiss, didn't care about anything except trying to come. I was *so close.* "Maybe I am in love with her," I heard Rubio say.

I felt him grin against my cheek, then he jerked and both of them were scrambling away from me, off the bed. The bedside lamp crashed to the floor, plunging us into darkness. It took me a second to realize they were fighting, locked together, throwing punches and reeling across the room.

"Stop," I screamed. "Stop it!"

"You fucking prick," Liam growled. "You don't care about her. You don't love her. Don't kiss her like that."

"I'll kiss her however I fucking want to."

I screamed again as they tumbled to the floor. I heard fists and thuds, and hissed curses. The door flew open and Mem stood silhouetted in the light from the hall. I clutched the covers around my nakedness, not wanting him to see me in this situation. All the horny exultation I felt had dissipated into anxiety and shame. I watched as Mem pulled Liam off Rubio with a power belied by his size. When Ruby advanced, Mem held him off with one extended hand.

"You must leave now, Mr. Rubio," he said.

"Both of you leave," Liam yelled at me and Ruby over Mem's shoulder. "Both of you, get the fuck out of my house. Get the fuck out!" He grabbed up a paper from the table behind him and tore it in his fingers. "Don't fucking come back," he said, flinging the pieces toward me.

I fled, leaving the comforter behind. I found the back stairs and tripped down them in the darkness, until I came out into the noise and activity of the play room. I struggled into my bra and got tangled up pulling my dress over my head. I was crying so hard from the shock of Liam's outburst, I couldn't make my fingers work. Then Rubio appeared beside me, already dressed, and helped me pull the skirt down over my sore ass cheeks. We were both cast out, beating a retreat.

"Ash-lee. Is okay. *Tudo bem, querida*," he said, touching the tears on my face. "I'll take you home."

"No," I said. "No, no, no." I broke away from him and ran toward the stairs, taking them two at a time. When I reached the first floor, I darted across the crowded living room like demons were chasing me. I heard Rubio calling out behind me but I didn't stop. I was getting the fuck out of Liam Wilder's house, because it was a horrible, horrible place where horrible things happened.

This time, I was never coming back.

Chapter Seventeen:
Because, Of Course

I came awake to the smell of coffee and the sound of dishes clattering. I blinked up at the concrete ceiling soaring above me and then across the loft apartment to the chrome-glistening kitchen. Rubio loped across my field of vision, his dog-printed pajama pants riding low on his hips.

I sat up and stretched, and collapsed again into the comfort of his cloudlike counterpane. He was only a couple years older than me, but he had the most elegant apartment ever, and this comforter... The white cotton softness bunched up around my shoulders like a hug.

Rubio came over and sprawled next to me. There was a faint, shadowed bruise beside his eye. "You owe me a back rub, Sleeping Beauty. I slept on the couch."

"That was very gentlemanly of you," I murmured as he turned onto his side. I knew he'd slept on the couch because I'd woken from four or five nightmares of Liam screaming at me. All last night seemed like a nightmare. I barely remembered how I'd ended up at Ruby's place. I didn't want to remember any of it, not yet.

Instead I concentrated on Ruby's muscles as I squeezed and stroked the planes of his back. It didn't feel sexual to massage him. Last night, at Liam's house, I hadn't really been having sex with Ruby. It was Liam I

184

craved, Liam who still had way too much control of my heart. I'd been trying to prove to myself that I could move past him, but all I'd learned was that I still wanted him. I thought maybe he cared for me too, at least until the end, when all hell broke loose.

"Ohhh," Ruby sighed. "Keep going. My lower back."

I massaged down to knead the little dimples above his ass. "You have a really nice place," I said, looking across to his wall-sized window.

"Nah. Is small. I never buyed much furniture."

"I like it. It's streamlined and clean-looking. I like the whole loft thing for you, although I pictured you with a bigger place. At first I thought Liam's house was your house."

"Hmm." He shuddered as I dug into the sides of his spine. "I'm not rich like Liam. Not too rich. I send most of my money to my family in Brazil. They need it more than me."

I knew from bios and clippings that Rubio had grown up poor, in a Rio *favela*, but it never occurred to me that he supported his family now. "Do you miss them?" I asked.

He turned to me, lying back and resting his head on one arm. "I go there sometimes, when I have the time." He stroked fingers over my tangled bed-head. "I think you have pretty black hair, like a Brazilian girl. I miss Brazil. Is hot there. Here, it's so cold."

"Is that why you have these big, fluffy comforters?" I asked, squirming deeper into his nest of blankets.

"I have them because girls like them," he said with a grin. "Hey, you okay today? How's your ass?"

"It's fine. A little tender, but I'll live." I couldn't hold his gaze beyond a moment or two. "Ruby, about last night... You and me...it's not... I can't..."

He made a dismissive sound. "I know. Was just playing, between friends."

I studied the rigid set of his mouth. "If you want to cast someone else in your ballet, I'll understand."

"Why would I do that?" His pout deepened. "Really, you're best for the part. I think all the money Liam gave me, I'm going to give it back to him. I don't need it."

"He doesn't need it either."

"A charity then. What charity you want, Ash-lee? You say, and I'll give the money in your name."

185

He waited for my answer, his hand lying beside mine on the comforter. Perhaps The Great Rubio was worth my adoration after all. I thought about it, turning my cheek from his pillow. "Maybe something...some charity to help victims of child sexual abuse."

I never intended to reveal any of that to him. I probably wouldn't have, if our gazes hadn't met across the space between us. He was silent a moment, then he made a soft sound and touched my fingers. "*Merda.* I'm sorry."

"It's okay," I said, looking away. "I'm better now. All of that is in the past. Liam helped me move past it for good."

"Oh. I wondered what was going on with you two. He never told me anything about you, nothing. But last night, I knew something bigger was going on."

"God, last night." I sat up with a groan. "Thanks for letting me stay here at your place."

"It was my fault, last night. I was bad. I push him sometimes. He'll get over it."

"He won't get over it. He was mad at me, not you."

"No, he was mad at himself. He gets that way. Sometimes, in his head, he is just..." He made some scattered gesture with his fingers.

"How long have you known Liam? How did you meet?"

"He helped me once in a bar fight. Four or five years ago now. Protected my pretty face," he said, breaking into a grin. "This was before he had his own play room for me to be wild in. After that, he was a friend who put up with me, and so we became closer. With guys, you know, friendship is just knowing each other. Accepting each other's weirdness."

"Like last night?"

"Last night was not about me and him." He turned his dark, piercing gaze on me. "Until now we were always 'bros before hos,' but you changed him. Since you met him, he is not the same."

"What do you mean?"

"I mean, I think he fell in love for you. I don't think he ever loved anyone before, any woman. I know he didn't. But now he does. Ash-lee, you know, it is really messing him up."

I felt a terrible pain in my soul, because I wanted so badly for that to be true. "I don't think he loves me. I tried to get closer to him, tried to tell him how much I cared for him, but he didn't want any part of it."

"But you see how he acts? Brooding and yelling, and hanging out at the theater all the time? He wants you."

"Wanting and loving are different things," I argued. "Just because we want each other doesn't mean we should be a couple, that we're 'in love.'"

"You're wrong," he said, wagging a finger at me. "He is in love with you. Sometimes I love you, Ash-lee, and sometimes I want you, but I am not *in love* with you. He is."

I collapsed back onto the pillows, unable to deal with his glib confession. What did love mean, anyway? "It doesn't matter now," I said. "Liam threw me out of his house. He told me not to come back."

"I called you a whale once, and an asshole," he pointed out. "I didn't mean it. People say things they don't mean sometimes." He walked around the bed and pulled me to my feet. "The question is, do you love him? Enough not to listen to his mean stuff?" He patted my face. "Don't worry about it now, girl. Was a difficult night, yes? It happens. Come have coffee. Eat something."

After he fed me breakfast, Rubio walked me the two blocks to my place in the late morning sun. We talked about *Waking Kiss* and some of the other ballets being choreographed for the showcase. Amazing that in a few months' time Rubio had gone from an untouchable god to this...this friend. He really was my friend. I turned to him at the door to my building.

"You know, Ruby, about last night... It was great up until the end. There was a time I would have given anything for your attention, so it was special to me. I know it was just crazy sex games to you, but I'll always remember your kindness, and the care you took to make it good for me."

He made a face. "I didn't take any care."

"Yes, you did. And I think..." I caught his chin and made him look me in the eyes. "I think someday, when you fall in love, all hell's going to break loose for some poor girl. And for you too."

He gave me a lopsided grin. "Why don't you worry about your own problems, lady? Hey, I see you later at the theater. After the performance, we practice. Back to business, yes?"

"Back to business. Yes." God knew I wanted to get back to business. He gave me one of his nice, grabby hugs and I went up the stairs to shower and get ready for work. When I got to my floor, Mem was standing outside my door.

"Ashleigh. Good morning," he said.

He looked so serious that I felt a pang of distress. "Is everything okay? Is Liam—"

"Mr. Wilder is fine. Sleeping off a long night. I am only here to ensure you got home safely, and that you sustained no lasting damage in last night's fracas."

Fracas. What a word. "I'm fine," I said, digging my keys out of my bag. "I wasn't involved in it. Do they fight like that a lot?"

"No," Mem said. "Not very often. May I come in, just for a moment?"

"Okay. But my place is a mess."

"It is no matter."

I let him in, flushing at the jumble of clothes on the floor, my unmade forest bed and the blanket structure I'd rebuilt last week. I scratched my forehead and threw my bag onto the table. "Sit anywhere you like."

He sat on the edge of the couch while I went to the kitchen. "Can I get you something? Coffee? Tea?"

"No, thank you. I can't stay long."

I walked over and sat on the couch with him, feeling flustered and a little defensive. "In case you're wondering, I stayed at Rubio's last night, but I didn't sleep with him."

Mem made a quelling gesture. "Do not feel you must make an accounting of your private life to me. I observe but I do not judge. I have observed a growing bond between you and Mr. Wilder."

He said it as a statement but it was more of a question. "We grew close recently, yes. He was helping me with some of my problems. My many issues," I added with a tight laugh.

"What happened last night?"

His calm, direct question wasn't accusatory. I blinked and tried to think about what had happened, because I wasn't totally sure. "I don't know what made him go off, Mem. Jealousy of Ruby? But me and Liam were never in a relationship. That was his requirement, not mine. I would have liked something...something deeper, but last week, Liam said we were done." I stood and paced over by my bed, tracing the notches in one of the sculpted tree trunks. "But then Rubio asked if I wanted to come with him to the party this weekend and I probably shouldn't have, but I did. It was partly because I wanted to see Liam. To show him I didn't need him, maybe. Even though..." I was babbling. Epic ramble. I turned to Mem with a frown. "I didn't come with Rubio, though. He's just a friend. I mean, we aren't—" I thought about Ruby's words earlier that morning. "We aren't in love."

Mem studied me a moment before he spoke. "Are you in love with Mr. Wilder?"

I didn't answer at first, but then I met his gaze and nodded. "I have been for ages now, but it doesn't matter. He doesn't want me. I played with him and Rubio last night to show that I could be like him. That I could keep things sexy and impersonal the way he does. I thought it would take a load off his mind." My forced laugh sounded a little maniacal. "I wanted to show him that I was super-independent now, and capable, and okay. Even though I'm not."

I batted at the bed curtains, waiting for Mem, the all-knowing shaman, to figure out this mess. Unfortunately, he looked as unsettled as me.

"You know, Mr. Wilder uses women as you use those curtains." He nodded at the sheer panels of silk. "To keep the demons away. He is not, perhaps, the man he presents himself to be."

"What do you mean, not the man he presents himself to be?"

"I mean that, like you, he has a past. It often influences his actions. I would tell you to ask him about it, but he would not tell you. I would tell you myself, but I promised not to."

"So you can't tell me anything, except that he has demons."

"I can tell you that you should not take his actions personally. That you should not blame yourself for his shortcomings. I can also give you this."

He held out a card with gold-embossed edges. It was an Ironclad card, like Liam's business card, but with another name on it. *Ronan Wilder.*

"Liam's father," said Mem. "If you wish to help Liam fight his demons, perhaps you will utilize that card and pay a visit to Mr. Wilder first. The elder Mr. Wilder, that is."

I stared down at the bold print. "Why do you call him Mr. Wilder? Why don't you call him Liam?"

"Liam is not his real name."

I looked up in surprise, and then I remembered. "Oh, that's right. *Ishi.*"

"His real name is Eric."

Eric?

Mem touched the back of my hand. "*Ishi* is a good man, and he always will be, but as I told you, he has no people. It haunts him, day and night. Go to his father. He can explain it all better than me."

"But I don't know his father. He won't know who I am."

"I imagine he will."

I chewed my lip. I was curious now, and a little freaked out. I wanted to help Liam—*Eric?*—if he had demons, especially after he'd helped me overcome mine. But it seemed I didn't even know who he was.

"I assure you, Ronan Wilder is a very kind man," said Mem. "He is a good father. He will want to help his son."

"I don't know much about good fathers." I stared through the shifting sheen of my bed curtains. "I never had a father, really."

"I never had a child. But in some way I like to take care of everyone." He held out a hand as he stood and I crossed to take it. It felt strong and cool. "It is your choice, Ashleigh, if you wish to save our *Ishi*. If you don't, eventually someone will. But I hoped…" He paused and withdrew his hand. "Well, I should not meddle. It is a terrible vice of mine."

With those words, he gave another of his strange little nods and disappeared out the door.

* * * * *

The next day I called Mr. Ronan Wilder's office to talk to him. The brusque woman who answered identified herself as his secretary and asked what my call was in regards to. In regards to? I had no idea how to answer that. I panicked and hung up. I called later that day hoping to get a different person. I didn't. I launched into a made-up story about needing to hire a bodyguard, but I chickened out when she asked for my information. I'd hung up twice now; there was no way I could call again.

All of Monday I vacillated. I couldn't reach Liam's dad directly, and I couldn't reach Mem for advice without possibly running into Liam. I wasn't ready for that confrontation yet. I wanted to know about these demons, about this Eric thing Mem had dangled in front of me. My curiosity eventually got the best of me, and I headed to Knightsbridge on Tuesday, to talk to a man I didn't even know.

Damn Liam. These were my free days, and I was spending them tracking down answers that might, just might, fix the disconnect between us. Then again, they might not. All the way to Ironclad's offices, I fought the urge to turn tail and run home. *He helped you. Maybe you can help him.* I remembered Liam as I'd seen him last, enraged, grappling with Rubio, yelling at me to get out. I looked up at the high-rise where the offices were located, steeled myself, and walked to the elevators in the lobby. No one questioned me, no one stopped me.

Halfway to the twenty-fourth floor I realized that I wasn't just heading to his father's place of work, but Liam's too. I knew he normally worked from home, but what if he happened to be here today? I'd have to play it off and pretend I'd come here to see him. It struck me then, how very much I wanted to see him, even with all the confusion between us, and the way we'd parted ways.

Bolstered by that thought, I entered the double doors to Ironclad's impressive headquarters. The entire back wall was a sheet of security glass. Two male receptionists looked up from behind a long, sturdy-looking edifice that I supposed was a desk. Wait. Were they receptionists or security guards?

"Can I help you?" asked the one closest to me.

"I'm a— I'm a friend of Mr. Wilder's. Uh, Ronan Wilder, not Liam," I added quickly.

The man was clean cut, blond and short-haired, in a suit. He gave me a tight smile. "Is he expecting you?"

"Yes," I lied. The other guy watched me. I could tell they both knew I was full of shit. I backtracked, stammering in embarrassment. "N-no. Well. I just need a moment of his time. He'll want to see me." They looked at each other. I had a sinking feeling I was about to be thrown out. "Please, just ask him. Ask if he has a moment to see me. My name is Ashleigh Keaton."

The first one stood and I waited to be shown the door, but instead he went to one of the office doors behind him. He gave me a look that let me know he was definitely doing me a favor. "One moment, please."

"Thank you," I said in relief. I waited, wondering who was checking me out from behind the glass. I was dressed in my version of professional, non-troublemaker, office-type wear, which was black slacks and a pale blue sweater with a silk scarf. It had taken me twenty minutes to get the scarf to look right. Dancers didn't wear these things.

The door opened again, and Blond Security Guy emerged with another gentleman. Oh shit, I was in trouble. This couldn't be Liam's dad. The man was short, maybe 5' 6", with ruddy pale skin and a stocky frame. He moved toward me to apprehend me—but then he smiled and held out his hand. "Miss Keaton. What a pleasure to finally meet you. I'm Ronan Wilder."

Or, maybe it could be his dad. "Mr. Wilder," I said, taking his hand. "I'm sorry I didn't make an appointment. If you're busy—"

"I'm not busy. I have some time, if you don't mind joining me for lunch?"

"Um. Sure. I mean, thank you." I followed him back through the door, into a maze of cubicles and desks. "Is Liam here?"

Mr. Wilder looked over his shoulder at my anxious tone. "Am I to understand this is a hush-hush operation?" I didn't see any of Liam in Mr. Wilder's appearance, but I heard him in the man's dry humor and the casual lilt of his voice.

"Sort of hush-hush," I said.

"Well, don't worry. He's not here at the moment." Mr. Wilder ushered me into a large corner office. I was momentarily distracted from my mission by the panoramic city view.

"We, uh…" I stared in awe at the floor-to-ceiling windows. They were even bigger than the window-wall in Rubio's loft. "We recently had a break up. Well…" I turned to him, determined to be honest. "Me and Liam were never really together. But we were close."

Mr. Wilder gestured me toward a spread of take-out containers on his desk—grilled salmon, rice, and oriental-style green beans. "Please, help yourself. They always order too much." He handed me a plate and I took a little bit of everything, then seated myself in a nearby chair.

"I knew you were close," he said once he set about serving himself. "I mean, Liam mentioned you to me, more than once. He seemed concerned about you."

I looked up at him with a green bean hanging out of my mouth. "What did he say?"

"Nothing. Or rather, as little as possible, which is why I grew curious. He did tell me you're a dancer."

"Yes. We met through a mutual friend. Fernando Rubio."

"I know Ruby," he said. "And I know Mem, who told me you might be visiting. I'm actually very close to my son."

I pushed rice around with my fork, spearing it with some fish. "I was wondering if you could answer some questions about him for me."

"It depends," he said. "Do you love Liam?"

192

The question was blunt and direct. So was my answer. "I'm here, aren't I?" We faced each other across the desk. "I love him, Mr. Wilder, but I'm not sure I know who he is. Mem told me his real name is Eric."

Mr. Wilder nodded. "His name was Eric once. Not anymore." He picked up his plate and brought it around the desk to the chair beside me. "What can I get you to drink?"

"Water, if you have it."

He brought me a bottle of Evian and cracked open a Diet Coke for himself. "I suppose it would be best to start at the beginning. I'm not Liam's real father, but I'm the only father he's ever known. I adopted him, legally, when he was twelve. I was working as a cop in south L.A. at the time. Tough beat, tough streets. I responded one night to a six-person homicide. Five children dead, and one mother, and one living child hiding behind the sofa with a gun. Liam was that child."

I almost choked on a mouthful of salmon. "He— He shot them?"

"Liam shot his mother," Mr. Wilder said. "But it was in self-defense. Liam's mother had six children by six different fathers. She struggled with illiteracy, drugs, mental illness, you know the story. And being poor, this whole family of children slipped through the cracks." His expression darkened. "Back then Liam was Eric, and he was the oldest. He went to school when he could, when he wasn't helping with his siblings. Somewhere along the line—not from his mother—he learned morality and compassion. From the age of seven or eight, he pretty much parented the five younger kids, and his mother too. Perhaps you've experienced his obsession with caring for others."

I nodded, my chest heavy with emotion. I'd experienced it firsthand.

"His mother was never the most stable influence, and after the last baby, she developed serious post-partum depression. What we know of that night, we know through neighbors, forensic evidence, and what Liam told us. I took that report." He stopped a moment, as if to collect himself. "To make a long story short, his mother decided she was going to leave this world and take all of them with her. She started with the baby, a gunshot to the head. She shot all of them, youngest to oldest, while Liam pleaded with her to stop. He blames himself, you know," he said, looking at me. "To this day, he believes he could have saved them somehow. After all, he was their parent. They depended on him for everything."

I put down my plate. My throat was too tight to eat anyway, and tears pricked behind my eyes. "He never told me any of this."

"He never tells anyone. He'll be angry that I told you. At any rate, to complete the grisly tale, he was the last one in his mother's crosshairs and he fought for his life." Mr. Wilder leaned back in his chair, his lips flattening to a grim line. "Obviously, he won."

"My God," I whispered.

"And then he hid behind the couch from the police. He thought he'd be blamed for her death, and for the deaths of his brothers and sisters." Mr. Wilder closed his eyes a moment. "I can never describe to you what it was like to come upon that scene. It's a horror no one should ever know. I left police work shortly afterward, started my own security business. And I adopted Liam. I couldn't look into that child's eyes and hand him over to the foster-care system, not after the life he'd lived. We left L.A. and moved to New York. Liam entered counseling, chose a new name, a good Irish name like mine, and started a new life. They were difficult years, don't get me wrong. He struggled with his past, but I tried to keep him oriented toward the future. He was homeschooled because he couldn't stand crowds, or other kids, or any relationships at all for many years, except for me, who he barely tolerated, and Mem, his teacher."

"Oh. That's why they're so close."

"Mem was a blessing, a godsend." Mr. Wilder picked up his plate and started eating again. "He taught Liam academics, but he also tutored him in martial arts and self-defense. Liam needed a way to feel safe again. As for me, I tried to heal him emotionally. I tried to make the world seem like a sane place. As he grew older he became interested in my work, and with his instinct to protect, security was a natural career for him. We moved to London when Liam was twenty-one and went into business together. Within a couple years, Ironclad exploded, went worldwide. You know, Liam will protect a client like a rabid dog. He'll protect anything weak or damaged, unless..." He sobered, studying me. "Unless it's someone he loves. Or, let me put it this way. Liam does not allow himself to love anymore. Because, of course..." He spread a hand in a helpless gesture. "Look what happened last time."

I sat in silence. All this time I'd thought myself the damaged, love-deprived child. Liam had watched the violent deaths of his siblings and then shot his own mother to save himself. The bleakness of it defeated me. I put my head in my hands.

"I know it's a lot to process, Ashleigh. I know it's horrible, nightmarish. I think he turned out pretty well, considering."

"Yeah," I muttered.

"I think what happened with you is that you got a little too close to his heart. Honestly, we've been waiting for this. Me, Mem, his stepmom, all of us who love him. We've been waiting for you. For someone capable of piercing that iron barrier of women and partying and stoicism and making him feel something."

"I'm not that person." I shook my head miserably. "I didn't pierce that barrier. He pushed me away."

"He's survived so much. I'm sure he can survive love too, if someone forces him to do it. I'm sorry for all you're going through, but there's an opportunity here."

I took a sip of water. I felt so confused, so overwhelmed at everything Mr. Wilder had revealed.

"I just…I can't believe he hid all this from me," I said.

"Do you feel angry? Betrayed?"

"No. I mean, I understand why he hid it. I feel awful that he went through all that. But he was the one…" I looked at Mr. Wilder. "He was the one who wouldn't let me hide, the one who pressed me until I told him about the bad things that happened in my past. I exposed everything to him, really deep, dark secrets that I'd never told anyone else."

"So Liam was the first person you confided in?"

"Yes."

"Why him?"

I stared down at my plate. "Because he pushed me, I guess. And because I trusted him. I guess he was the first person who made me feel safe enough to do it."

"Maybe," Mr. Wilder said slowly, "you can be that person for him."

Chapter Eighteen:
Fear and Anger

I didn't think about Ashleigh. I refused to. Instead, I plunged myself into work. Work and partying, my eternal shelters. I skulked around the play room Saturday night but chose not to play with anyone. Rubio wisely didn't show up. Maybe he was with Ashleigh. I didn't know and I didn't care. Ruby knew when to hang around me and when to stay away, which was a key part of our friendship.

Because I couldn't fucking stand him sometimes.

It wasn't jealousy. I wasn't jealous over Ashleigh or anything like that. It was manners. You didn't fucking kiss girls during threesomes, not like that, and he knew it.

But Ruby was the least of my problems, and Ashleigh…she was past tense. I didn't need complications like that in my life, not with a new office opening next month in Amsterdam and the ongoing clusterfuck in Washington, D.C. I had real shit to worry about. So I wasn't pleased when, Monday at noon, my phone buzzed on my desk.

Little Ishi is here.

I glanced at the message, pushing down the sudden, crippling desire to see her. She was here. She was right downstairs.

I'm busy, I typed. *Send her away.*

I didn't read the next text, or the third. When he texted the fourth time, I pushed back from my desk and headed for the stairs. I had no hard feelings toward Ashleigh, I just needed her to move on with her life so I could move on with mine. I found her with Mem in the living room, sitting on the couch in a cute little black and white dress. She had a pink rose in her lap, balanced across her knees. It pained me to look at it, just like it pained me to look at her, so I glared at Mem instead.

"I was working. I was right in the middle of something."

"Ashleigh has come to see you."

"Yeah, I got that. You texted me four fucking times."

Rude. Very rude of me. I flicked a glance at Ash, pale and agitated beside him. Mem gave me a scathing look. "Why don't I leave you two alone?" he said.

He touched her hand and stood to go. Neither of us said a word, even after the door closed behind him. Ashleigh fingered the stem in her lap while I sat in the chair across from her, leaning my head back with a sigh.

"I'm sorry I disturbed your work," she finally said. "But I needed to see you. To talk to you. I wanted to bring you this."

I didn't take the rose when she held it out to me. I felt embarrassed for her. "Very nice gesture," I said instead. "Great sense of symmetry you have."

She put the rose on the couch beside her and pushed her hair behind her ears. She didn't seem angry or offended by my coldness. No, there was something else in her gaze, some enduring tenderness. I needed to stomp out those tender feelings once and for all.

"Look," I said in a hard voice. "You have to face when something's over. I don't want you coming over on Mondays anymore. From the way you acted last Saturday, you're cured. More than cured."

She lifted her chin. "There was no reason to wig out on me and Rubio. We're just friends."

"I don't care either way," I lied. "I told you from the start we were going to keep things casual. No strings attached, for both our sakes."

"Maybe so, but I don't want to do that anymore. I think the whole idea of it is sad."

"You know what's sad?" I asked, nodding toward the flower. "That rose I brought you, to replace the other one—it wasn't from the performance. I bought it at a florist near my house and gave it to you

197

because I wanted to get you into bed. Because I wanted to fuck you. That's all I really wanted from the start."

I waited for anger, for histrionics, but she only asked very calmly, "That's all it ever was? All the stuff you did for me? Just to get laid for one lousy weekend? Wow." She grimaced. "I'm sorry for you then. No wonder you're so angry."

"I'm not angry. I just want you to understand—"

She stood, raising a hand to silence me. "I understand. I understand a lot more than you know. I understand that you have problems and they make you act like a jackass. That's what I came here to talk to you about but now I'm feeling pretty negative toward you so I think I'll just go. Oh, and..." She shoved the pink rose into my hand. "You can take this and give it to someone else. Whoever it is you want to fuck next. Maybe this time it won't be such a fucking hassle for you. Good luck."

Her little tirade aroused me. Why did she have to arouse me with everything she did? When she started across the living room toward the door, I reached out to stop her. "What did you mean about my problems?"

"I know why Mem calls you *Ishi*," she said, turning back to me. "Someone finally had the courtesy to explain what the fuck is going on with you."

I regarded her suspiciously. "What do you mean, what the fuck is going on with me? Nothing's going on with me, except that you can't seem to move on."

"I talked to your father."

Her words took the wind right out of me. I stared at her. "You didn't— How— You don't even know my father."

"Mem gave me his business card. I went to see your father and we had lunch, and he told me where you came from and everything you went through when you were a child named Eric. And now I *know*."

God damn it. I was going to kill Mem, the prying, manipulative ass. Her voice softened and her pale eyes searched mine. This is exactly what I hadn't wanted, her sympathetic gaze seeking out the damaged, broken little boy inside me. "I'm sorry, Liam. If I had known—"

"I didn't want you to know." I would punish them both for this, Mem and my father too. My past was my past. It was something I'd left behind, something that had no place in my current life. I felt stricken. Exposed. "My dad shouldn't have done that. He shouldn't have told you. I don't share that with anyone, ever. It's nobody's business but my own."

"But Liam—"

"You shouldn't have gone to see him. It was none of your fucking business!"

"None of my business?" Her fragile sympathy turned to anger. "It's none of my business, really? When I told you everything about me? When you pried it out of me, sneaking around and looking into my past? I told you everything, every horrible, wrenching detail, and you hid everything from me, everything that makes you the person you are. Everything that makes you—that makes you"—she threw out her arms angrily—"behave this way! You even use a fake name. Jesus, Liam! Or should I say Eric?"

"Don't call me that." I bent the rose stem and flung it over toward the kitchen. "I took a new name, yes, to start a new life. My dad and my therapist agreed that I should do it. I didn't want to live in the past."

"You completely erased yourself. How is that healthy? How come I had to be fixed and you didn't?"

I balled my hands up in my hair. "You asked me to fix you! Because you couldn't have sex, remember?"

"And you can't have love. Or any relationship besides being someone's dominant. Someone's casual sex partner. Are you really happy like that?"

I shook my head. "Stop it, Ashleigh. Just stop."

"You made me face everything. You made me accept what happened to me and move on. So how come you don't have to? Why won't you give me a chance to help you now?"

"Because I don't want your help. I don't need it." I took her arm and dragged her toward the door. I had to get her away from me before I lashed out again. "I have work to do. You need to go."

She dug in her heels, struggling against me. "Don't box me out, Liam. Talk to me. God, what your mother did to you was so much worse than what my father did to me. *So* much worse, but you never said anything. You never shared anything with me."

"Because you didn't need to know. Damn it, Ash. I put that shit away a long time ago."

"I only wanted to know *why*," she said, her eyes wide and pleading. "Why you pushed me away. Why you keep these rigid walls around you. I understand the pain, the impulse of hating yourself. Of believing it was your fault when it wasn't really. I understand how risky it feels to let someone in when your trust has been broken so badly—"

I spun and walked away from her, back toward the living room. I wasn't prepared to have this conversation, not with her, not with anyone. "Leave my past alone," I said, putting distance between us. "I don't want to talk about it."

"I want to talk about it." She followed after me, like a dog yapping at my heels. "We need to talk about it, because I love you."

"No."

"I do. I love you, whoever you are, whatever your past. I fell in love with you and I want you to love me back. Nothing bad will happen. Just affection and caring between us."

She was there, right there, with her intent, pretty face and her tearful eyes. She terrified me. What she was offering terrified me. I fended off her hands when she reached for me. "You don't love me," I said. "You loved the sex. That's all we had together. Sex."

"I love you, Liam. I've loved you forever, since the start. Since you told me in the dressing room that everything would be okay. Since you waited outside my door that night to be sure I locked it. Since you paid off my teacher's school and made love to me at your cottage and…and bought me that goddamn bed. Your denials won't change anything. They just make both of us frustrated and unhappy." She reached out and took my hands. "Trust me, please. Love doesn't have to be a tragic thing."

She didn't understand. She didn't understand anything. It had nothing to do with her or my brothers or sisters, or my mother, or anything except the pain of loving someone. It had to do with the danger, the horrible risk, and the way you couldn't control any of it. I pulled away from her, wishing I had a blanket fort to hide in. Safe walls, luminescent stars. "I don't want to love anyone," I yelled. "Why can't you respect that?"

"Because I love you," she said just as angrily. I refused to look in her eyes or process the fact that she was crying. Everything about her petrified me. Her intensity, her emotion, and the bond between us that I couldn't seem to break.

"Why can't you love me, Liam?" she asked, prodding me. "What are you afraid of?"

I breathed the word, because I couldn't say it. "Everything." I forced myself to look into those eyes, the deep blue-gray pools that had compelled me from the start. "None of it's real, you know. Boundaries and control. Consent. All that shit I taught you about. In real relationships, it's not there."

200

I turned away from her, drawn back to another time, another place. I remembered shock and helplessness, gunshots, the horrible blood and the silent intensity on my mother's face. I never meant to hurt my mother. It sounded so stupid, that I hadn't meant to hurt someone I'd shot in the face, but it was true. It just happened, a desperate incident outside of any consent or control. I squeezed my eyes shut, willing the memories away. "I can't, Ash. I can't. Will you please just go away?"

She slid her hands around my neck. I stood stiff, frozen. "Liam," she said against my lips. "You won't hurt me. You helped heal me. You're a wonderful, caring person and I love you. Won't you let me help you now?"

"You have to go," I said, pulling away from her. "I have work to do."

"Liam—"

"Enough!" I bellowed in a voice I'd never used with her before, an even worse voice than I'd used with Ruby that night. "The answer to your question is no. I won't let you help me. I'm—I'm—" I cast around for words to express the way I felt. "I'm fine exactly the way I am. I don't need your fucking help. That was wrong of you to go see my father, to go sneaking around behind my back. You think you can fix me? Maybe nothing's wrong. Maybe the problem is you. That I don't trust you, that I don't like you, and that I don't really want you. Did you ever consider that?"

She blinked at me once, twice. "No, I didn't," she said, her voice cold and sharp as an icicle.

"Well, maybe you should." I pointed at the door. "If you don't mind, I'd like you to leave without saying anything else. If you need a ride home, talk to Mem about it."

And I left her standing there, because I couldn't bear to look at her any more.

* * * * *

Mem touched my arm as he drove me home through the busy streets of London. "You must forgive me, Ashleigh. This is all my fault."

I shook my head, twisting my hands in my lap. I'd taken so much care to dress up and look pretty for Liam. And the flower, ugh. I'd pictured an emotional scene that ended with him falling into my arms, thanking me for my concern and maybe even professing his undying love for me.

Nope. It hadn't gone like that at all.

"It's not your fault," I said to Mem. "At least he knows now that I understand. I wanted to see if it changed things, but it obviously doesn't."

"It changes more than you know."

"But those things he said to me at the end—"

"He did not mean them. He loves you and it frightens him terribly."

I covered my face as more tears squeezed from my eyes. If Liam loved me, it was the bad, destructive kind of love that made you want to hurt whoever it was you cared about.

"So what do I do now?" I asked from between my fingers.

"I think there is nothing to do." Mem stopped at a light and looked over at me. "I believe the next move must be his."

I studied his dark, steady eyes. He seemed to know everything about everything. I wanted to beg him, *What? What will his next move be?* I hoped it wasn't to file a restraining order against me. "Maybe we're not meant to be together. It shouldn't be this hard to love someone."

"It shouldn't, but sometimes it is. Both of you have the cards stacked against you, as the saying goes." He looked down at the gearshift of Liam's sporty car. "I was sorry, by the way, to hear of your father's passing."

I snorted. "I wasn't sorry. I drank a whole bottle of wine to celebrate."

He looked at me until the light turned green, and then moved back into traffic. "Do you think you will ever be able to let the anger go?"

Anger? I never thought of myself as being angry. I was the victim, the person betrayed, the powerless one. But he was right. I carried around a lot of anger and hate, not just for my father, but my mother too. It took up a great deal of space inside me, but their sins seemed too horrible to forgive. "I don't know," I said to Mem. "I don't think I can ever let it go completely. Is that bad?"

He shrugged. "You will never forget the wrongs done to you, but anger, like guilt, can poison an entire life." He pulled up to my building and put the car in park, then took a deep breath and looked over at me. "You must strive to exorcise your demons, you and Liam both. You cannot change the past, but you can change the future."

"I'm trying. I've been changing a lot, but how can I make Liam change if he doesn't want to?"

"You ripped off the bandage. It was a good start. He'll need time to stop the bleeding, time to try to put it back on again, and then…"

"And then what?" I asked, desperately needing answers.

"I don't know. I'm not sure he'll ever be fully healed, but I also know he's not happy the way he's living. He deserves a love-filled life."

"A love-filled life," I echoed. "Maybe with us, two wrongs can make a right."

"There is nothing 'wrong' with either of you," Mem said. "You're a very strong, brave woman, and Liam is a caring man. Give him a little time to bleed. All of us, deep down, have some survival instinct. At some point, he'll realize he's weakened from lack of blood. Or lack of love."

"So I have to wait? I can't do anything?"

"I'll watch over him in the meantime. I won't let him come to harm."

I didn't want to wait, but I knew from experience you couldn't force someone to get better until it was time. It had taken a certain degree of desperation for me to reach out and ask Liam for help.

I gave Mem a hug and a nod of solidarity. "Tell Liam to come to me when he's ready. Tell him I'll be waiting for him, however long it takes."

* * * * *

I skulked around my big echoing house, feeling wrung out and battered. I avoided Mem on principle, and I skipped out on my usual Sunday dinner with my dad. They'd both betrayed my trust, under the guise of "helping me." I was so damn sick of the whole helping thing I was about to bust. I'd worked through my issues as a child and come to a place of peace, and I didn't want to open up that can of worms again. The status quo was easier, and I was mostly happy with my life.

Except that life didn't include Ashleigh.

Fucking hell.

I understood the hypocrisy of my actions, believe me. I'd done far more snooping around on her than she'd ever done on me. Hell, I'd even broken into her apartment once, but I only ever did those things to be a friend to her. I hadn't waved a flower in her face afterward, demanding honesty and trust and love.

Her words haunted me as I drifted through the week. I heard them during the day while I worked, and in my dreams when I slept. *Why can't you love me, Liam? What are you afraid of?* Bedlam and loss of control, for starters. Blood and screaming. The grinding, devastating burden of not being enough. Not being enough brother, not being enough son. *I understand the pain, the impulse of hating yourself. Of believing it was your fault when it wasn't really.* But that wasn't the issue, whether or not it was my fault. The issue was the risk inherent in love, especially love for someone like Ashleigh, who'd already been hurt so badly.

It was impossible, all of it. I went to Amsterdam to work on the new office, thinking distance could smother my feelings for Ashleigh, but it didn't. I dreamed of her every time I managed to sleep.

I hoped Ashleigh would find someone else to love while I was away, I really did.

But no, I didn't.

Hell, I didn't know what I wanted. I was still frantically lying to myself.

Chapter Nineteen:
No Boundaries

The knock came on a stormy, rainy Monday. It was twelve noon on the dot and that's how I knew, after three weeks of waiting, that Liam Wilder was at my door.

I was still in my pajamas, reading in bed like I always did on rainy days. I put down my book and sat up very straight. Three weeks, and I'd suffered through every fucking day of it, exchanging anxious texts with Mem and fending off Rubio's probing questions about "Liam's deal." I knew Liam had been traveling, but I hadn't known he was back.

He knocked again and I vaulted out of bed and threw the door open. He looked the same, towering and sexy and handsome, but also different. More vulnerable beneath his good looks. He was in jeans and a white button-down top that lent him an aspect of purity. There were dark circles under his eyes.

"Hi, Liam," I said. There were a million other things I wanted to say—*I've missed you. How are you? Will you fall in love with me, please?*—but he already looked on the verge of fleeing. "Do you want to come in?" I asked instead.

"Yeah," he said, letting out a breath. He moved past me into my place, the same way he had the first time he came here. "Are you busy? Do you have a minute?"

"I've missed you," I blurted out. I closed the door and leaned back against it, as if I had the power to stop him if he wanted to go. "Great sense of symmetry you have." I glanced at the clock. "It's noon on Monday."

"I'm here for a session," he said with a tight smile. "No, not really. I just got back in town this morning. I've been in Holland."

"I know."

"We're opening an office there."

"I know. Mem told me."

He paced the length of my apartment and back, like a wild, trapped thing. He turned toward the bed and then away from it, running his fingers through his hair. He turned back to look at it again. "That looks nice. Pretty. I never saw it here once it was set up. I never came over here. I was too...afraid." He shook his head and spread his arms. "I told you I might hurt you. Right from the start, I warned you."

"Ruby did too," I murmured. "I thought you were worth the risk."

His eyes shot up at that word. *Risk.* I'd struck a nerve—and he was all nerves. I frowned and crossed to him. "You're making all of this too complicated, Liam. You really are."

He retreated, moving behind my bed. He was so tall he could lean his head against the branches. "I know I'm making it too complicated," he said. "I know I had no right to be angry at you for looking into my past. I shouldn't have said the things I said. I came here to apologize."

I watched him, trying to read his expression. Was it going to be a goodbye apology, or was he going to let me love him despite the fear and guilt he carried around? I knew he loved me. I knew it when I opened the door. I could see it now in his tense shoulders and his tortured gaze.

"So, I'm sorry," he said, gripping the branches like the bars of a cage. "I'm sorry for everything I did. It had nothing to do with you and everything to do with my own issues. And I realize now..."

He stopped and took a deep breath. "You realize now...?" I prompted when he didn't speak.

"I realize now that I need you, and I want you, but..."

I felt soaring hope, and joy, but there was a *but.* "But what?"

"I can't promise..."

Oh God, he was killing me. "You can't promise what?" I asked, climbing onto the bed and walking over to him so we were face-to-face.

"I can't promise anything." His eyes went very wide. A muscle ticked in his jaw. "I can't promise jacked-up shit isn't going to happen, or that we'll be happy every day of our lives. I can't promise everything will be okay."

I took his face in my hands. "I don't care."

"You should care," he said sharply. "I'm scared as hell. But Mem has all his sayings, you know. And he's always said to me that love solves everything. He's said it for years now, but I never believed it."

"I believe it. You proved it to me before I even knew you were doing it, before I could admit I was falling in love with you. But I'm in love with you now and there's nothing I can do about it. That's the way it is and the way it's going to stay."

I could hear his palms squeaking over the metal as he gripped the branches harder. If he wasn't careful he was going to yank one right off. "But are you in love with the old me?" he asked. "The one who put on the act, who pretended he had his shit together?"

I stroked his cheeks, stifling a smile. "You've never had your shit together. You never fooled me. Well, not for very long."

He let go of the bed and grabbed my hands. "But what—what if I can't get it together?"

"You need to let go of these fears," I said, leaning my head to his. "You're so strong and patient. So caring. If anyone deserves to be loved, it's you. So now…" I brushed my lips across his in a whisper. "Now it's your turn to be brave."

I let out a long, slow breath, right against her mouth. I wanted to disappear inside her where I could be sheltered and safe. I wanted to let go of my fears but they'd dogged me for so long. They felt comfortable and normal. They mitigated all risk.

"Ashleigh…" I shied away from her. I felt like I was standing on some precipice or some threshold I was afraid to step through, but she was on the other side and I needed her. She held me as I fought with myself, held me with complete trust…and no fear.

I'm all up inside your boundaries now, aren't I?

Yes, Ashleigh. You really are.

Her arms tightened around me as she pressed her cheek to mine. I breathed in the scent of her blackberry hair and felt the pulse beat strong and steady at the base of her neck. And somehow, as I listened to her breathe and thought about our time together, and how much she'd changed when she was brave enough to try, I realized that maybe I could change too. That maybe I had to change to survive. Hope bled into me and some dormant part of me shuddered to life, some deadened, hardened thing that I supposed was my capacity to love. I was terrified to love this woman but it didn't matter.

I already loved her.

It was already done and accomplished, tied up in a neat bow just like her toe shoes. Denying it, evading it didn't make it any less true.

She kissed me, so, so tenderly, her lips feathering across mine, and then she kissed me harder, urging me to respond. I cupped her face and pressed my mouth to hers, drinking in the sweet, remembered scent of her. After holding her away from me so long I was ravenous to get closer. I pushed her back onto the mattress, stroking fingers over her soft, silky pajamas, over familiar curves and planes. I let go of control and fear and something else swept in to take their place. Surrender. Capitulation.

Peace.

My arms locked around her waist and we kissed with the intensity of lovers parted for a hundred years. A thousand years. It seemed like an eternity that I'd denied what I felt for this woman. "Are you sure?" I asked, pushing back her hair. "Are you sure you want me?"

"I want you like crazy." She leaned to me, nibbled at my lip and then bit it hard. "Just love me, okay?"

Oh, I could love her. I *had* to love her, because not loving her had almost destroyed me. I couldn't get enough of her now and I think she felt the same way, since she was wrestling to hold onto me. I slid my fingers under her waistband while her hands scrabbled at my shirt buttons. We undressed each other in a frenzied tangle of limbs and clothes, but then I felt her tense and I forced myself to slow down. I didn't want to scare her, not in this moment. I gentled my movements and stroked her face. "I'm sorry for hurting you, baby. For pushing you away. I'm sorry. I was afraid. I was..." My throat closed up. The words were a little hard to say. "I was dead inside."

"No more apologies," she said, pressing her fingers against my lips. "I just want to be with you. I need you. We need each other."

I caught her hands in mine and trapped them over her head. "Open for me," I coaxed in a low voice. "Show me." I pressed her thighs apart with my knees and reached down to guide my cock into her tight wetness. "I love you," I said as I moved into her. "I love you. I love you. *I love you.*"

She kissed me while I babbled out all the pent up words in my heart, and then we set about making love without any walls between us. No boundaries. Half the time I held her down and half the time I let her go only for the joy of pinning her down again. Every place she touched me hummed with pleasure, with completion. The bond between us had never been severed, only twisted and stretched until both of us were doubled over in pain.

No more pain, though, not for either of us. I whispered promises to her as we moved together. To love, to trust. To never be away from her again. When I felt her go wild beneath me, gasping in her release, I gathered her in my arms and emptied myself inside her. Not just my billowing, clenching orgasm, but the fears and memories that haunted me. Over time, we could make new memories to replace the bad ones.

As long as she forgave me for being such an asshole to her. I was pretty sure she would. She was kissing me again.

* * * * *

I spent the next few weeks starting over with Ashleigh. I brought her flowers, took her out to long, romantic dinners, and spent hours in her Sleeping Beauty bed. I texted and called when we had to be apart, and I told her all the time that I loved her. In other words, I acted like a total obsessive sap, but she didn't seem to mind.

There were difficult days too, when I withdrew because it was the most familiar course of action. There were times I said things I didn't mean, and did things to push her away, but she didn't accept that anymore. We'd have a rip-roaring fight and work things out. We developed a system of boundaries and consent that worked all the time, for both of us. And yes, we did BDSM scenes, very hot ones, but we also put it aside sometimes and got lost in the physical sensations of sex.

There was a lot of sex.

It wasn't like before though, when I used sex to anesthetize myself. Now I used it to feel closer to her. Ashleigh worried about the women who still came on to me, but I wasn't tempted by them, not in the least. I didn't miss the one-night stands and bed-hopping, because that had all been driven by desperation. I never wanted to go back to feeling like that again.

In time, she learned to stop worrying about the party friends, in the same way I learned to stop worrying about Rubio. Did I think Rubio wanted Ashleigh? Yes, I knew he did. His entire ballet had been inspired by her. Did I think he would admit it, now that he realized how much Ashleigh loved me? Even Ruby wasn't a big enough asshole to do that.

Perhaps the best outcome was that Mem finally stopped calling me *Ishi* and started calling me Liam. He stopped calling Ashleigh *Little Ishi* too. We had a home and family now—each other. All my life, I'd spent so much energy trying to remain detached, trying to make myself into this model of a person who was powerful and untouchable. My heart, especially, I had wanted to keep out of reach, safely locked away in my chest.

Ashleigh had my heart now.

I held her one night in her bed, after some grasping, groaning sex, resting beside her with my nose nestled in her sleek black hair. "You smell like roses," I whispered.

"Pink roses?"

I glanced over at the framed rose on the wall, the one she kept as a reminder for us both. "Every rose in the world," I murmured. "Everything."

She turned her head until her cheek pressed mine. "You're so romantic."

"Maybe. Yes. And horny."

She squirmed as I lifted her hands and told her to grab the branches of the headboard. I reveled in her soft, plaintive moan as I set about molesting all my favorite parts of her. Her delicate shoulders, her shapely breasts, her hips and waist. "Why did you really get me this bed, Liam?" she asked as I stroked between her thighs.

"To fuck you in it."

She gave a wild peal of laughter, looking up at the twisting branches. "I mean, did you buy it because it looked like the bed in *Sleeping Beauty*? Did you think to yourself, *Oh, I'm Mr. Moneybags and I'm just gonna buy this girl a crazy freaking bed so I can blow her mind*? Was it that kind of thing?"

"Yeah. Pretty much." I tickled her just to hear her laugh again. "And because I thought you deserved a safe place to sleep."

She grabbed me, squirming away from my teasing fingers. I tsked and returned her hands to their place on the headboard. "Be a good girl. Let me do what I like to you."

"I don't like tickling." She shimmied away again as I went for a sensitive spot on her thighs. This time when I grabbed her hands I held them.

"I've been thinking we should move this bed into my house," I said. "Along with all your other stuff. And you, if you're willing."

She stopped struggling and gazed at me, her beautiful face lighting in a smile. "Really?"

"Really. I want to be with you all the time. If you're ready, I'm ready to make the commitment." I glanced across the room, at her messy blanket structure. "You can bring your fort too, if you want. Mem might steal it, though." I caught her fit of giggles in my mouth. "What?" I said, pulling away from her. "He'd probably use it for some of his meditation shit." I reveled in her laughter, fighting my own smile, but I was dead serious. I wanted her to move in with me because I wanted to sleep beside her every night.

"You're sure?" she said, sobering. "You want me at your house? All the time?"

"I want it to be *our* house. We can put a fort in every room. Blankets everywhere, whatever. Just come be with me."

She gave me a shy, sweet smile. "Now that I have you, I don't need the fort anymore, but I'll definitely bring the bed."

"And the leotards and tights clipped over the shower rod. Bring those too, because I love having to bat those out of the way every time I want to take a shower."

"Of course, yes. They're coming."

"Okay, good."

She laughed again and nestled right against me. "I love that you accept me as I am."

"Amen," I said out loud, or maybe to myself. Ashleigh was the answer to a prayer I hadn't even known how to put together. She was all up in my boundaries, and it was a wonderful thing.

Epilogue:
Waking Kiss

My costume for *Waking Kiss* was a lovely, flowy gray-blue confection, the same gray-blue as Liam's guest room. The same gray-blue of my eyes, he pointed out when he saw it.

I didn't stay in the guest room anymore, though. I stayed in Liam's bedroom in Liam's house. In Liam's play room, whenever we had the time to play. He even bought a Pacman machine for me, being Mr. Moneybags and all. We were planning a wedding in the summer, after the company tour, something small and fun with my dance friends and Liam's family, and Rubio as best man, of course.

But that was later, this was now. Premiere night. There were several new choreographed pieces besides *Waking Kiss*, but I thought Rubio's was the best. I might have been a little biased.

"Stop pacing," Liam said as we hung out in Ruby's dressing room beforehand. "You're both going to be great."

The room was full of pale pink roses. Wall to wall, which was nice, because they'd become my favorite color of rose. My carrel in the corps dressing room overflowed with them also. Liam never made small gestures, but then he was a big-hearted man.

I pushed down nerves and did some stretches using Liam as a brace. Rubio went up in one of his signature handstands, his sleek matching gray-blue costume glittering under the vanity lights.

"How does the world look from down there, brother?" Liam asked after thirty seconds or so.

"Upside down." Ruby flipped back to his feet. "Now right side up again."

It was nice of Liam to keep us talking, to try to help us relax, but until this first performance was under our belts we were both going to be a bundle of anxiety. That's the way it was when partners made an official stage debut. Although this wasn't the first time we'd danced onstage together…

"You sure you got the right pointe shoes?" Ruby asked me. "Nice and quiet?"

I made a face at him. "I'm sure. Have I had noisy shoes even one time since that night I danced *Sleeping Beauty* with you?"

"If you did, I'd tell Liam to punish you. So be careful, girl," he said, wagging a finger at me.

I shuddered. Punishments were no laughing matter when it came to Liam. Fortunately I didn't earn them too often in our power exchange games.

Yves stuck his head in the door. "I'm heading back out to the seats," he said. "*Merde* to you both."

We waved to the director and then Rubio crossed the room to take me in his arms. "*Muitos abraços,*" he said. "Many hugs, and *merde*, and all of that. Thank you for dancing with me. I am very excited for this."

I hugged him back, not worrying that Liam was watching. We'd worked through all those issues in the weeks following our ill-fated threesome. Me and Rubio were strictly friends, partners, while me and Liam were something much deeper. Two damaged people who were healing one another. Two lovers forever connected by unbreakable bonds.

"I'm glad now I didn't ask Heather," Ruby said against my ear. "So glad. You are the very best dancer here. You helped me reach this day, Ash-lee."

"You did it all," I insisted.

"You did it too."

"Don't make me cry," I said as he pressed his cheek to mine. "It'll mess up my makeup."

A moment later, the three of us walked out to the backstage area, since me and Ruby's ballet was right after the intermission. I hopped up and down on my toes and shook out my hands. I was nervous but I had something to prove to myself, and to Liam, and to Rubio and Yves and my fellow dancers. I had to prove that I didn't want to be invisible anymore, that I didn't need to hide from malevolent demons under the bed.

I wanted to show everyone the joy I felt, the struggle I'd overcome. I tapped my toe boxes on the parquet floor. Quiet. Nice and quiet. The stage manager gave us a sign and we headed out to strike our opening poses behind the curtains, but then I ran back and grabbed Liam's face and kissed him. His soft hair tickled my cheek and when I drew back, his eyes held mine.

"*Merde*," he whispered. "I love you."

I didn't have time to reply, not with the stage manager hauling me toward Rubio, but my smile said everything brimming in my heart. *I love you, Liam Wilder. You're my white knight, my lock breaker who promised everything would be okay.*

You're the prince whose kiss awakened me after a hundred years. The wait was nothing.

This is for you.

THE END

A Final Note

I hope you enjoyed this first story in my City Ballet series. The storyline came to mind after I stumbled across some writings about Ishi, who was a real person. I won't relate his story here, but it's worth a Google. In essence he was the last survivor of his native tribe, a man with no remaining loved ones and no home. I thought about all the people in the world who moved through life lonely and damaged, survivors of various tragedies. I imagined two such people finding one another—and healing one another—and ended up with the story of Liam and Ashleigh.

This was, at times, a difficult story to write. I owe a huge debt of gratitude to my editors and beta readers, who helped me find the distance I needed to analyze and make improvements: Renee Regent, Linzy Antoinette, Lina Sacher, Tasha L. Harrison, J. Luna Scuro, Lanie S. Flin, Melissa, Melisa, Doris, and of course my wonderful editor Audrey—without you this book would not have been as good.

Finally, I must thank my Brazilian reader and friend Maryara for inspiring me to write my bad boy, Fernando Rubio, and for helping me with the Portuguese language in this book. If you enjoyed Rubio's complexity and spirit, you'll be happy to learn he's the subject of my next book, *Fever Dream*. As Ashleigh predicted, Rubio does fall in love with "some poor girl" and all hell does break loose. I hope you'll read the first-chapter excerpt from *Fever Dream* following this note.

As always, thanks for reading me, reviewing me, sharing your thoughts about my stories, and offering me such unwavering support. I appreciate your encouragement more than words can say.

An excerpt from *Fever Dream,* the next story in the City Ballet series, available in late 2013

Fernando Rubio vaulted up the stone steps to the white town house, his stormy Brazilian temper in full effect. He drew back a fist and banged it on his friends' front door.

"Liam. Ashleigh! Ash-lee! I have some words for you, damn it. I know you're in there. Open up."

The door swung wide and a dark-haired, elderly man peered out. "Mr. Rubio. What a pleasure to see you."

He pushed past Mem and stalked into the house. "Where are they?"

"They are downstairs. They undoubtedly"—Mem slipped around the front of him—"*undoubtedly* wish for privacy at the moment."

Rubio waved a hand, heading for the Wilders' BDSM-equipped basement. "No matter what they're doing, it's nothing I haven't seen before."

"Mr. Rubio, if you would kindly wait in the living room—"

Ruby ignored Mem's polite but pointed protests and continued to the lower floor. He stopped halfway down the stairs, scanning Liam's play room in the dim mood lighting, until he located the naked couple. Oh…God. "That's disgusting!"

At his barked exclamation, Liam turned to search for him with a frown. "Do you mind? Timing, my friend. Very bad timing."

"You are both disgusting."

The tall, long-haired man wrapped his arms more tightly around his petite partner. "What are you so offended by? I'm kissing my wife."

"Exactly. You have this entire den of depravity, sex toys and BDSM furniture," he said, waving a hand around the basement, "and you are standing there kissing her."

"Not only that—we just *made love*," his friend said, teasing. "Tender, sappy, emotional, gaze-into-each-other's-eyes kind of love."

"With lots and lots of kissing," Ashleigh added.

"Ugh." Ruby spun and started back the way he'd come. "I'll wait upstairs. You're both..." He searched his mind for an adequate insult. "You're both completely disgusting." He waved a finger at Ashleigh. "And you! I am furious with you."

He turned his back on her apologetic expression and took the stairs two at a time. There was nothing she could say to excuse her behavior, nothing he wanted to listen to, anyway.

Mem greeted him when he arrived back in the living room. "Would you care for some refreshment, Mr. Rubio? Coffee? Tea?" He took in Ruby's dour expression. "Something stronger?"

"I don't want anything," he snapped, "except to unsee what I just saw." Oh, and for Ashleigh to not leave the theater. He wanted that more than anything. They'd been working together for four years now, collaborating and achieving new heights of artistry with each ballet. He collapsed onto one of the living room's leather couches and put his head in his hands. How could she leave him now, after all they'd created together? After all the work they'd done?

A few moments later Ashleigh appeared from below, clad in Liam's black tee. At least he assumed it was Liam's since it hung to her knees. She hugged the shirt around her waist and crossed to sit next to Rubio on the couch.

"Well?" he said. "I am waiting for your explanation. Why are you leaving City Ballet?"

"I'm not leaving. I mean, I'm not leaving London." She leaned forward, rubbing her knees. "I'm just taking a break from dancing."

He felt unreasonable anger at her offhand tone. "A break? No. You are quitting the company. That's what Yves told me after class. Why didn't you warn me? You didn't tell me nothing until today. Then, boom."

She lowered her head, her black locks falling forward across her cheeks. "I couldn't tell you. I didn't know how to tell you, so I let Yves do it."

"Well, I almost punched Yves in the face." He pointed at her. "That would have been your fault."

She touched his hand on the cushion between them and then wrapped her fingers around his. "I'm sorry. I didn't know what to say. I don't know what to say to you, even now."

He felt choking emotion. Cold betrayal and loss. Ashleigh was his favorite ballet partner. They danced almost everything together, in perfect, comfortable harmony. "Why?" he asked. "What I do? I'm sorry."

"It's not you."

"I know I'm rude sometimes. I know I always touch your tits and pretend it was an accident. I know, it's bad. I won't do it anymore, I swear."

"It's not that," she said, squeezing his hand tighter. "I've loved working with you. You have to know that. These past few years have been a dream for me, both personally and professionally." Her blue-gray eyes communicated the same pain he felt, the pain that had devastated him when Yves broke the news an hour ago.

"Why?" he whispered. "Why, then?"

She let go of his hand and picked at the hem of Liam's shirt. "I'm tired, okay? Ballet has always been easy for you because you're a natural, a phenomenon. It's a struggle for me. I want to... I want to try something different."

Liam joined them with two beers. He sat on the arm of the couch beside his wife, holding out one of the bottles to his friend. "You realize you're being a total pussy about this, right? A pathetic crybaby pussy?"

"Stop it," Ashleigh said, reaching over to her husband. "You don't understand. It's hard for dancers to lose a partner. Over time you develop this really transcendent bond, almost like brother and sister."

Or husband and wife. Rubio had secretly pined for Ashleigh years ago, when she was dating Liam. Sometimes he still did, even though his friends were happily married and completely devoted to each other. Ashleigh turned back to him, pleading with him to understand. "You taught me so much about ballet and artistry, so much about performance. I feel horrible leaving you, but...me and Liam are having a baby. I'm three months pregnant. I won't be able to dance next season because of that."

Rubio's eyes went wide. What the hell? A baby? "Is this a joke?" he sputtered. "Your belly is completely flat."

"I'm not showing yet, but believe me, I'm pregnant. Remember how I kept throwing up on the summer tour?"

Ruby put his hands to his head. "*Jesus Cristo*. Why you need a baby? I need a partner! What about that?"

"Watch your tone with my wife," Liam said.

Ruby turned to jab a finger at him. "This is your fault."

"Everything is everyone else's fault, huh?" said Liam. "Maybe it's your fault. You introduced us, if you'll remember."

"Yes, but I didn't imagine all this kissing and getting married and making love and…and *babies*."

Liam shrugged. "That's what grown-ups do."

Ashleigh frowned at her husband and turned to Ruby, edging Liam out of the conversation.

"There are a lot of talented dancers you can partner with at the company. I'm sure Yves will let you dance with whoever you want."

"Except you," he groused. "I can't dance with you."

"A few months from now I'll be big as a whale. Right? You won't want to dance with me."

Ruby couldn't stop the half-smile. "Don't try to be cute. Don't be funny. I'm angry at you."

"I know. I'm sorry." She leaned to him, opened her arms and hugged him tight. Rubio waited for her to start laughing, to tell him this was all a joke. She didn't look pregnant. She didn't feel pregnant, but Ashleigh, his favorite partner, his soul-mate partner, was pregnant and he didn't know what he was going to do.

"Maybe I'll quit too," he grumbled against her neck. "Maybe I'll stop dancing. Maybe now it's time."

She pulled away from him in horror. "No, you can't. Don't even say that."

"Pussy," Liam muttered from behind her.

"You have years left to dance," she said, truly alarmed. "You're only thirty years old."

"You're only twenty-eight!"

"It's different with men and women. You're stronger than me and..." She put her hands over her belly. "I really want to have this baby right now. It's time for me to do this. I feel it in my heart."

"Stop begging him to understand, hon," said Liam. "It's Ruby, remember? He's obnoxious and self-centered. He'll never understand the impulse to start a family, but eventually he'll get over it. Won't you?" Liam shot him a dire look.

Ashleigh dropped her head onto Rubio's shoulder. "I just feel like...this is the time. I should have told you," she said, lifting her eyes to meet his gaze. "I should have warned you we were making these plans but I didn't want you to be angry."

"Well, I'm angry."

"But Ruby—"

"I gave you so much, Ash. So whatever. Maybe I forgive you someday, but not now. No."

At those words, tears filled her eyes. She jumped to her feet and stalked from the room.

Liam sighed, sliding down onto the couch. "Very nice. Making a pregnant woman cry. I hope you're proud of yourself."

"What did I say?"

"What did you say? God, you're an idiot." Liam snatched away his beer. "I would make you go apologize to her, but that would probably upset her more. Plus the pregnancy hormones are making her really erratic and I can't guarantee she won't kick you in the neck." He leaned forward and fixed Ruby in his potent amber stare. "But seriously. If you're going to keep coming over here, if you're going to attend the play parties on Saturdays, you're going to have to cut her some slack. She's pregnant and it can't be undone."

Ruby eyed his friend, noting the subtle tension in his voice. "You and her planned this pregnancy? Or it just happened?"

Liam rubbed his forehead. "It was kind of planned. It kind of just happened. She wants a couple kids, and..." He covered his eyes and kneaded his palms into his eye sockets. "I'm going to be okay with that."

"You're going to be, or you are?" Liam's silence was deafening. Ruby sighed and took back his beer. "Ashleigh is a good girl, you know. She won't be like your mother."

"My mother had postpartum depression. Any woman can get it. Ashleigh too."

221

"Okay. But if she does, you'll be there to help. It won't be the same."

"I know." That was all he said. *I know.* He stood and started toward the stairs. "I better go see if she's okay." He turned back to Ruby and gave a regretful half-shrug. "Look, I'm sorry you're losing your partner. I don't mean to be a bastard to you, but I'm on Team Ashleigh. I have to be. I'm asking you friend to friend, and I really hope you hear me: Let her go."

"I will," he sighed. "I don't have a fucking choice, do I? But who the hell am I supposed to dance with now?"

"It doesn't matter who. You're the best ballet dancer in the world, Ruby. Pick someone. Don't be a fucking pussy, for fuck's sake."

With those words, his friend went up the wide marble staircase to comfort his wife.

Follow Annabel's blog (annabeljoseph.com) and Twitter (@annabeljoseph) to learn more about the upcoming release of *Fever Dream*.

About the Author

Annabel Joseph is a multi-published BDSM romance author. She writes mainly contemporary romance, although she has been known to dabble in the medieval and Regency eras. She is known for writing emotionally intense BDSM storylines, and strives to create characters that seem real—even flawed—so readers are better able to relate to them. Annabel also writes vanilla (non-BDSM) erotic romance under the pen name Molly Joseph.

Annabel Joseph loves to hear from her readers at annabeljosephnovels@gmail.com.

Made in the USA
Lexington, KY
14 September 2013